A former journalist on the *Daily Mail* and *Evening Standard,* and social editor of the *Tatler* for ten years, writer and broadcaster Una-Mary Parker has crafted a dramatic and compelling novel of romantic suspense. Her previous international bestsellers have been translated into eleven languages, are available from Headline, and have been highly praised:

'[Una-Mary Parker] is on the cutting edge between Ruth Rendell and Judith Krantz. She's a writer to watch' *Chicago Tribune*

'Romance and suspense with an unexpected twist' *Sunday Express*

'Freshness, convincing dialogue and capacity to sustain one's interest' *Sunday Telegraph*

'This novel has everything – intrigue, romance, ambition, lust . . .' *Daily Mail*

'Una-Mary's bestselling formula succeeds yet again' *Daily Telegraph*

'A book to keep you turning the pages' *Prima*

Also by Una-Mary Parker

Sweet Vengeance

Una-Mary Parker

HEADLINE

Copyright © 2000 Cheval Associates Ltd

The right of Una-Mary Parker to be identified as the Author of
the Work has been asserted by her in accordance with the
Copyright, Designs and Patents Act 1988.

First published in 2000
by HEADLINE BOOK PUBLISHING

First published in paperback in 2001
by HEADLINE BOOK PUBLISHING

10 9 8 7 6 5 4 3 2 1

ISBN 0 7472 6197 0

Typeset by
Letterpart Limited, Reigate, Surrey

Printed and bound in Great Britain by
Clays Ltd, St Ives plc

HEADLINE BOOK PUBLISHING
A division of Hodder Headline
338 Euston Road
London NW1 3BH

www.headline.co.uk
www.hodderheadline.com

'She sleeps and as her eyelids droop
A veil of innocence descends.
Misleading mask! – so free from sin
That none would guess the truth within.

'She sighs and with each gentle breath
Her lips seem to be smiling.
Beguiling smile! – that seems sincere
On waking's but a false veneer.

'She turns with movements like a child.
A hand outstretched for comfort.
By day that hand will seize and take
All within reach for its owner's sake.

'At dawn that innocence will go
With that first flutter of her lids.
On waking – if she'd but retain
The look that does not search for gain.'

One

'Well! Here we are at last. Isn't it wonderful? Aren't we going to be happy? Thank God we've sorted out everything at last.

'I knew this was the only way, you see. After all the argument . . . When you rejected me – Christ! You've no idea how much that hurt. I couldn't believe it at first. How could you do that to me? Jesus, I was spaced out for weeks . . .

'I never stopped missing you, though. Funny, isn't it, how you build pictures in your mind? Imagining all sorts of nice things happening: being together, having long talks, laughing at the same things . . . then you get so disappointed when it doesn't happen.

'It was like that with me. Always painting pictures of our life together. And always disappointed when it didn't happen. Like when you said "No".

'Oh, Jesus Christ, there's so much I want to say to you. Things I want to tell you. You do *know I love you, though, don't you? Love you more than anyone in the world . . .*

1

'This is the moment I've longed for, for such a long time. And there's no turning back now, is there? We're together at last and that's how I hope it will always be.

'Just you and me.'

The first flicker of unease slid into Joanna Knight's mind at a quarter to nine when she realised Arabella hadn't turned up for work. As she was renowned for her punctuality that was odd for a start. She normally arrived at eight-thirty sharp. By nine o'clock Joanna's unease had become concern. Yet she kept thinking her mother would surely come flying into the showroom at any second, blonde hair skimming her shoulders, hot blue eyes blazing with enthusiasm, her glossily painted mouth curved in a teasing smile. 'You know I'm never late, darling. The traffic was terrible,' she'd say.

So why was her mobile phone switched off?

By that point the fashion correspondent and film crew from B-Sky-B were getting restless. Further offers of coffee didn't pacify them.

'Do you think she'll be here soon?' Dominica asked. 'We do have to interview another designer this morning. We can't wait much longer.'

It was the eve of London Fashion Week and Dominica Shepherd, one-time model turned TV presenter, was getting edgy.

'I know she's on her way,' Joanna replied, still sure at this point that it was true. 'Let me call her housekeeper to check what time she left home.'

While Dominica and the crew hovered restlessly, Joanna rushed back to her desk and grabbed the phone.

Melosa answered after several rings.

'Mrs Webster she left as usual,' she told Joanna in her halting English. 'She take Louise to school. Like she always.'

'What time did they leave, Melosa?'

'When they always . . . at a quarter after eight.'

'Thanks.' Joanna replaced the receiver slowly. That wasn't good news. Every morning, like clockwork, Arabella left her Kensington flat at eight-fifteen, dropping off Louise at her day school on the way and then driving straight to work in Pimlico Road, arriving on the dot of eight-thirty.

Her couture business Arabella Designs occupied what had previously been a corner shop with accommodation on two floors above it. There was an exclusive atmosphere about the place now. Glass swing doors led into a comfortably sized salon with changing rooms, and a large window in which today three evening dresses were displayed overlooked the street. Workrooms and offices were on the upper floors where twenty seamstresses and a PA-cum-secretary worked, and where Joanna, dealing with public relations, also had a tiny office.

She glanced at her wrist watch. It was nine-fifteen. Not earth-shatteringly late by normal standards, but very late by Arabella's.

Joanna closed her office door with her foot while she made her next call to Rutlands. No point in letting everyone hear what was happening.

'This is Joanna Knight,' she explained when she got through to the small private school. 'Has Louise Webster been dropped off with you this morning?'

'Yes,' replied the school secretary in surprise. 'Mrs Webster was one of the first mothers to arrive, but then she usually is.'

Next Joanna rang Equus in the Brompton Road.

'Is Arabella Webster there, please?'

There was a momentary pause while the receptionist looked at the appointments book. 'She's not booked in for today. Is that her daughter? Thought I recognised your voice. Your mother had a shampoo and blow-dry yesterday so I don't expect we'll see her for another couple of days.'

Joanna pressed the mouse on her desk, flicking up the details of Arabella's personal file on her screen. Dentist . . . doctor (she was having treatment for hypertension) . . . osteopath . . . health club . . . chiropodist . . . where was Joanna supposed to *start*?

At that moment her office door opened and a bone-thin, brittle-looking woman in her early-forties shot in from her own office diagonally across the landing. Eleanor was Arabella's PA and showroom manager.

'What's happening?' she asked urgently. 'Is Arabella all right? Why isn't she here?' Her sharp white jaw glinted like exposed bone against the black of her dyed hair. She glared at Joanna as if she was responsible for her mother's absence.

'I don't know,' Joanna replied, dashing past her and running down the flight of narrow stairs to the ground floor. The grey and white showroom, furnished only with a rail holding a couple of dozen garments, several modern chairs and a low glass-topped table on which

4

stood an arrangement of white flowers, was dazzlingly bright under the television lights. Suddenly they were switched off.

'It's getting too bloody hot in here,' she heard one of the crew grumble as she picked her way across the cables that snaked over the grey carpet.

'I'm afraid we're going to have to go,' Dominica said regretfully. She glanced at her gold wrist watch. 'We're running late and we've got to get to Fulham. This is a helluva week . . .'

It took the crew much less time to pack up and go than it had to set up.

'Fuck!' Joanna said to herself as she raced back upstairs. She'd worked so hard to get that TV interview and now she wondered if they'd bother covering the actual show. There was nothing so fickle as the media. As she reached the landing she heard Eleanor's voice. The door to her office was open and she was talking to someone on the phone.

'. . . Arabella's new collection is absolutely revolutionary! A complete departure from anything she's done before, using leather, metal, feathers, tiny mirrors and silk imported from China. This is the first time she's put on a big show during London Fashion Week and there's been a massive response to the invitations.'

Here Eleanor's voice dropped confidingly and Joanna strained to hear what she was saying.

'Of course she dresses a lot of very famous women: pop stars, Hollywood actresses *and* certain members of the royal family. They love her designs, especially for foreign tours such as . . .'

5

Joanna frowned. Arabella never mentioned the royals to the media. It was a very sensitive issue. Great offence could be caused if they thought you were taking advantage of their patronage. She was on the point of interrupting Eleanor's flow, because apart from anything else talking to journalists was *her* job, when Rosie McDowell, the head seamstress and workroom manageress, who'd been with Arabella from the beginning, came down the stairs from the workroom.

'Is your ma here yet?' she asked anxiously.

Joanna shook her head.

Pink and plump like a full-blown example of her name, Rosie regarded Joanna with motherly concern. 'There's a problem with the black and gold evening dress. I've got to ask her if she's planning to put beaded shoulder straps on it or black satin rouleau ones?'

They'd all been working for weeks now, getting the collection ready for Friday's show, and pressure was mounting. Everything had to be perfect. Arabella liked to check every stitch and no one, not even Rosie, dared make final decisions or adjustments without her express permission.

Arabella was now nearly an hour and a half late and Joanna was developing a splitting headache. 'I'm really worried. God, I hope she hasn't had an accident!'

'Maybe someone else wanted to interview her, sudden like? Perhaps for the radio?' Rosie suggested helpfully.

Joanna shook her head. 'Sky was one of the most important interviews of the week. She'd never have let them down if she could have helped it.'

Joanna Knight had never intended to be her mother's PR. When she'd left boarding school, with nine GCSEs and four 'A' levels, including an A* for art, Arabella had sent her off with a group of friends to travel around the world during her gap year. That had been great and Joanna had really enjoyed touring around India and Thailand, eventually ending up in Australia and New Zealand.

Back in London, living in an attic flat in Pimlico, she was all geared up to start a three-year course at St Martin's School of Art, where she considered herself lucky to have been accepted. It was all she'd ever really wanted to do, but her mother suddenly decided she had other plans for her. And somehow, because no one ever refused Arabella anything, she ended up getting what she wanted.

'Darling,' she'd said one weekend, having invited Joanna to her flat for Sunday lunch, 'd'you know what I'd like, more than anything else in the world?' Her expression was wistful.

'What's that, Mummy?' Joanna had been nineteen at the time, and believed that her mother already had everything a woman could possibly want.

Arabella, slim and tanned, golden and sexy, reached out and took Joanna's hand, ignoring her bitten nails and slightly plump fingers. 'More than *anything* in the world, sweetheart, I'd like you to work with me in the business. We're going places, you know, darling. The company's growing. I want to build it up so that I become as famous a name as Coco Chanel. I know we have a long way to go and the first thing I'm going to

7

need is someone to invest in me. Have faith in my talents, so I can become a big player on the fashion scene.'

Joanna sat looking less than *soignée* in her slightly grubby T-shirt and baggy trousers and stared at Arabella, too astonished to speak.

'*Me*?' she croaked, alarmed. Why should her mother want her involved in such a glamorous lifestyle? High fashion wasn't Joanna's scene at all. She'd always done everything Arabella wanted, usually for the sake of peace, but she was the ugly duckling of the family, the budding artist, not caring how she looked in case she lost street cred among her peer group – and here was her mother asking her to become a part of the *fashion* industry? 'But I'm going to St Martin's.' She reached for her wine glass and took a gulp.

Arabella set such store by beauty. It was what her business was all about, of course. Making women of all ages look as beautiful as possible. She was a beauty snob, in fact. Plain people didn't interest her. That was why Joanna was secretly sure her mother favoured her half-sister Louise, nine years old and fine-boned, with blonde tendrils of hair flowing wispily around her heart-shaped face. Her bright blue eyes were fringed with black lashes. Her lips always looked as if she'd just been eating raspberries. Louise should be the one eventually to join Arabella in the business. Not Joanna. She'd taken after her father, Jeremy Knight; tall and strong-looking, with capable hands. She never bothered with make-up although acknowledging that her eyes, grey like Dad's, were quite nice and that her dark hair, cut short more for convenience than style, was all right.

'I *can't*, Mummy,' she said childishly, aghast at the prospect. 'I'd never fit in.'

Arabella frowned at being opposed. 'Of course you'd fit in,' she said almost crossly. 'You're my daughter. Who else would I want to do my PR? You're so good with people and I'll soon teach you the ropes.'

Although they were alone because Louise was spending the weekend with her father, Eric Webster, Arabella leaned closer across the dining table and lowered her voice confidingly.

'I need someone I can trust, my darling. You and Louise will inherit the business eventually, in any case. So why not become a part of it sooner rather than later?' She squeezed Joanna's hand, giggling like an excited young girl now. 'We'll have such fun! Seeing you every day will be heaven. I can hardly wait.'

'But I don't know a thing about PR. I've always wanted to go to art school. It's what I want to do,' she'd argued rebelliously.

Arabella drew away, lifting her long mane of blonde hair off the back of her neck with both hands and then letting it drop to one shoulder. 'And who pays the rent of your flat?' Her tone was cold. 'If it weren't for me you wouldn't be able to afford one room in Earl's Court on the pocket money your father gives you.'

Joanna flushed, knowing it was true.

'I don't know why I should go on subsidising you if you're going to be so unsupportive of me. And what happens when you leave art school? The world is full of impoverished artists. Am I supposed to go on financing your lifestyle then? Look, sweetie,' Arabella continued, changing tack, 'I wouldn't ask you if I didn't genuinely believe you'd be wonderful at the job. I'd so like to have you near to me. All those years when you were away at boarding school were . . . well, I missed you.'

'You had Louise.'

'She's just a baby. *We're* on the same wavelength, darling . . .'

In the end, of course, Joanna had given way. Just like everyone else did where Arabella was concerned. Before she knew it she'd been enrolled on computer and business studies courses, had gone on to work in an established PR firm to gain experience, and then eighteen months ago had arrived to start work at Arabella Designs.

On the desk in her new office she found a bouquet of pink roses, with a card on which was scrawled: '*Welcome, my darling. I'm so happy you're here. Fondest love. Mummy*'.

It was now twelve-thirty. After a chaotic morning the place was suddenly quiet, the showroom deserted. The ladies who shopped had become the ladies who lunched. There were few passers-by in Pimlico Road to admire the dresses in the window. Even the workroom was quiet as the girls stopped for sandwiches and coffee and a glance at the *Sun* or *Mirror*, knowing they'd be working late again tonight. Eleanor had gone to bank some cheques. There was still no word from Arabella.

Feeling too keyed up to eat, Joanna fetched herself a bottle of water from the fridge in the galley kitchen and wondered what to do next. After the tension of the morning, during which she'd contemplated phoning the local hospitals to see if her mother had been in an accident, the sudden silence unnerved her. She longed to phone her boyfriend, Freddie, with whom she was now living, but he worked as a pupil barrister and was in court all day today so she decided to phone her father. Jeremy and Arabella hadn't communicated since she'd walked out on him after four years of marriage, but he and Joanna had stayed close and she loved her step-mother, Victoria, a warm-hearted, domesticated woman who made huge fragrant casseroles and baked her own bread.

She tapped in the number of *Metropolitan* magazine and asked to be put through to the advertising department.

'Hello?' It was wonderful to hear Jeremy's rich and reassuring voice.

'Hi, Daddy, it's me. Listen, I'm worried about Ma. She hasn't turned up for work and I don't know what to do. I've checked all over the place but there's not a sign of her. She's already missed a vital TV interview, and she's supposed to be doing another with the *Daily Telegraph* this afternoon. I don't know what else to do.'

'She can't have gone far, Jo,' he said calmly. 'This is her big week, isn't it?'

'Yes. People have been ringing all morning, wanting to talk to her. What the hell can I say? Apart from she's busy, she's tied up at the moment, she's out, she's with an important client . . . I'm running out of excuses,' Joanna added desperately.

'Well, don't panic, darling,' he said comfortingly. 'Could she have gone to the site of the show? It's being

11

held in the grounds of the Natural History Museum, isn't it? Maybe she's got carried away discussing the arrangements? You know what she's like better than I do now but I'm sure she's still a perfectionist. If the cat-walk's three inches too short she'll insist on its being rebuilt.'

'But I don't understand why her mobile has been switched off all day. I've phoned the model agency, Cartier, Jimmy Choo, the make-up people, *everyone* who's involved, and no one has heard from her.'

'Mmmm.' Jeremy was silent for a moment, deep in thought. 'If it had been anyone else . . .'

'*Exactly!*'

'Have you phoned the local hospitals to see if she's been admitted to the casualty department?'

'No.' Joanna spoke in a small, terrified voice. 'I thought about it but then I figured we'd have been told if anything had happened.'

'I'll do it now, love. Try not to worry. I'm sure there must be a perfectly simple explanation. People don't just vanish like this and you know your mother – she's a born survivor. I'll get back to you in a few minutes.'

Joanna leaned back in her swivel seat, exhausted and now tormented by visions of her mother lying injured or in a coma, suffering from a stroke or a heart attack, maybe even . . .

Eleanor returned from the bank, breathless and flustered. 'Have you heard anything? Has she arrived?'

Joanna shook her head. 'Are you sure she didn't leave a message on your desk, or even in the workroom, explaining why she couldn't come in today?'

Eleanor looked distressed, her bony hands working nervously. 'Of course she didn't. I'm terribly worried about her, Joanna. She's been working so hard, getting this collection ready. She's under enormous strain . . . but she always tells me where she's going, what she's doing, who she's seeing . . .' Her eyes brimmed and she added abruptly, 'I always know where to find her. And as her so-called publicity agent, you should too.'

Joanna flushed, feeling like a scolded schoolgirl. The phone on her desk burst unnervingly into life. She grabbed the receiver.

'Arabella Designs. Can I help you?' she said automatically.

'It's me, Jo . . .'

'Oh, Dad!'

Jeremy's voice sounded carefully measured. 'No news, which is good. I've been on to the casualty departments of all the main London hospitals but no one of your mother's description has been admitted.'

'Thank God for that.' Joanna felt a surge of relief. 'So what should I do now?'

'My advice would be to wait until later on today to see what happens. If she hasn't turned up by the late-afternoon, I think you should tell the police. Report her as missing.'

'Missing?' Joanna repeated, stunned. Out of the corner of her eye she could see Eleanor's horrified expression as she stood listening to their conversation. 'What do I say, Dad? I thought you could only report small children who went missing right away? Don't you have to wait at least forty-eight hours if it's an adult?'

'Not necessarily. This is an important week for your mother, isn't it?'

'The most important week of her career.'

'Then I think you should do something about it if you haven't heard from her by five o'clock.'

'OK.' She was filled with anguish and anger in equal measure. How dare Arabella put them all through this worry when they were already stressed? What the hell was she playing at?

It was two o'clock. Joanna glanced at the day's schedule and realised tonight was the big reception at Lancaster House to launch London Fashion Week, hosted by the Prime Minister and his wife. Vivienne Westwood, Catherine Walker, Amanda Wakeley – they'd all be there; the guest list read like the *Who's Who* of the fashion world. Arabella had been ecstatic when she'd received her invitation and her excitement had been almost touching, like a young girl's, as she'd planned what to wear. What a wonderful photo opportunity it was going to be, too, Joanna thought worriedly. It would be really disappointing if she failed to turn up in time.

At four o'clock pandemonium broke out in the workroom as the seamstresses started squabbling. Snatches of conversation filtered down the staircase to the offices from the floor above.

'We'll never be finished at this rate . . .'

'What did Arabella say we were to do with these silk roses?'

'I don't know. She ought to be bloody here, instead of leaving it all to us . . .'

'. . . just get on with it!'

'How the hell can I get on . . .'

'Don't you talk to *me* like that!'

'But doesn't anybody know where she is?'

Raised voices replaced the usual soft whirr of the sewing machines. A door slammed. Then there was silence. Rosie will sort them out, Joanna reflected hopefully. She was fully aware that many of the workroom girls disliked Arabella because she could be sweet one moment then capricious and exacting the next, so no one quite knew where they stood. But all of them were anxious to keep their jobs in a business that was dependent on the whim of clients' tastes. Top designers with a celebrity clientele went bankrupt with shocking regularity. It happened again and again just as they, and everyone else, thought they were financially established. Arabella always managed to keep the business afloat somehow but only just, and no one felt very secure in their job.

A few minutes later Eleanor put her head round Joanna's door. 'Everything's under control now,' she announced. 'I know Arabella would have wanted them to keep working, so I've told the girls what to do. They were making such a fuss about trimmings and Rosie has no control over them. Anyway, everything's underway now so when Arabella gets here she'll have nothing to worry about.'

Joanna knew she ought to be thankful that Eleanor had taken the initiative, but she was worried. In Arabella's absence, it was Rosie's job to be in charge of the work-room. To interfere was to undermine her authority.

When Joanna had come to work for her mother eighteen months ago Eleanor had been deeply affronted. She made it obvious she considered it to be sheer nepotism, and at every opportunity had tried to put Joanna down.

At that moment the phone started to ring again.

'Excuse me,' said Joanna, politely and pointedly.

Eleanor departed, looking crestfallen.

Joanna grabbed the receiver and suddenly a wave of relief swept over her as she heard a dear familiar voice.

'Oh, Freddie! I'm so glad you rang. I think something awful may have happened . . .'

'Babe! What is it?'

'Ma hasn't turned up for work and no one knows where she is. I'm really worried, Freddie. I just don't know what to do.'

'That's not like her, is it? Have you checked every-where?'

'Yes, and Daddy has been on to all the hospitals. It's as if she's completely vanished.' A tear rolled down her face and plopped on to her shirt. She rubbed at the stain fiercely.

'Oh, Jo darling, what an absolute nightmare.' He paused as if deliberating. 'Could she have gone to see any of her family? Perhaps someone's been taken ill and she had to rush off . . .'

'You know she doesn't have any family now. Both her parents died years ago and she's an only child.'

'And this is her big week, isn't it?'

16

'Tell me about it. I've been fending off the media all day.'

'Shit! What a bummer. God, I wish there was something I could do. The court adjourned early today but I've got to go back to Chambers and God knows when I'll finish tonight.'

'OK,' she said wistfully. 'I'll ring you if I have any news.'

'Try not to worry, babe. Knowing Arabella, I'm sure she's all right . . .'

The other phone started to ring. 'I've got to go, Freddie. See you tonight.' Calls were coming in thick and fast from journalists who'd suddenly realised they had a deadline to catch. 'Fuck! Fuck! Fuck!' Joanna swore as she grabbed the receiver again and again. She'd already fixed up newspaper, magazine, radio and television interviews for Arabella for the next four days, and blanket coverage of her show. What the hell was she supposed to say to everyone if her mother failed to turn up?

At four-thirty she put through another call to Melosa, partly to make sure she'd collected Louise from Rutlands but also to ask, one more time, if she'd heard from her employer.

'She no call me,' Melosa said nervously. 'What happen, Jo? Where she gone?'

'I don't know. Listen, Melosa, don't say anything to Louise. I don't want her upset. If she asks for her mother, just say she's busy at work. I'll come over now and see Louise before she goes to bed. This isn't your evening off, is it?'

'No. I stay here.'

17

Thank God for that! 'OK, Melosa. That's fine. I'll see you shortly.'

Joanna made one last call before she left the office.

'Dad? There's been no news. Nothing.'

'Have you told the police?'

'Not yet. I thought I'd do it now. Go in person and take a photograph of Ma with me.'

'Good idea. Is there anything I can do, Jo?'

Some unknown terror inside her was fast taking shape, being brought to a head by the decision she'd made. 'Nothing, Dad,' she replied, forcing herself to sound calm.

'Take care, sweetheart. Keep me posted.'

'Yup. 'Bye, Dad.'

Late afternoon, Monday 13 September

When Joanna arrived at Belgravia police station the officer on the front desk listened as she burbled nervously, and then, after taking down her name, asked her to wait a moment while he fetched someone who could take down all the details.

Joanna sat on a hard bench in the entrance hall, with the unreal feeling that she was taking part in an episode of *The Bill*. The more she thought about Arabella's not showing up today, the more incredulous she felt. Her mother had been planning this week for years. To have her own show, attended by the fashion world was all she'd ever wanted. She'd married Jeremy Knight when

18

she'd been seventeen, after a whirlwind love-at-first-sight romance, and Joanna had been born ten months later. For a while, in spite of living in a small studio flat in Fulham, they were deliriously happy. Sometimes they stayed in bed all day, making love, listening to music and reading aloud to each other. Jeremy had charm, good looks and a romantic disposition, but at only twenty-two himself, he was not yet earning much at J. Walter Thompson, although his future in advertising looked promising.

At first Arabella, with no family of her own, hadn't cared. She'd bought cheap fruit and vegetables from the barrows in the North End Road, where the stallholders knocked a few pence off because she was so fresh and pretty with long blonde hair and a willowy figure. She was always friendly and smiling, too, and they were soon calling her Bella and shouting, 'Mornin', love,' when she appeared, carrying her baby in one arm and holding her shopping basket on the other.

Storm clouds were gathering, though. At first Jeremy tried to ignore her growing discontent and dissatisfaction when she couldn't have all she wanted. They had fights over getting a car, going on holiday, getting a bigger flat. Nobody could live on sex and air, she screamed. So he got a job with another agency, where he earned a bit more money, but still she wasn't satisfied. Her love for beautiful clothes was becoming a passion and as they couldn't afford the sort of dresses she yearned for, Jeremy bought her a sewing machine and suggested she start making her own.

Without realising it, he'd started her on a career that

had taken her to the top, and within four years of being married, deprived himself of a wife. One day, Arabella upped and left, taking Joanna with her. Women had started admiring what she was wearing and so, capitalising on her own stunning appearance, she started dressmaking for others. Soon she had to take on two seamstresses and move to a bigger flat. By word of mouth her business grew; someone offered to back her so she could expand even more; within a few years she'd taken on Rosie McDowell to manage the workroom staff and Eleanor Andrews to organise the showroom and secretarial side.

Joanna lived with her mother until she was eighteen, being left almost entirely in the care of a live-in nanny until she was nine and then sent to boarding school. When she'd been twelve, she'd been shocked by her mother's unexpected second marriage to a professor of history, Eric Webster, by whom she'd had Louise, now nine. This marriage hadn't lasted either. Arabella had left Eric, amidst much acrimony, three years ago. Joanna had to admit that her mother had never been predictable, and that today might just be another example of her waywardness.

'Would you like to come this way, Miss?'

Joanna looked up. A tall, beefy uniformed policeman with sandy hair and an earnest expression stood looking down at her.

'Detective Sergeant Chambers will see you now, Miss.'

'Thank you.' She followed him along a corridor and into an interview room. A minute later she was joined by a young man in a grey suit, dark blue shirt and striped tie. He looked tired and harassed, and as he took the seat on the opposite side of the table he let out a deep sigh.

'Miss Knight?'

Joanna nodded.

'I gather you wish to report a missing person.' Chambers drew a note pad towards him and a ballpoint from the outside breast pocket of his jacket.

Trying to be brief, she gave him all Arabella's details. 'I hope,' she said, suddenly wondering if she'd been right to come to this place where serious crimes were being dealt with day and night, 'I'm not making a fuss over nothing, but it's *so* unlike my mother to go missing, especially at a time like this.' She'd already told him about Arabella's fashion business.

'Do you know if she took her passport with her? And what credit cards she usually carried?'

'I've no idea, but I can find out,' Joanne replied.

Chambers pursed his full lips and doodled on the pad. 'How is her health?'

Joanna looked up sharply. 'She's very well. Actually she does suffer from hypertension but the doctor has given her medication for that and she's fine otherwise.'

'Any other problems?'

'No. She's very active . . . after all she's only forty? . . . nearly forty-one.'

'What about depression? Does she suffer from that?'

The question took Joanna aback. 'No, that's the last thing she suffers from. She's extremely up-beat and enthusiastic. Has a wonderful life, really,' she added, thinking that if her mother worked hard by day, she also played hard by night.

'Can you give me the name of her doctor, please? We have to check on these things, you know.'

Joanna flushed, appalled at the inference behind his question. 'She certainly hasn't committed suicide,' she retorted hotly. 'That's the last thing that could have happened.'

Chambers scribbled on unperturbed. Then he glanced at her again, his eyes looking heavy as if he needed a good night's sleep. 'Has she any enemies?'

'I don't think so . . . no, I'm sure she hasn't.'

'Has she ever mentioned being stalked? Getting anonymous letters? Mysterious phone calls?'

'What *is* this?' Joanna burst out indignantly. 'My mother may have had an accident, lost her memory or . . .' Her voice faded away and she found herself regretting the fact that Freddie had been unable to come to the police station with her.

'These are routine questions, Miss Knight. We have to eliminate everything that's of no consequence. You have a different name from your mother. Does that mean she's re-married?'

Joanna nodded. 'Her first husband was Jeremy Knight, and her second Professor Eric Webster.'

'And she lives with the Professor now?'

'They're divorced,' Joanna replied succinctly.

'Just one more question. Who is the last person to have seen her this morning?'

'A teacher at Rutlands, the day school my half-sister goes to.'

★ ★ ★

Joanna hailed a taxi to take her to Emperor's Gate, where Arabella had bought a maisonette for herself and Louise when she'd left Eric. It was on the first and second floors of a house in the widest part of the cul-de-sac, overlooking a triangle of trees and grass surrounded by heavy wrought-iron railings. This was an old-fashioned, genteel part of Kensington, set apart from the commercial hustle and bustle of the Cromwell Road, and at first Joanna had been surprised by her mother's choice. Surely she'd have preferred a smart pad in Mayfair or a mews house in Knightsbridge?

But when she went to see it she realised the large Edwardian rooms, with their high ceilings and long windows, made a perfect setting for Arabella. Here, away from Louise's father, she could create a stylish backdrop for herself. Here she could entertain in the way she liked, informally but grandly, placing enormous silk cushions on the floor for guests to lounge on by the light of dozens of white candles, while waiters handed round succulent morsels and topped up everyone's champagne glasses.

Louise had finished her supper and was watching television when Joanna arrived.

'Hi, Jo!' she shouted in greeting, flinging herself affectionately into her half-sister's arms. 'I didn't know you were coming.'

Joanna hugged her back, seeing her mother as she must have looked when she'd been a child.

'Hello, Bunny. What have you been up to today?'

'The usual things.' Louise giggled. 'And I made a pussy cat for Mummy.'

'A pussy cat?'

Louise showed off her attempt at pottery. 'It's been fired,' she announced proudly.

Joanna cradled it carefully in the palm of her hand. 'It's beautiful. I love its fur.'

'Our teacher showed me how to make it look like hair. You make the marks in the clay with a pin.'

'That's really clever.'

Louise beamed at her praise.

'Where *is* Mummy?'

Joanna's heart contracted, dreading this moment, afraid she might convey her own anxiety to this trusting child.

'Mummy's really tied up with work,' she replied with as much conviction as she could muster.

'Can I phone her?'

'Well,' Joanna glanced at her wrist watch, 'the phones will have been switched over to the answering service at this hour, so there's no point. Never mind, I expect she'll be back much later, although you may be asleep by then.' God, how can I lie to her like this? she wondered. 'Why don't you go and have your bath? Mummy wants me to look out some papers for her.'

As soon as Louise left the room, Joanna hurried to the desk where Arabella kept her passport in a drawer. It was still there, valid until 2003. A quick search among her designer handbags in her bedroom closet failed to yield any credit cards though. But that was not surprising. Her mother never left home without them.

'Can you stay for a bit?' Louise asked, coming into the room glowing and scrubbed in her pyjamas.

24

Impulsively, Joanna put her arms around the little girl and kissed her warm cheek. 'I thought you'd never ask.'

'Would you like some coffee?' It could have been Arabella, the society hostess, talking.

'No, thanks, Bunny. I'm almost drowning in it as it is. By the way,' her voice was a study in casualness, 'did Mummy say if she was going anywhere special after she'd dropped you off this morning?'

Louise's face lit up. 'Yes. I wanted to go and see Daddy, too, but she said I had to go to school.'

Joanna looked at her, stunned. 'Your daddy?'

'Yes.' Louise gave her deliciously rich, throaty giggle. 'Not *your* daddy!'

Christ! Why hadn't Joanna thought of that before . . . except that it was so unlikely. 'But . . . why was she going to see him?' Arabella and Eric hadn't talked for months, except through their solicitors.

'About money, I think.' The child's expression was comically knowing. '*You* know. He doesn't give us enough. Mummy's always having to ask.'

Joanna sat in incredulous silence. It had never occurred to her that her mother might have gone to see Eric. She always got Melosa to make the arrangements when Louise spent a weekend with him, or else Eleanor.

'You're absolutely certain about this, sweetheart? Where was she going to see him?'

Louise looked surprised. 'At our old home, of course.'

'Are you sure?'

Louise nodded. 'Daddy never goes out in the morning. I told her to give him my love. I'm spending the weekend with him, you know,' she added in a grown-up voice.

'Right.' Joanna felt bewildered. So – if Arabella had visited Eric this morning, where had she been for the rest of the day?

'I'd better be going,' she said, rising.

'Can't you stay any longer, Jo?'

'I would really like to, Bunny, but there's still so much work to do for the show on Friday.'

Louise hopped from one foot to the other as she went with Joanna to the door. 'Mummy says I can see the show. Will there be lots and lots of people there? Are Mummy's clothes wonderful? Are they all glittery, like a Christmas tree?'

Joanna stooped to give her a kiss. 'They're dreamy.'

'Cool!'

After hurrying along Emperor's Gate, Joanna turned right into Cromwell Road. The bright amber light of a taxi for hire shone in the darkness. She hailed it, telling the driver to take her to Warwick Square.

Reaching for her mobile which always seemed to end up at the bottom of her capacious bag, she dialled Eric Webster's number.

He answered immediately.

'Eric? This is Joanna. I believe my mother came to see you this morning?'

His voice was brittle. 'Yes, she did.'

'What time was this?'

'What do you mean . . . what time? Why do you want to know?' He sounded outraged.

'Because she hasn't been in to work today. Louise told me she intended to drop in to see you on her way.'

'So? If you know that, why are you asking me?'

Joanna's lips tightened. Eric was being as obnoxious as usual. A mean-spirited man whom her mother had married for one reason only – his late aunt had left him a beautiful house, filled with antiques, and six million pounds. Memories of miserable school holidays when she'd lived with her mother and him came flooding back. He'd never liked Joanna or been kind to her and was always sarcastic about her school reports. Once she even overheard him telling her mother that it was a pity her daughter was stupid as well as plain.

She took a deep breath, confident enough to stand up to him now. 'Because I want to know if she told you where she was going after she left you.'

'Since when has Arabella ever told me what she was doing?'

'How did she seem this morning?'

'What the hell is this interrogation for?' he snapped furiously. 'Stop bothering me, Joanna. I have better things to do than talk to you.' There was a click. He'd put the phone down on her.

'Fuck you!' she swore angrily. She heard the taxi driver chuckling.

'Fallen out with your boyfriend, have you?' he asked in a friendly fashion, glancing over his shoulder through the opening in the glass screen.

'No, my boyfriend's a god! I was talking to my ex-stepfather,' she replied with a grin.

'A god, eh? Have you told him that?'

'Of course I have.'

'He's a lucky feller then. Wish my missus would call me a god!'

'She probably thinks it.'

'D'you reckon? Could have fooled me, mate. She'll be out playing Bingo while I'm driving around all night, trying to make a living.' But he sounded as if he didn't really mind.

Joanna felt warmed by how normal his life sounded. He was probably the only breadwinner. Wife with a weakness for a bit of a flutter. Children grown up now but maybe still living at home, giving their mum some of their wages towards the housekeeping. How safe, she thought. How wonderfully, comfortably safe.

Then she put through a call to the police station, and as DS Chambers had gone off duty, asked them to pass on the message that the last person to have seen Arabella Webster that day had not been the teacher at Rutlands but her ex-husband, Professor Eric Webster.

When Joanna heard Freddie's key in the lock, she rolled off the sofa, from where she'd been watching *Newsnight*, and ran to his arms as he stood in the doorway. He was tall and thickset with candid blue eyes and light brown curly hair. And the widest and most genuine smile she'd ever seen. She found herself enfolded in his arms in a bearhug but he was kissing her with the utmost tenderness, as if her face was fragile.

'Any news, babe?'

'Not really. Come and have something to eat. I've kept some Chicken Tandoori warm for you. I'm afraid it's only a takeaway but it's better than nothing.' Joanna led him by the hand into the kitchen.

'Have you eaten?' he asked, concerned by how pale she looked.

'I had something earlier,' she replied vaguely. 'I've spoken to the police again. I found Ma's passport in her flat, so she obviously hasn't gone abroad, which is something.'

He took his supper into the living room and, settling himself in the one big armchair, put his plate on his knees. Joanna switched off the television and poured herself a glass of Perrier then went back to her place on the sofa. Then she told him about Eric. 'He was rude as usual, and finally hung up on me,' she added.

'Eric seems to get off on being nasty,' Freddie observed.

'He's an old bugger. It's as simple as that.' Her voice was low from exhaustion and stress.

Freddie had his own opinion of the relationship between Arabella and Eric – gleaned from what Joanna had told him. He was in no doubt that if Arabella disliked her husband, he really hated her. And Jeremy had told him that Eric had often referred to Arabella's 'shallow, rackety lifestyle' so it was not surprising they didn't get on. Apart from the twenty-three-year age difference, the relationship between dry and intellectual Eric and sparkling and temperamental Arabella had always been explosive.

When Freddie had finished his Tandoori he put his plate on the floor and stretched his arms above his head, yawning.

'Jesus, I'm knackered. And if I'm tired, how must you be feeling, babe?'

'I'm too scared to feel tired.' For a moment she covered her face with her hands. 'Freddie, if she'd had an accident or been taken ill, we'd have heard by now, wouldn't we? So what can have happened? People don't just vanish into thin air.'

He folded his arms across his chest and tried to fight a feeling like a heavy weight on his head, pressing down on his eyelids. 'Let's look at all the possibilities, good and bad,' he suggested in a matter-of-fact voice. 'Has her car been found?'

'I don't think so.'

'Suppose she'd felt unwell while driving to work? What would she have done?'

Joanna frowned. 'Stopped the car, I imagine,' she said after a moment. 'Then used her mobile to get in touch with one of us.'

'And suppose she was too ill to?'

Her eyes widened in horror. 'You mean, unconscious? Oh, my God, and she's got high blood pressure! Suppose she's had a stroke? She may be sitting in her car some-where . . .' Joanna jumped to her feet. 'I've got to go and look for her. Can I borrow your car, Freddie?'

'I'll come with you.' He was already struggling into his overcoat, fishing in his pocket for his keys, making his way towards the front door of their flat. He was desperate to get to bed and sleep, but it was obvious Joanna was in a state.

They set off in Freddie's Volvo, making straight for Eric's home in Milner Street. If Arabella had gone to see him directly after dropping Louise off at school, this was at least a starting point. As they drove slowly past,

Joanna noticed all the curtains were drawn and there wasn't a chink of light showing anywhere. The house had a deserted, uncared for look, as if it missed its dazzling mistress who, even late at night, used to keep the curtains open and some lights on, revealing the glittering chandeliers in the main room.

'Why are we going all around the block?' Joanna asked. 'She'd have driven straight to the office when she left Eric.' They'd been spending several minutes circling the nearby streets, looking for the dark green Jaguar with its customised AD 1 UP number plates.

'I was thinking,' Freddie explained diffidently, 'that maybe she's still in her car. It's always possible the police haven't spotted it yet, I suppose.'

'Let's try Moore Street and Halsey Street as well, then,' Joanna said despairingly. It had started to rain, a cold drizzle that reflected the shadows on the shiny road and added to the desolation of the night.

It was now one o'clock in the morning, and there was an empty chill in the deserted streets.

'Did your mother take the same route to Pimlico Road every morning?'

'I don't know, but when she lived with Eric she'd head for Sloane Street, via Cadogan Square, then round Sloane Square, down Holbein Place and at the end turn left into Pimlico Road. On a good morning it would only take about six minutes.'

'Then let's do it.'

They drove slowly, straining to see a green Jaguar. At last they turned into Pimlico Road and drew up outside Arabella Designs. Joanna looked at the building and the

31

three dresses, spotlit now, in the window and it seemed a hundred years since this morning.

'I can't bear it,' she sobbed, bursting noisily into tears. Her mother was missing. Missing! The word hit her as if she'd been struck a physical blow. She was crushed. For a moment her vision was blurred and she felt as if she had pins and needles in her head. Somehow, seeing the premises closed for the night, silent and deserted as she'd never seen them before, brought the whole situation into razor-sharp reality. Freddie leaned over the gears and held her tight.

'What happens now, babe?'

She shook her head. 'I don't know.'

'Let's go home. There's nothing more we can do until the morning and you need some sleep.'

Two

Joanna was the first to arrive at the showroom. It was seven-forty-five. Switching on all the lights, she checked for e-mail and then went up to the empty workroom. It was eerily silent. The sewing machines were still; the irons switched off, their soft hiss of steam extinguished. Four rails of clothes stood at the far end. Each hanger had a number attached to assist the dressers with the running order of the show. Joanna checked them against the list in her hand. Midnight-blue lace encrusted with tiny mirrors . . . ivory silk overlaid with chiffon . . . black velvet with ostrich-feather trimmings . . . crimson pleated taffeta . . . emerald green grosgrain with a suede jacket . . .

She touched them all, lightly and reverently. This was the best collection her mother had ever created. Joanna's pulse quickened, partly in dread, partly from excitement. Such a big show was always going to be nerve-wracking but without Arabella it was going to be terrifying.

No sooner was she seated at her desk than Eleanor

33

arrived, anxiety and nervous tension obvious in every line of her face.

Without taking off her coat, she charged straight into Joanna's office and stood looking down at her, her hands shaking. 'Is there any sign of Arabella? I phoned her flat . . .'

'There's no sign of her,' Joanna replied bleakly. 'The police are circulating her description . . .'

'The *police*!' It was almost a shriek. 'We don't want it getting out that she's not around. Who told the police anything?'

'I *had* to tell the police, Eleanor. My father thought I ought to, and so did Freddie. Something awful may have happened to her.'

Eleanor stared at her. 'Yes, I know.'

Then she averted her face as if she did not want Joanna to see her expression. 'Well . . . I'll get on with everything,' she said, turning to go to her own office. 'There's still a lot to do.'

Joanna settled to check over the seating plan for the show. Three hundred people were expected; fashion press and celebrities had to have seats reserved for them in the front row, and the photographers and TV cameras had to be given a prime position. When Jeremy phoned her at nine-thirty, she felt as if she'd already put in a day's work.

'Hello, darling. Have you heard anything?'

'Nothing. The police are circulating her description but I'm scared, Dad. She's been missing twenty-four hours now.'

'What did they say?'

'They asked me if she was depressed. It was as if they were suggesting she might have committed suicide, but you don't believe that, do you?'

'Never in a million years,' Jeremy retorted with conviction. 'She's not the type. She's too self-absorbed.' He well remembered how, when she'd walked out on him, she'd taken everything she could lay her hands on. He'd been left with an empty flat, a stack of bills and a note saying she wanted to get on with the rest of her life. 'I really wouldn't worry on that score, Jo,' he added, a touch dryly. 'It's the last thing she'd do. Why don't you and Freddie come to supper tonight? Maybe we can put our heads together and come up with some ideas?'

'I'd like that.'

'I suppose . . .' He hesitated. Joanna had always rather put her mother on a pedestal, as most children do, and he'd never liked to disillusion her. Nevertheless a thought had occurred to him, knowing Arabella as he did.

'What?'

'It's just an idea, but is it possible she's gone off with someone?'

'Gone off with someone?' Joanna repeated incredulously. 'What? *This week?*'

'She was always impulsive, darling,' he said gently.

'Yes, but . . . Oh, I refuse to believe that. She's been working eighteen hours a day to get the collection finished. She hasn't had time.'

Surely she'd have suspected something if her mother had a new man in her life? But then Arabella had never discussed her personal life with her daughter.

★ ★ ★

The rest of the morning was spent on the phone. BBC TV News, Global TV, Reuters television division, Fox News Channel for the US, Sky News, Galaxy TV, and Brighter Pictures all wanted to confirm their coverage of the show. In terms of PR Joanna felt she'd done a fantastic job. But supposing Arabella was still missing?

Around noon the calls mysteriously stopped. Exhausted, Joanna made herself a cup of coffee and left a message on Freddie's mobile that he was expected for dinner at her father's house if he finished work on time.

A minute later Eleanor barged into her office, her angular face bleached white. She was holding a noon edition of the *Evening Standard*.

'Look at this!' she said agitatedly. She dropped the copy on to the desk, and pointed at the front page. 'If this is your doing then I think it's terribly bad publicity. It's the worst thing that could possibly happen.'

Stunned, Joanna gazed at the large photograph of Arabella taken at a party a few weeks before. Above it the headline screamed: TOP DESIGNER GOES MISSING, and in small type below: *on eve of show*.

'But how did they know?' she said in a shocked voice. It made a farce of the arrangements she'd been making with the press for the past two hours.

'If the police are circulating her description, the press are bound to pick it up,' Eleanor said worriedly. 'This could ruin the show now. What are the backers going to say? What about the interviews you've fixed for . . .'

Even before she finished her sentence, the phones started ringing again. They continued ringing for the next three hours. That a leading fashion designer should vanish on the eve of her show during the capital's main fashion event became the sensation of the afternoon. Joanna quickly learned that every TV station was carrying the story and every tabloid was working on a layout for the front page of tomorrow's edition.

It was then that she was hit by the most astounding thought. She dismissed it almost as soon as it struck her, but it kept recurring, filling her with confusion.

Was it possible . . . could it be possible that Arabella had staged her own disappearance as a publicity stunt?

Afternoon, Tuesday 14 September

'There's a policeman here to see you,' Eleanor announced. It was nearly four o'clock and Joanna felt stunned by lack of sleep the previous night, too much coffee, nothing to eat, and this extraordinary new thought that she couldn't get out of her mind.

'What's happened?' She leaped to her feet, suddenly alert with dread. They always sent the police round in person when there was bad news. Had they found Arabella? Was she . . .?

Her heart was racing as she ran down the stairs to the showroom. A young uniformed policeman was standing in the middle of the elegant feminine setting, looking lost and out of place.

'Miss Knight?' he asked tentatively.

Joanna nodded, dumb with fear. She stared up at him for what seemed like years and then he spoke.

'The station has radioed me to come and tell you that they've been trying to contact you for several hours but all your phone lines are busy. Will you ring them, please, and ask for Detective Inspector Walsh?'

So it wasn't the terrible news she'd feared. Or was it?

'Do you know why they want me to phone?'

'I'm afraid I can't say, Miss.' Or won't say? His bland expression gave nothing away.

'Thank you,' she said automatically. Back in her office again she tapped out the number of the police station.

'You wanted to get hold of me?' Joanna asked, having introduced herself when she'd got through.

DI Walsh sounded calm and controlled. 'Yes, Miss Knight, we did. Can you let us have any personal papers, bank statements, etc., that your mother may have kept in her flat?'

'Yes, all right. Shall I bring what I can find to the station?'

'Yes, please. Can you also see if she took her cheque book with her?'

'Yes, I will. Have you any news at all about her?'

'It's too soon to say but we are covering every eventuality,' Walsh replied evenly.

'You haven't found her car?' Joanna asked, desperation creeping into her voice.

'Not so far.'

There was nothing more to say. Feeling sick, she promised to get back to him and then she hung up.

'What's happening?' Eleanor asked, coming into her office. 'What do the police think could have happened? Oh, my God, this is absolutely terrible. I'm so worried.'

'I just have to go to Arabella's flat to check on a few things,' Joanna said shortly. 'I won't be long.'

'Don't worry about hurrying back. I've had a talk with the girls in the workroom and everything's under control.'

As the taxi hurtled Joanna in the direction of Emperor's Gate, she tried to think calmly of all the reasons why Arabella might have gone away. To get urgently needed extra fabric? Trimmings from a special source? It didn't make sense.

Melosa greeted her anxiously. 'Is your mother back?'

'I'm afraid not, Melosa. I suppose you don't know if she had any plans to go on a trip?'

The housekeeper shook her head, wringing her hands. 'I no idea. Louise, she keep asking for Mummy. "Where Mummy?" she say this morning. I take her to school. I fetch her soon. "Where Mummy?" she want to know.'

Joanna nodded her understanding. 'The police are looking for her and I hope there'll be some news soon.'

As she spoke she walked into the cool elegant drawing room with its long windows leading on to the balcony, and original Edwardian fireplace. Arabella had decorated it with rich terracotta wallpaper and white linen soft furnishings. The flowers she'd arranged in crystal vases over the weekend were still fresh, filling the room with their sweet fragrance. Then Joanna remembered today was only Tuesday. It might seem like weeks since her mother had disappeared but in reality it was only yesterday morning.

Seating herself at the pretty escritoire which stood

between the windows, she started going through the pigeon holes and drawers, knowing Arabella kept all her personal papers here. She felt uneasy going through her mother's things. It was like spying. When she came across bank statements, used paying-in and cheque books, letters from Arabella's friends, she bundled them into an envelope for Walsh, not liking to read them herself. They were private and did not concern her. Next she came to Arabella's Christmas card list, a batch of receipts, a collection of blank greetings cards, old diaries, snapshots taken on holiday, and a book marked 'Entertaining'. In this she had listed the dates of the various parties she'd given, who was there, what she gave them to eat and drink, and at the bottom what she'd worn for the occasion. Joanna smiled. How typical of her mother not to want guests to see her in the same dress twice.

With a pang she realised how achingly she was missing her, although Arabella could be the most infuriating person on earth. There had been moments when Joanna fervently wished she'd never agreed to work in the company, and moments when the loss of a career as a painter had rankled deeply. She'd always be 'Arabella's daughter' now; never a person in her own right. Sometimes these love-hate feelings left her confused but at this moment she was quite clear about how she felt. She missed her mother and she desperately wanted her back.

She thought she heard a noise and turned in her chair with a chill feeling she was being watched. But there was no one there. Melosa had gone to collect Louise and she was alone in the flat.

When she emptied the desk, pushing everything into a big plastic bag, she moved on to where Arabella kept her business files, just in case there was anything personal among them. These were kept in a drop-in filing system which had been fitted inside an antique black lacquer Chinese chest. It stood to one side of the fireplace with a table lamp and several ornaments on top.

Joanna lifted the brass catch of the lid. Arabella was always losing things so it was never locked. She surveyed all her mother's business papers, which for some reason she preferred to keep at home. Everything was neatly organised under various headings. Finding nothing of a personal nature, she closed the lid again, and for a morbid moment felt as if she were closing the lid of a coffin. Telling herself not to be so fanciful, she scribbled a hurried note for Melosa and left, anxious to get away from the desolate emptiness of a home that was usually filled with light and laughter.

At the police station she handed everything to DI Walsh. 'Thank you. We'll let you know if we hear anything,' he said. 'Try not to worry.'

Outside in the street Joanna hailed a taxi and then switched on her phone, hit by the bleak awfulness of the situation. She tapped the recall button for Freddie's number. He was walking back from the Law Courts to Chambers in Bedford Row.

'What's happening, babe?'

'I've been to Ma's flat, collecting her personal papers for the police,' Joanna said, then burst into tears. 'Freddie, I'm going mad with worry. She's all over the newspapers. The police don't know *anything*. Where in God's name is she?'

'Try to stay calm. I'm sure there must be a perfectly good explanation. What can have happened to her between Kensington and Pimlico, for God's sake? And during the rush hour, too, when there are hundreds of people about who would have seen something? She must be somewhere, Jo.'

The taxi was drawing up outside Arabella Designs. A cluster of press photographers was hanging around the entrance.

'I've got to go, Freddie. I'm arriving at the showroom and it looks as if it's under siege by reporters. I'll talk to you later, OK?'

As Joanna stepped out of the cab the paparazzi surged forward en masse, blinding her with their flashlights and jabbering loudly.

'Any news of Arabella, love?'

'Have you heard anything?'

'Any idea where she's gone?'

'Look this way, love.'

'How serious is it?'

Cameras were thrust in her face. A buzz of voices assaulted her ears. She dashed across the pavement, head down, and put out her hand to push open the door of the showroom. It was locked.

'Fuck!' she said under her breath, rapping on the glass with her knuckles.

The photographers closed in around her threateningly. She felt trapped. She banged again, louder this time. Why was the fucking door locked? It never was normally.

Eleanor appeared and began undoing the bolts as if there was all the time in the world. Joanna pressed her hand against the brass handle, the door suddenly flew open and she almost fell into the showroom.

Eleanor slammed the door shut behind her, ramming home the bolts again. 'I had to lock it,' she said defiantly, 'otherwise I'd have had those dreadful people crawling all over the place.'

'You could have called my mobile to warn me,' Joanna snapped back. She was dangerously near breaking point. That rampaging mob of press men had shaken her badly.

There was worse to come. She'd no sooner got up to her office than Rosie tapped on the door, looking hot and bothered.

'I don't want to make trouble, Joanna,' she said in a low voice, 'but I won't stand for Eleanor coming into the workroom and telling everyone what to do. We're all worried about Arabella's disappearance, and we do realise the collection has to be finished in time. But if she goes on and on, nagging the girls, there'll be trouble. She's got no business to be in the workroom at all.'

Joanna looked at her sympathetically. 'What would you like me to do, Rosie?'

'Can you come and give them a bit of encouragement? Reassurance, like. They're all fond of you and it will calm them down a bit if you have a word.'

'Yes, of course. I'll come now,' Joanna replied, wondering what on earth she was supposed to say. Climbing up the stairs after Rosie, they nearly bumped into Eleanor on her way down.

'Everything's running smoothly,' she announced importantly.

Joanna pretended she hadn't heard. As she entered the busy workroom, twenty women stopped what they were doing and looked at her warily. They sat, in white overalls, at long tables covered in protective white sheeting to keep the garments clean. They varied in age from nineteen to sixty, and the older ones she'd known since she was a child. She faced them squarely now, a tremulous, almost tearful smile on her face. Rosie stood to one side and then Joanna noticed Eleanor sidling back into the room, too.

'I just want to say . . .' she began falteringly '. . . we're all under a lot of stress at the moment and I'm so grateful to you for working hard to get the collection finished. I don't know what's happened to my mother but I hope we shall have some news soon. The police are doing everything they can. Meanwhile it's obvious the show must go on, it's . . . it's what she would want.' Her throat clogged and for a moment she couldn't continue.

'What she's trying to say,' Eleanor stepped forward with brisk assertiveness, 'is that we've all got to pull our weight. The clothes *must* be ready by Thursday and that may mean some of us have to stay late. I suggest that Rosie makes a list of exactly what needs to be done and then we can prioritise the work so that . . .'

Rosie was glaring angrily at her. 'Excuse me, but I don't think there's any need for you to translate what Joanna just said. Go on, love,' she added, nodding to Joanna who had flushed crimson.

She bit her lip and continued earnestly: 'I just wanted

to thank you all. I know it's going to be a fantastic show, and I know how grateful Arabella always is for how hard you all work. I hope she'll be here on Friday night – it's what we all hope. But in the meantime . . . thank you so much.'

One or two of the workers wiped away emotional tears, remembering her when she'd been a solemn little girl with plaits, very much in awe of her dazzling mother. How dignified and mature beyond her years she seemed now. The younger ones looked at her with grins of approval, thinking she was a bit of all right.

Eleanor marched back into her office, hurt that her efforts to represent Arabella had been rebuffed.

'Thanks, love,' Rosie whispered to Joanna, patting her arm.

DI Walsh called DS Chambers into his office at five o'clock.

'We're drawing a blank on the disappearance of Arabella Webster,' he announced. 'There's obviously more than meets the eye to this case. I'm going to authorise a national appeal to encourage members of the public to come forward if they have any information. We'll put up posters with her photograph everywhere, and have it announced on TV and radio. We're also going to carry out over a hundred interviews with members of her staff, her friends, and people in her immediate circle. She's a big cheese in the fashion world. Seems to know everyone, from hairdressers and photographers to journalists and models. I'll want your assistance on this one, Chambers. We're going to have to go through every aspect of her life with a fine-toothed comb.'

For the first time since Walsh had known him, Chambers' face seemed to light up.

'Very good, sir. That should be interesting.'

'It'll certainly be that,' Walsh rejoined dryly. He'd already got an inkling of what Arabella Webster was really like.

Joanna fetched a bottle of Evian from the fridge in the galley kitchen and took it into her office. The clear purity of the chilled water slid down her throat, soothing and calming. It was not knowing what had happened to her mother that was driving her crazy. She glanced at her watch. In a few minutes it would be time to leave.

Then her door swung open and Eleanor stood there, an almost wild look on her face.

'I'd appreciate it if you didn't interfere in the running of the business,' she stormed, tears in her eyes. 'You're only here because . . . well, your mother was kind enough to give you a job. But I've been here for twelve years and I've known her for much longer. You must let me decide how the workroom girls are to be handled. You undermined my authority just now.'

Joanna recoiled, shocked by the other woman's open hostility. She'd never liked Eleanor, not even when she'd been ten and Arabella had taken her on, explaining that she was an 'old school friend'. The woman's enmity had shown itself even then, as if she'd been jealous of the child. Now it was undisguised and raw.

'I certainly didn't mean to do that, Eleanor,' Joanna said peaceably, 'but the last thing we need right now is trouble in the workroom. Rosie is actually in charge there and I think we must leave it to her.'

'But your mother isn't here to gee them up,' Eleanor retorted, 'and they're not going to have everything finished in time for the show unless they get on with it.' She was, Joanna noticed, bordering on the hysterical.

'They are, Eleanor. They've never let us down yet.'

'But let me just say, I don't think Rosie *is* getting the best out of them. She's . . .'

'She's fine.' Joanna was determined to appear calm even though she felt unnerved by this outburst.

The tears were rolling down Eleanor's cheeks now and she was slapping her forehead and waving her arms about in frustration and anger.

'But *listen*, Joanna, it's *vital* . . .' Then she turned away with a muttered oath and slammed the door behind her. Joanna could hear her feet clumping noisily across the landing, and then there was another bang as she slammed her own office door.

Joanna drank Evian straight from the bottle and subsided into her chair. What the hell had come over Eleanor? Did she know more about Arabella's disappearance than she was letting on? Surely not! And yet . . . She seized the phone and tapped in her father's number. It was answered immediately.

'I thought it might be you,' Jeremy told her. 'Any news, darling?'

'Nothing really. I just rang to say I'm going to drop in and see Louise on my way over to you this evening. Melosa says she's really missing Ma, so I thought I'd cheer her up.'

'Poor child. You're going to have to . . .' Jeremy stopped. There'd be time enough to make those arrangements later. 'Anyway, we'll see you later on, Jo. Can Freddie make it?'

'He certainly hopes to.'

'Great. 'Bye, darling.'

'Joanna!' Louise flung herself at her half-sister as if she hadn't seen her for months. Then she clung to Joanna's hand, her little face a frozen mask of misery. 'Where's Mummy? Everyone at school said she wouldn't be coming back.'

'Oh, sweetheart.' Joanna led her to the living-room sofa and, drawing the child down beside her, wrapped her arms around her.

'Pay no attention to what people say. You know, and I know, that Mummy would never run away and leave us.' She looked earnestly into large blue eyes ringed with sooty lashes. Arabella's eyes. 'Mummy loves you very, very much . . .'

'And you, too!'

Joanna hugged her tighter, her throat suddenly constricting. 'Yes, and me too, darling. So we've got to be brave until she returns. This is a very big week for her and I'm sure she's only dashed off to get more fabric or some special feathers or . . .'

'But not fur.'

'No. Not fur. Unless it's fake fur.'

Louise nodded approvingly. She looked a little less tense. 'But why can't the police find out where she is? She can't have gone far. Melosa says they'll put up pictures of Mummy in the underground.'

Joanna frowned, damning Melosa for her big mouth. And for getting the wrong end of the stick. She didn't want Louise to know the full seriousness of the situation and blamed herself now for not warning the house-keeper.

'Don't pay any attention to what Melosa or anyone else says.'

'I tried to phone Daddy when I got back from school but there was no answer. I left a message on his machine.'

'I expect he's busy lecturing.'

'I hope Mummy comes back before I spend the weekend with him. I don't know what clothes to take.'

'I can help you, darling. Have you had supper?'

Louise nodded. 'Can you stay the night?' Her voice was thin and wobbly.

'Would you like me to?'

Louise's mouth quivered. 'Yes. I don't like being here with just Melosa.'

'Then I'll stay. Is it OK if I go and have a quick supper with my daddy first and then come back?'

Relief washed over the child's face and she visibly relaxed. Then she nodded vigorously. 'Can Freddie come for the night, too?'

Joanna grinned. 'We can't do without Freddie, can we? OK, I'll tell Melosa we're coming back after supper.'

'You can borrow one of Mummy's nighties,' Louise said, pink with pleasure.

There was a moment's silence, broken by Joanna saying breezily: 'Thanks, sweetheart, but I'll have to go home to get my toothbrush anyway.'

The idea of wearing her mother's nightdress had suddenly caused a saying to spring into her head: 'Dead men's shoes'.

In Cromwell Road she hailed the first taxi she saw. 'Portsea Place, near Marble Arch, please,' she told the driver.

Victoria Knight opened the front door and immediately embraced her stepdaughter. 'Dear girl,' she said warmly. 'I'm so sorry about all this. What a terrible time you're having. Come in. I expect you could do with a strong drink.' She led the way down a flight of dark winding stairs to the basement kitchen of the little terraced house. Her ample motherly figure was encased in a beige wraparound skirt and a ribbed white tee-shirt. Her greying hair was bundled up on top of her head and her face, its features etched with deep laughter lines, was devoid of make-up. If Jeremy had deliberately decided to marry a woman who was the exact opposite of Arabella he couldn't have chosen better.

They found him pouring out glasses of wine at the kitchen table.

'Jo, my darling!' He hugged her with one arm and handed her a glass with the other. 'Get this down you,' he said, seeing how emotional she was. Then tenderly he guided her into a kitchen chair.

She sipped the chilled white wine and leaned her elbows on the table. 'It's at moments like this that I wish I still smoked,' she said wryly. But already she felt better, safer, in this unpretentious home.

Jeremy and Victoria were the epitome of a comfortable, homely couple who enjoyed the simple things in life. With no children of their own, they had an adored Border Terrier called Caspar, shared the cooking, listened to jazz music and read widely. Joanna had spent a lot of time during her school holidays with them, and it was the only real experience of family life she'd ever known. She smiled at her father as he settled his rotund figure into a chair on the opposite side of the table, and noticed that even when he was serious, his florid face and grey eyes seemed to radiate good humour.

'Tell us what's happening?' Victoria urged gently as she set bowls of nuts and olives on the table.

'I don't know where to start.' Joanna took another sip and Jeremy immediately reached over the table and topped up her glass. 'Mummy has completely vanished,' she continued, 'without trace. There's no sign of her car, either. Nothing. She can't have gone abroad because I've found her passport. The last person to see her was Eric, early yesterday morning. He says she left his house after fifteen minutes and I can only suppose she got into her car to come on to work. But then what? It's an absolute nightmare. Louise is asking for her all the time, and I've promised I'll stay with her tonight. I've had trouble with Eleanor, who's been upsetting Rosie. And as for the media!' She ran her fingers through her short hair so that it stuck out in tufts. 'It's a *bugger*!' she added vehemently.

'They've been on to us,' Jeremy said grimly.

'Who?'

'The press, wanting to know if I'd seen her recently. Whether we were still on good terms. What did I think had happened? God, they're a bunch of morons.'

Joanna shrugged. 'The irony is I've been cultivating them all like mad for months to get maximum publicity for the show, and now I'm trying to get them to leave me alone.'

'Is there anything at all we can do to help?' Victoria asked.

'You only have to ask,' Jeremy added.

Joanna smiled at them, deeply touched. 'That's so kind of you. I think everything's under control. What's today . . . Tuesday? God, I'm losing track of time. There's still tomorrow and Thursday and the show's not until Friday. I'm worried about Louise, though. She's due at Eric's on Friday evening for the weekend and Melosa is due to have time off and I don't know how I'm going to . . .'

'No problem, dear girl,' Victoria cut in. 'We can look after her. Why doesn't she come and stay with us tomorrow? That would leave you free for the rest of the week, and we can take her round to Eric's on Friday evening.'

Joanna felt a great weight lifted from her shoulders. 'Would you really?' Louise was very fond of Jeremy and Victoria and even fonder of Caspar. She'd be very happy spending a few days with them.

'That would be perfect for another reason,' Joanna continued. 'The other children at school are frightening her with tales of mothers who disappear and never come back. I'll phone the headmistress and tell her I'm keeping Louise at home until . . . until . . .' Her voice broke and sudden tears spilled down her cheeks. She covered her face with her hands.

Jeremy rose. 'Come here, my sweetheart.' He strode round the table and pulled her into his arms. He rocked her as if she was still a child. 'You'll be all right,' he kept saying softly. 'You'll be all right.'

As she lay in bed with Freddie later that night in the spare room of Arabella's flat, Joanna remembered her father's words. He'd said she'd be all right. But he hadn't mentioned Arabella.

Three

AGAINST A BACKGROUND OF TWO BROKEN MARRIAGES AND A METEORIC RISE TO FAME . . .

The next morning the sensation of Arabella's disappearance was on the front pages of all the tabloids. Pictures of her taken at glitzy parties, looking stunning in one of her own designs, smiled out at millions of readers as they sat in trains or on buses on the way to work.

When Joanna arrived at work the phones were already ringing. They kept on ringing all day. Concerned clients, in shocked society voices, expressed shock and asked what was going to happen. Media people, in a variety of accents, demanded quotable sound bites and kept asking Joanna what she thought might have happened.

At noon Rosie came downstairs from the workroom. She'd obviously been weeping. 'It looks bad, doesn't it?' she said mournfully, coming into Joanna's office and pointing to the stack of newspapers on the desk.

'I know,' she admitted. 'I wish they hadn't sensation-alised it all, though. It makes it seem much worse than it probably is.'

Rosie shook her head. 'She's been missing for three days now. It just isn't like her.'

That was what everyone was saying. Arabella was so reliable. You could set your clock by her. She was never late for anything. Joanna found these clichéd remarks deeply depressing. Especially as she knew they were true.

Rosie broke into her thoughts. 'You'll be representing her at the show, won't you?'

Joanna looked startled. 'I haven't thought about it.'

'You must, lovey. If you don't, Eleanor will be pushing herself forward.'

'But . . . does anyone have to represent Ma? And what would I have to do?'

Seeing Joanna's shy face filled with dismay reminded Rosie of how she'd always been in her mother's shadow up to now, too scared to assert herself. 'What Arabella would be doing if she was here. You've already made a start by talking to the girls yesterday. You just need to lead the band, that's all.'

'*All?*'

Rosie nodded, round face pink and earnest. She pointed her finger up to the workroom above.

'I'm telling you, love, those girls won't be ruled by Eleanor. I've never said it before because it wasn't my place and your ma won't have a word said against her, but the girls and I can't stand her. If she starts interfering on Friday, there'll be trouble. You've got to take control of the show. We're all behind you, y'know. Every one of us.

We think you're a little wonder, with your ma missing and all, still here at work like the rest of us.' Tears glistened in the deep wrinkles around her eyes.

'I'll try and do my best,' Joanna said in a small voice. The responsibility of taking her mother's place only added to the burden she was already under. Too many people were already depending on the success of this show, including the backers, and now on her.

'I know you will, love,' Rosie said softly. 'You're a real little trouper, that's for sure.'

'Joanna, I was thinking . . .'

They spun round. Eleanor was standing in the doorway, looking agitated. Joanna wondered how much she'd overheard.

'Yes, Eleanor?'

'Basically, we need to have absolutely everything over in the marquee by early tomorrow evening.'

Joanna frowned, but she was sure of her facts. 'Pick-up time is seven o'clock Friday morning . . .'

'That won't be soon enough,' Eleanor replied fretfully. 'Can I just say . . .'

Rosie stuck her hands on her hips, glaring angrily. 'We're not *allowed* into the marquee until the day of our show. You know that, Eleanor. We've all been told that from the beginning. Anyway, everything's arranged.'

'But can I point out . . .' She was almost bursting to say her piece.

'Rosie's right,' Joanna confirmed in her quiet way. 'Arabella said we had to adhere to the tight schedule set by the organisers because we have to fit in with all the other designers who are showing.'

Eleanor let out a long breath of frustration and stomped off. Rosie looked at Joanna with raised eyebrows, and Joanna nodded slowly. Rosie was right. She'd have to take charge. For some reason Eleanor was taking Arabella's disappearance worse than anyone.

Evening, Wednesday 15 September

With Louise happily tucked up in Jeremy and Victoria's spare room, Caspar sleeping at the foot of the bed, Joanna kissed her goodnight and then after thanking Jeremy and Victoria for looking after her half-sister, returned to her own home. This was a three-roomed attic flat in Warwick Square which she'd shared with three girlfriends before Freddie had moved in with her, and she loved its airy height, level with the tree tops in the central gardens.

Stacks of dirty dishes, an unmade bed, damp towels abandoned on the bathroom floor, and dead flowers in a vase on the living-room table made her realise she hadn't had time to do anything here since Arabella had vanished. She found keeping the flat nice, or 'nesting' as Freddie teasingly called it, soothing and therapeutic. He was going to be home late again tonight so methodically and to a background of music she washed up, mopped the kitchen floor and threw out the rubbish, put clean white sheets on the bed, tidied the bathroom, and finally dusted and hoovered around. She found it was as good as a workout.

Hot and sweaty, she slipped into a scented bath,

warmed herself a tin of tomato soup, as Freddie had said he'd grab himself something to eat, and then slid between the fresh sheets with a book, to await his return. The mundane physical activities of the evening had helped to calm her down.

It was nearly eleven o'clock when she heard his key in the lock. 'Hi-ya, babe!' he said, coming straight into the bedroom. He dropped heavily on to the side of the bed then leaned forward, pressing his weight against her chest and kissing her firmly on the lips.

'Hi,' she replied softly. 'Are you OK? You have eaten, haven't you?'

He sat back, grinning. 'I had a giant takeaway pizza and a gallon of coffee and now I'm buzzing like a hive of bees.' He'd phoned earlier in the evening to see if there was any news, but nevertheless asked her again.

She shook her head. 'Nothing. The police station must be sick of the sound of my voice. I ring them practically every hour and it's always the same. "Nothing to report, I'm afraid, Miss." ' She leaned back against the pillows and closed her eyes for a moment. 'I wish I could wake up and find the whole thing had been a hideous nightmare.'

He rose and started taking off the layers of clothes he wore to guard against the icy conditions of the Law Courts, especially on a Monday when the heating had been turned off for the weekend.

'What's morale like at work, babe?'

'Eleanor's being manic but what's new?'

'Why is she kept on, for God's sake?'

'I've no idea. Ma says she's invaluable. She makes the

clients' appointments and they seem to like her, probably because she fawns all over them. She does the accounts and deals with the salaries. She pays the bills and writes letters. Ma will never get rid of her.'

He glanced up sharply but Joanna's face was averted and he couldn't see the expression in her eyes. He had his own private opinion about what had happened to Arabella. But from the way she was speaking of her mother in the present tense, Joanna obviously didn't share it.

'Things any competent girl of twenty could do,' he remarked lightly, flinging his shirt into the corner. 'How long has she been with the company?'

'Ages. They were at school together. I can't imagine their ever being friends, though. They're so different.'

'Eleanor hasn't been married, has she?' His black socks and then his underpants followed his shirt.

'No. She's never had a boyfriend, either.'

Freddie smiled quizzically. 'A touch of the Mrs Danvers, perhaps?'

'I've never thought about it,' said Joanna in surprise. 'I've always looked upon her as a devoted employee. Though not devoted to me as I've discovered,' she added dryly.

He disappeared through the door and she could hear sounds of splashing and the hiss of the shower.

'How is the case going?' she shouted.

'Relentlessly,' he shouted back. 'I'll be in court for at least another couple of weeks.'

'Poor you.'

'At least we've got the weekend coming up.'

Joanna rolled on to her back and thought about the weekend. The show would be over. The pressure at work would lessen. Her father had said Louise could go back to stay with them for as long as she liked, after her visit to Eric. But there'd be no respite for Joanna unless there was news of Arabella. The torment would continue. The tension would mount. She was locked in purgatory and there was no escape.

The splashing stopped and Freddie emerged from the bathroom, smelling of soap and toothpaste. Joanna smiled at him, loving him, grateful to him, dependent on him as she'd never been before.

His candid blue eyes impaled her with their intensity. In the silence of their bedroom the charged air was hot and oppressive.

Sharp desire suddenly tugged deep inside her, almost taking her breath away. 'Oh, Freddie, I love you . . .' she said, reaching out for him.

'Move over, babe.'

He slid into bed beside her. His lips brushed her mouth. His legs, as he wrapped them around hers, were strong and muscular. He started kissing her deeply, hungrily, and in moments she'd lost her sense of self, wanting only to be a part of him. Then he entered her swiftly, like a shaft of golden light in an otherwise grey landscape, and she felt complete.

Night, Wednesday 15 September

'What a long journey, wasn't it? Or so it seemed. It must have seemed long for you, too, and tiring . . .

'That's all behind us, though. We're here and we're safe. No one will ever part us again. I'd rather die . . . d'you know that? I mean it. I'd rather die than be parted from you again . . .

'But why am I talking in this depressing way? It's never going to happen. I'm tired, I suppose. That's why I sound a bit down.

'Ha! A bit like looking forward to Christmas and all the presents . . . and then when it happens it's a sort of anti-climax . . .

'Not that having you here with me is an anti-climax. Far from it! Don't get me wrong. It's tiredness, that's all. After the initial euphoria, I'm bound to be tired.

'You've nothing to fear, you know. You do realise that, don't you? I'm going to look after you from now on . . . as you've never been looked after before. I'll bring you flowers every day . . . do you like flowers? I knew you would. D'you like music, too? I love music as long as it isn't sad. Nothing in the minor key is for me, thank you very much. Starts me feeling miserable right away . . .

'They say music is the food of love. D'you believe that? I'm not so sure. I think poetry might be. I think I'll get a book of poems that we can read together . . .'

Morning, Friday 17 September

'All I have to do is make sure the running order is correct and that each model is put into the right outfit,' Joanna kept repeating to herself, as she arrived at the showroom at six o'clock on Friday morning. Rosie was already there, checking the numbers attached to each plastic-shrouded garment. Shoes and hats were in boxes. The jewellery, loaned by Cartier, would be taken directly to the marquee just before the show, by security guards who would stay to watch over it.

Then Eleanor appeared, breathless and hyper, her movements jerky with nervous tension. 'Is everything ready? Oh, I wish to God Arabella was here.'

'We're all ready,' Joanna replied calmly. 'Rosie is doing a final check.'

Eleanor ignored her. 'Rosie, are you sure you've packed the feathered wraps?' She looked wildly around the workroom. 'They were hanging with the evening dresses yesterday.'

Rosie stood staring challengingly at her. 'Everything's packed. Numbered. Listed. We have fifty copies of the list. All we need now are the models and jewellery. All right?'

Eleanor flushed, glancing at Joanna as if seeking support, but she was checking her own boxes of press releases and programmes for the invited audience. She'd often assisted at Arabella's intimate shows, held in the cosy showroom downstairs, with clients sitting on little gilt chairs hired for the occasion. This was going to be different. Today's show, held in the giant marquee erected for the occasion, would be neither intimate nor cosy. Arabella had sent Joanna to watch a rival's show the previous year, not wanting to appear herself because it would look like snooping. It had been a revelation. She'd come away impressed and intimidated by the sheer scale of the slick and professional production. Now she knew what to expect.

In a space like a dark aircraft hangar, there'd be a catwalk 140 metres long, stretching like a runway down the middle, white and shiny, high and narrow, lit by dozens of dazzling spotlights suspended from an overhead network of iron girders. Hundreds of chairs would be lined up in rows, flanking the sides and one end of the runway, each with a much-coveted Reserved ticket on the seat. Especially in the front row. That was reserved for the top VIPs such as fashion editors from the smarter magazines and newspapers and the hottest names on the current celebrity list; they would expect to be as much photographed as the models.

It would also be hot and stuffy. The crowds, jammed in together with only standing room at the back for some, would be in a fever of excitement. The music would be deafening and funky. And then the show would start. Models with heavily painted expressionless faces and strange hairstyles would move with the liquid precision of water being poured into a glass. They could have been programmed by remote control so perfect were their move-ments. Searing the air with strobe-light effects, dozens of flash bulbs would click with blinding brilliance. Then the TV cameras, with their own lights blazing, would zoom in on a particularly outrageous garment, focusing on the model's crotch or breasts. Meanwhile the fashion press would be scribbling frantically, devouring the garments with their eyes, like starving refugees sighting bread.

That was out front. What sort of hellish chaos reigned back stage? Joanna wondered. Within a couple of hours she'd find out. And there'd be no Arabella to coax, calm and control everyone.

Joanna rushed to lock herself in the loo, trying to stem the flow of tears, part terror, part grief, that were suddenly overwhelming her. A small child inside her was crying: 'Mummy, where are you? Please be here, today. Please.' While the adult was saying: 'Pull yourself together, for God's sake. You're the PR of Arabella Designs. You *can't* fall apart.'

She blew her nose, splashed her face with cold water and ran a comb through her hair. Loud rapping on the loo door startled her.

Eleanor shouted, 'Joanna? Are you in there? The van's arrived to pick up everything.' The day which should have been a triumph for Arabella had begun.

'Make-up, Joanna?' asked a girl in a pink overall. She was carrying what looked like a mechanic's tool box. There was ten minutes to go before the show started and the atmosphere of nervous anticipation was almost tangible. All the models had been painted, powdered, had glitter sprinkled across their eyelids, and deep plum lipstick applied to their mouths. A team of hair stylists had then moved in to curl and crimp, twist, pleat, braid and lacquer the girls' hair. Now they were getting into the first outfits to be shown. The right shoes. The right jewellery and accessories.

Out front, several hundred people were crammed into the hot, perfume-laden air of the marquee, greeting each other loudly and flapping their programmes about. In a seat, right by the catwalk, Louise sat spellbound in her school uniform, eyes as round as an owl's taking in everything.

Joanna was unnerved to find herself suddenly the centre of attention.

'Make-up?' she echoed, frowning stupidly.

'You're representing Arabella, aren't you?' the girl in the overalls asked. 'Rosie told us you were her daughter, and as she's not here, you'll have to go on at the end, won't you?'

Joanna recoiled, appalled. 'Oh, no! I couldn't possibly do that. I'm only the PR for the company.'

'Everyone's expecting you to go on,' the girl said confidently, pushing her into a chair, brushing her short hair back from her face and giving it a quick spray of lacquer. Then she started pressing foundation on to Joanna's face with a small triangular-shaped sponge.

'But who . . .?' Joanna felt really panicked now. It was bad enough having to ensure the show went smoothly, but to go on to the catwalk at the end, surrounded by all those tall, thin, long-legged beauties!

'I can't,' she said in a small voice.

'Yes, you can and you must,' said a warm and friendly voice in her ear. Rosie was smiling gently down at her. 'You must do it. For Arabella's sake.' Seeing Joanna was about to get emotional, she added sternly: 'What's she going to say when she gets back if you don't do it proper, like?'

It did the trick. Joanna nodded resolutely. 'Not too much make-up, though,' she told the girl. She was already wearing a black crêpe trouser suit designed by Arabella.

'Can anyone lend me a pair of earrings?' Her mother had always said they were essential, especially with short hair.

A pair of gilt clips were produced from the box of costume jewellery. The finishing touches were made to her face: 'Just a *little* blusher,' the make-up girl begged.

Joanna looked at herself in a mirror, ready for the part she must play. Nevertheless, and in spite of her head telling her not to be a fool, her heart kept lurching as she looked around, half hoping Arabella would suddenly emerge from between the rails of clothes, laughing and saying: 'Of course I'm back, darling.'

Someone thrust a large white envelope into her hand. She ripped it open with shaking hands. It was a Good Luck card, signed by all the girls in the workroom.

The show was starting. The music was blaring out. The twelve models stood ready in the wings for their first entrance. Joanna moved over to them, folding the card and tucking it into her pocket. No time to think. No time to get emotional. This was the moment of calm before the storm broke. Months of planning and work were about to blossom into fruition. Everything was ready for the off. The only person missing was Arabella.

It all passed in a mad blur of clothes being ripped off, shoes kicked away, more clothes pulled over heads, numbers from the running order yelled, millions of pounds worth of jewellery clasped round necks and wrists, false hair pieces pinned on, and hats jammed down to eyebrow level. Armed guards kept watch. Make-up artists hovered, ready to do running repairs. Models screamed at dressers. Dressers shrieked at Eleanor as she kept getting in the way. Sometimes the applause drowned the music and sometimes the music drowned the applause, in a sunburst of ever-changing lighting effects.

Without thinking, Joanna found herself doing exactly what Arabella had always done. She checked each model before she went on. Adjusting a collar a millimetre. Tweaking a hat a fraction forward. Straightening a skirt. Lifting a train so the fabric flowed like a waterfall. And then finally, smiling encouragingly at each girl and murmuring: 'Beautiful . . . you look gorgeous . . . fantastic . . .' so that the model swept on to the runway brimming with confidence.

Eleanor watched Joanna, as she had been doing all day, with undisguised annoyance. Rosie and the dressers kept elbowing her aside as if they were protecting Joanna, their future Queen Bee, and it made her blood boil with jealousy.

The finale was a bridal dress designed on the lines of a slim Grecian robe, cleverly draped and moulded to the body with fine silver cord. The applause reached a crescendo, crashing like Atlantic rollers in wave after wave. Then the models, laughing and jostling around Joanna, edged her towards the catwalk, linking their arms through hers, preparing to sweep her out in front in spite of her nervous protestations.

'Wait!' shouted a high-pitched voice. Joanna spun round and a large bouquet of roses was shoved into her hands by the youngest seamstress in the workroom. It was almost too much but there was no time to pause, no opportunity to gather together her inner resources. She was led out on to the runway to be met by a roaring cheer of approval that seemed to sweep over her like a tornado. Dazzled by the blinding spotlights, dazed by the thunderous applause, she managed to look confident though she'd never felt more like hiding away in a dark corner. Beside the exotic and glamorous models she felt painfully awkward and plain, but she was the one the audience loved because she looked like a real person. That was her appeal. There was shout after shout of 'Bravo!' Not, she knew, because she'd designed anything or even sewn a stitch, but because she was Arabella's daughter, that was all. She knew the difference. No one would applaud her for herself.

But how they loved her! All the editors, the buyers, the clients, the media, even the sophisticated celebrities, seeing a fresh-looking young woman in a black trouser suit with her short hair shining and a tremulous smile on her face. They thought she looked both vulnerable and determined. Everyone knew what she'd been through that week because she'd become front-page news, too, and everyone guessed there'd be worse to come.

'She's being so brave!' A hardened fashion writer wept unashamedly. A cynic nearby scoffed, 'She's only getting a sympathy vote. It's probably all a publicity stunt anyway. And it's worked. Arabella Webster was just a society dressmaker this time last week and look where she is now!'

'You're wanted on the phone, Joanna,' someone called out.

'Who? Where?' she asked, looking around. The scurry of departing models and dressers packing up the collection was like bedlam. Everyone wanted to get away and there was chaos.

'Over there, in the organisers' office.'

Joanna hurried over to where a section of the marquee had been screened off. Here there was frenzied activity as everyone with a query seemed to be bombarding the clerical workers with questions. The organisers had installed a land line for the week. As soon as she appeared, someone pointed to where the phone was.

'Thanks.' She picked up the receiver, wondering which journalist wanted more information, more pictures, an interview about Arabella.

'Hello? Joanna Knight speaking.'

It was a man's voice. Ordinary, unexceptional, educated and instantly forgettable.

'I hope the show went well because it's the last one Arabella intends to do,' he said bluntly. 'She has other interests now.' There was a click as he hung up.

Joanna stood staring at the instrument as if someone had thumped her in the middle of her chest. She turned to the secretary nearest the phone.

'This . . . this c-call for me,' she stammered. 'Did he say who he was? What d-did he say?'

'Sorry,' said the young woman apologetically, 'I wasn't paying that much attention. It's like a madhouse in here.' She put her head on one side for a moment, then she shook it. 'No. I'm sure he didn't say who he was. I think he just said, "Can I speak to Joanna Knight?" That's all. Sorry . . .'

Joanna dialled 1471, but a recorded voice told her she was unable to give the caller's number.

'Is everything all right?' the secretary asked chirpily.

'Why don't you go straight home, love?' Rosie suggested when she heard what had happened. 'You'd better get on to the police. Tell them your ma's not really missing after all. She's . . . well . . . I don't know what to say.' Her mouth was tight. 'You've done your bit, and bloody marvellous it was, too, if you'll excuse my French. But we can manage now.'

This is all wrong, Joanna thought. We ought to be celebrating the fact that Arabella's alive but instead resentment and fury were welling up in her. How dare she go off and leave them all like this, without a word? What about Louise, asking for her every day? What about Joanna's own agony of mind? And what about the livelihood of all the people who worked for her? Arabella had done some pretty impetuous things in her life but this was wicked. Really wicked. Joanna bit her lip, wondering who to tell first.

'Your step-mum and your dad have collected Louise,' Rosie said, as if she knew what Joanna was thinking. 'And they told me to say they'll pick her up from the Professor's house on Sunday evening. OK, love?'

Joanna was nodding mechanically, only half listening. 'Where can she have gone? For God's sake, what can she be doing?' she burst out angrily. 'I'll never forgive her for this.'

'You are sure . . .' Rosie hesitated. 'Well, why don't you see what the police have to say? Go home where you can make those calls in peace. If this gets out whilst you're still here, there'll be a stampede, mark my words.'

'You're right.' So far neither Eleanor nor any of the girls knew what had happened. 'If I have any news,

71

Rosie, I'll ring you at home later.' Impulsively Joanna flung her arms around the motherly figure and hugged her. 'Thank you for everything. I don't know what any of us would have done without you this week.'

Rosie patted her shoulder. 'Now you take care of yourself,' she whispered.

Joanna didn't wait to get home. She hailed a taxi and asked to go straight to Belgravia police station. The more she thought about that call, the angrier she felt. Had that man really meant it when he'd said Arabella had 'other interests now'? What other interests, for Christ's sake?

She shot out of the cab when they arrived, dashed up the entrance steps to the building and into the hall.

'Can I see Detective Inspector Walsh, please?' she asked breathlessly at the front desk. 'It's very urgent. I'm Joanna Knight and it's about my mother.'

It was several minutes before he appeared, looking bland and smooth in a dark blue suit and a maroon tie.

'Good afternoon, Miss Knight. What can I do for you?' His blue eyes searched her face closely, as if trying to determine her state of mind.

'I've just had a phone call from a man saying my mother is alive and . . .'

'Alive?' he queried. 'Perhaps you'd like to come into the interview room and tell me exactly what's happened.'

She sat opposite him, feeling rattled and impatient, wanting to tell him about the call.

'Who was this man?' he asked as she started speaking again.

'I don't know. He rang the organisers at the show. He obviously asked for me and when I spoke to him . . .'

'What did he sound like?'

'What?' She frowned. 'Oh, ordinary. Just an ordinary sort of voice. Nothing special.'

'Any accent?'

'No.'

'Educated?'

'He didn't have an Oxford accent if that's what you mean. It was just . . . well, like a newscaster or someone who does the weather forecast.'

Walsh gave a faint smile. 'Nearly all of them have a regional accent, even if it's only slight.'

'The point is,' Joanna said, realising she was taking out her anger with Arabella on this man, 'it appears my mother's still alive. His actual words were "that's the last show Arabella intends to do. She has other interests now". It couldn't be clearer, could it? My mother's asked someone to tell us she's gone off somewhere and left us all in the lurch. I can't believe she'd do such a thing, even though she is unpredictable. I'm terribly sorry you've had your time wasted . . .'

Walsh raised one broad-palmed hand. 'Just a moment, Miss Knight. Would you recognise this voice again if you heard it?'

She looked at him in surprise. 'I suppose so.'

He rose. 'Just wait here.'

He was gone for some time. Did he know something about Arabella's disappearance that she didn't? Had he suspected, all along, that her vanishing act was the work of a selfish woman who didn't give a damn about anyone else?

When he returned he had DS Chambers with him.

'Listen to this,' Walsh said, 'and tell me if you recognise the voice. OK, Chambers.' The DS slipped a cassette into a tape recorder at one end of the table and switched it on.

'. . . He's innocent, you know. I've got all the evidence to prove that Dave was nowhere near Brick Lane that night . . .'

Joanna froze. 'Who's Dave?' she asked.

'Nothing to do with your mother, Miss Knight,' Walsh said quickly. 'I just want to know if you recognise the voice?'

'Yes, I do. At least, I think so. Can I hear it again?'

Chambers switched the tape on again.

'. . . and I thought you'd be interested to learn that . . .'

'That *is* him,' Joanna said positively. 'It's the way he pronounces "interested". He says "in-ter-es-ted". I remember now, he said my mother had "other in-ter-ests". Who is he?'

Walsh looked pained, and Chambers stared down at his feet.

'I'm so sorry, Miss Knight,' the inspector said gently, 'but that man is our ace hoaxer. Every time anything happens in this area he manages to get hold of all the parties concerned, as well as ourselves, then phones up without giving a name and talks a lot of nonsense. He's so well known to us that that's why we've got him on tape. He's a mischief-maker, that's all. That chap Dave he's referring to was sent down for four years for assault and battery and we had witnesses to prove it.'

As he saw Joanna's crushed expression, all the fire gone from her eyes, he continued: 'Your mother's case is very high-profile because of her fashion connections. It would be the easiest thing in the world for him to get the organisers' number today, ask for you, and then proceed to try and send you on a wild goose chase.'

'But *why*?' she asked brokenly. 'Why would anyone want to do a thing like that?'

'There are a lot of sick people about, I'm afraid,' Walsh said grimly. 'We'd give anything to catch him, but he's as slippery as an eel. Uses public phone boxes and never talks long enough for us to trace the call. I'm sorry to say there has been no sign of your mother since Monday, but we are renewing our efforts to try and find her.'

'And will you?' Joanna looked pinched and shivery.

He cleared his throat. 'I have to be honest and say that the longer she is missing, the worse our chances are of finding her. Alive, that is,' he added gruffly.

Joanna wondered if she had the capacity to feel any more shock and pain than she already felt. And now guilt was added to that. She'd actually believed her mother had gone off and left them all.

'I'm sorry to have bothered you,' she murmured, rising. 'I should have known she would never have done something like that.'

'There is just one more thing, Miss Knight. We've been getting several calls a day from Eleanor Andrews, enquiring about Arabella. Could she liaise with you, perhaps? We're very busy here, and if just you were to ring, it would be a great help.'

Joanna looked startled. 'I'm sorry. I'd no idea.'

Four

'It's amazing, isn't it, that Arabella managed to produce two marvellous children like Joanna and Louise?' Jeremy observed as he linked his arm through Victoria's. They were strolling through Hyde Park, taking Caspar for his afternoon walk. Golden leaves fell in showers and gathered in drifts around their feet as a breeze, bringing with it the first chill of autumn, stirred among the trees.

'I suppose it is surprising,' she agreed, tucking stray wisps of grey hair behind her ears. Over the years, bit by bit, he'd told her all about his first wife. And how, after she'd left him 'to do her own thing', making clothes hadn't been the only thing she'd done.

'Talk about naïve!' Jeremy said, watching Caspar charge after a squirrel. 'I believed then that her appearance and lifestyle were because she was making a fortune with her clothes business. It never struck me that she'd become extremely promiscuous, and was acquiring jewels and furs

77

and the odd envelope stuffed with cash from men with dubious reputations.'

'Do you think she got tired of it and that's why she married Eric – because he was rich?'

Jeremy looked around with sad eyes at the dying of the summer. In places the grass had grown high and frothy and Caspar looked as if he was swimming in a green sea as he rushed about.

'Time was running out for her, that was the problem. Then the husband of one of the women she made clothes for had a friend who dated Arabella pretty regularly. She was bleeding him dry, asking him to help pay Joanna's school fees, and God knows what else. He'd already given her a car, a mink coat, and a diamond necklace. The word spread and she had to stop, or her business would have collapsed. She kept a low profile for a bit, and then married Eric, who had no idea of her lifestyle at that stage!'

Victoria stopped to bend down and pick up a stick to throw for Caspar. 'You know,' she said, drawing her brows together thoughtfully. 'I couldn't do that. Sleep with men for money or gifts. Not even if I was starving. I don't think I could do it even if I had children who were starving.'

Jeremy remembered Arabella at seventeen, when he'd married her; she'd always appeared to enjoy sex, especially foreplay, but there had been moments when he'd wondered how much she really got out of the act itself. Although he'd believed she really loved him, it was almost as if the thrill for her came from having power over a man.

'I wish to God I'd been able to get custody of Joanna there and then, but I didn't have a proper home or earn enough to afford a child minder while I was at work, and so of course Arabella walked it. Looked marvellous in court, demure and motherly, and talked about baking cakes and helping Joanna with her homework, and the judge was totally taken in by her.' He reached out to take Victoria's hand and smiled into her eyes. 'If only I'd known you then.'

'Joanna does seem to have survived, though.'

'I think Arabella got a fright and stopped before Jo could fully realise what was going on. Added to which her mother sent her away to school when she was only a kid. I was very angry about that.'

Victoria watched Caspar capering, with an indulgent smile.

'Do you think Arabella's disappearance has anything to do with her past?'

Jeremy shrugged. 'God only knows.'

Morning, Monday 20 September

'Miss Knight, we have some information which may concern Arabella Webster,' DI Walsh informed Joanna when he phoned her shortly after she arrived at the office.

Her head swam and she could hardly speak. 'What? Have you found her?'

'The North Yorkshire constabulary have reported that a woman answering to Mrs Arabella Webster's description was found yesterday afternoon, wandering around the village of Grassington. She was very confused and seemed to have lost her memory.'

'Yorkshire?' Joanna felt light-headed with relief. She wanted to run up to the workroom and scream the good news to Rosie and the girls. 'Really? Where is she now?' Her mind was whirling – confused, ecstatic, bewildered, filled with triumph. It explained everything. The stress of the big show must have brought on a nervous breakdown. Last Monday morning, while they were all waiting anxiously for her to arrive, Arabella must have decided she couldn't go through with it. She must have driven her car . . . anywhere, just to get away. And loss of memory must have followed.

'The thing is,' Walsh continued, not sounding at all delighted, 'they haven't found her car. When she was picked up she seemed tired, but not as if she'd walked for a long way having abandoned her car somewhere. The woman in question doesn't seem to think she *has* a car. This raises a doubt as to whether or not . . .'

But Joanna was barely listening. 'Shall I fetch her? Where is she now? Still in this place . . . Grassington?'

'We do need verification that it is indeed Mrs Arabella Webster, so if you are able . . .'

'I'll go right away.' She'd get a train. A plane. Hire a car. She had to get to Arabella immediately. She'd be so scared if her memory suddenly came back. She'd wonder where she was and what had happened.

'I must warn you, Miss Knight, not to get your hopes up too high,' Walsh said almost sternly.

'Yes. Right.' She sounded distracted. 'What's the

address? Which is the nearest big town?'

'Skipton. But we have to remember Mrs Webster has been missing for seven days. And in that time none of her credit cards has been used, nor has she withdrawn any money from her various bank accounts. I must advise you to treat this situation with caution because it may turn out not to be your mother.'

But Joanna knew in her bones it was Arabella. Instinctively she just knew. 'Has anyone else been reported as missing? I mean, answering to my mother's description?' she demanded. 'If not, it must be her.'

'But this woman was only discovered wandering about yesterday. If she lives alone no one may have realised she's gone missing yet,' Walsh explained more gently. 'According to the doctor who examined her, she's most likely suffered a Major Amnesiac Episode in the past thirty-six hours.'

'A major . . . what?'

'Major Amnesiac Episode. It means a sudden and total loss of memory. It can be caused by a virus affecting the central nervous system. But of course we don't know if . . .'

'It would still figure, though. If my mother has suffered a nervous breakdown and gone into hiding somewhere, amnesia could have followed,' Joanna pointed out determinedly. 'Where is she now?'

'Skipton General Hospital. She's under observation and the specialist observing her condition is a Dr Joel Levene.'

'Thank you.'

Twenty minutes later Joanna was in a taxi on her way to King's Cross. It was already eleven-thirty. The traffic was so bad she didn't arrive at the station until shortly after noon.

Shoving a ten-pound note into the taxi driver's hand, saying, 'Keep the change,' Joanna ran on to the crowded concourse, deciding to pay for her ticket when she was on the train. Dodging people with babies in pushchairs, sidestepping old ladies with luggage trolleys, being whacked on the shoulder by students turning around suddenly with heavy rucksacks on their backs, she finally reached the centre. She looked up, frowning with concentration.

Departures . . . departures . . . She scanned the ever-changing board indicating arrivals and departures, searching frantically for the times of Leeds-bound trains. When was the next one? Would she have a long tortuous wait?

Suddenly she saw Leeds flicker up. Thank God. Her eyes flew to the top of the board. It left at 12.10. From platform 7. She had less than two minutes to catch it and platform 7 was some distance away.

Freddie came out of courtroom number 11 at one o'clock for the lunchtime recess. Time to stretch his legs and have a sandwich and a cup of coffee before returning in an hour. The long drawn out case of Marcus Cohen v. Helen Dougall was nearing its conclusion at last. The judge was due to sum up tomorrow. Freedom from sitting on wooden benches in a chilly courtroom while both sides argued their points seemed imminent.

He reached for his phone and tapped in the number of Joanna's mobile. The reception was appalling and he couldn't make out what she was saying through the crackling and intermittent cutting out. Hanging up, he tapped in the number of Arabella Designs. Eleanor answered immediately.

'Is Joanna there, please?' he asked politely.

'No, she's not,' Eleanor snapped back. 'She's gone rushing off on some wild goose chase. I don't know if she's even coming back today.'

'Where's she gone?'

'How should I know? I'm only trying to run this whole outfit single-handed, and we're snowed under with work.'

'Right.' For the umpteenth time he wondered why Arabella had ever employed the woman. 'Has she heard anything?'

'The police rang her earlier but frankly I'm too busy to get involved. Why don't you try her mobile?' Her bad temper was almost palpable down the line.

'I will.' With equal curtness Freddie pressed the red 'Off' button.

Joanna slammed the carriage door shut just seconds before the 12.10 pulled out of King's Cross. Her legs felt weak from the sudden exertion of sprinting, but her spirits soared with relief. She'd no idea how long the journey was going to take but at least she was on her way. Suddenly hungry, she walked through the rattling carriages to the restaurant car. Lunch would help pass the time and give her some much needed energy.

'Sorry, Miss, we're full up,' the waiter told her, and looking around at the neat tables, set with white linen and good quality cutlery and glasses, she could see what he meant. There wasn't a single spare seat. 'You should have booked, Miss. This is a very popular train.'

'Will there be a second sitting?' she asked, her mouth watering as she saw people enjoying plates of steak and kidney pie or grilled cutlets.

The waiter shook his head. 'I'm afraid not. There will be a trolley service going up and down, though.'

'How long will it take to get to Leeds?'

He didn't even have to think about it. 'A couple of hours.'

'As soon as that?' Good. She'd have to change at Leeds, but the next journey was only a short one.

On her way back to find a seat, she decided to return Freddie's call. Maybe the reception would be better now.

'Freddie?'

'Babe, where *are* you?'

'I'm on a train to Yorkshire.' She stood leaning against a shuddering window as the train hurtled towards the North of England.

'What the hell are you doing?'

Briefly she explained. 'I'll be back home tonight,' she added, 'hopefully bringing Mummy with me.'

'Jesus! That's amazing. Do they really think it's her?'

'Who else can it be? The description matches. It has to be her, Freddie.'

'That's wonderful. Keep me posted, won't you? I'll be out of court again at four-thirty, so call me then and let me know what's happening.'

'I will. Talk about relief, eh?' She suddenly realised she felt happy for the first time since last Monday. It was a strange sensation. A stroll along an almost forgotten shore after a tornado had uprooted everything, shattering her safe and cosy world. But she felt like treading carefully, as if she was recovering from some debilitating illness and feared breaking this new fragile bubble of euphoria.

Still standing in the corridor, so as not to disturb other passengers, she phoned Jeremy. With each passing mile that rumbled and rattled by, she felt stronger, more positive. Her manner with her father was almost defiant, as if daring him to cast doubt on her finding Arabella.

Instead he said: 'I'd have gone with you if I'd known, sweetheart.'

'There wasn't time, Daddy.' Of course there had been. She could have taken an afternoon train instead of rushing as if it were a case of life or death. Arabella was being looked after by a specialist in hospital. No harm could come to her now.

'I'm just desperate to get to her,' Joanna continued. 'I think I'll hire a car to bring us back. If she's had a Major Amnesiac Episode, she ought to be in a London hospital with a top neurologist.'

'How sure are the police that this is Arabella?'

'Everyone in Britain must know what she looks like by now. I suppose someone in Grassington recognised her and told the police.'

'And apart from loss of memory, how did they say she seemed?'

'Tired, but I think basically OK. Obviously very confused. Oh, Daddy, isn't it a relief? Rosie and the girls went crazy this morning when I told them. Anyway, I'll keep you posted, Daddy.'

'Please do, Jo darling.'

Jeremy replaced the phone and wandered into the little sitting room that led off the kitchen. He wanted to watch Sky News in case there was any mention of a woman answering to Arabella's description having been found. But he decided it would not be wise to mention it to Louise when she returned from shopping with Victoria. Better to wait until he had it confirmed by Joanna. Then they could start celebrating.

Having spoken to Joanna on her mobile, as she munched a damp ham sandwich and drank a cup of bitter coffee on the train, Walsh alerted the North Yorkshire constabulary to the time of her arrival. As a result, when her taxi drew up outside Skipton General Hospital, his counterpart, DI Ken Black, was waiting inside by the front desk.

'Miss Knight?' He wore a grey raincoat over his tweed suit and on his feet were a strong pair of brown brogues. Bluff, blunt and with a weather-beaten, hard-looking face, he shook her hand unsmilingly, nodding a greeting.

'Hello,' she murmured, suddenly nervous. She followed him into a lift and in silence they rose to the second floor.

'So . . . you've found my mother?' she asked him eagerly.

His expression was inscrutable. 'I don't know about that.'

'But Detective Inspector Walsh says a woman

answering to my mother's description . . .' she insisted desperately.

'We won't know until you've seen her whether it's your mother or not, will we?' he replied dourly.

The lift stopped and he led the way along a series of corridors, passing large public wards with rows of beds filled with tired sad faces and then a series of closed doors which she imagined must be private rooms. The almost tangible odour of all hospitals assaulted her nose. The hushed murmurs of sick people and the rubber-soled footsteps of nurses blanketed the sounds around her. A deep trembling had started up in her stomach and she felt sick.

DI Black suddenly stopped and looked through the open door of a small office where a ward sister was sitting, writing in a big black book. He cleared his throat and she looked up.

'We've come to see . . .' he began, but she jumped up from her seat and came forward with a knowing nod. Then she turned and smiled at Joanna who stood looking suddenly petrified.

'I'll take you along to see the patient,' she said smiling cheerfully. 'Come this way.'

The atmosphere was taut with apprehension. Joanna's mind was racing and her heart thundering. The sister opened a plain wooden door, its small glass window screened from within, and entered the room ahead of them.

Joanna had somehow imagined she'd find Arabella in bed, lying back against a mound of snowy pillows with her blonde hair brushed around her shoulders and the lack of make-up in no way diminishing her beauty. Instead she was sitting in an easy chair with her back to them, looking out of the window. She was wearing black and her hair was roughly pinned back. Joanna took a deep breath and stepped forward, realising her mother didn't seem to have heard them entering the room.

'Here's a visitor for you,' the sister said brightly. 'Are you going to say hello?'

The woman turned slowly and Joanna found herself looking into the face of a total stranger.

DI Black drove Joanna back to Skipton station in silence, never taking his eyes off the road, while she sat in the passenger seat, her face averted so he would not see the tears trickling down her cheeks and her attempts to sniff quietly, because she had no tissues with her. Her disappointment was crushing. She felt overwhelmed with despair. And angry, too, that she'd been given hope in the first place. Then she remembered DI Walsh's words of caution that morning. He hadn't been at all sure the lost woman was Arabella. He'd warned her several times but she hadn't wanted to know. She'd gone rushing off on her own, and now she was having to face this feeling of utter desolation on her own, too. Jeremy had been right. She should have taken him with her.

DI Black spoke. 'What time's your train?'

'I've no idea,' she said, more coldly than she'd meant to. 'I was planning to hire a car to take my mother back to London,' she added, feeling she'd been rude.

'I never thought it was her,' Black said flatly.

'Then why . . .' she flashed back.

He shrugged. 'The description fitted.'

Except that my mother is beautiful, Joanna thought. That other woman hadn't been beautiful at all. She'd looked old and haggard with the rheumy oyster eyes of an alcoholic.

'We have to pursue every possibility,' Black continued.

After another silence he spoke again. 'That picture you gave the London police – it was an old one, wasn't it? Sort of flattering, eh?'

She felt herself stiffen. 'It was taken a few months ago and she looks exactly like that. She's only forty anyway.' In her annoyance at his attitude, her tears stopped and she pulled her coat tighter around her.

They made the rest of the journey in silence and when he pulled up in front of the station, she jumped out of the car, thanking him politely.

'Good luck,' he called after her, but she was gone.

Evening, Tuesday 21 September

'You've lost weight, Jo darling,' Jeremy told her when she dropped in to Portsea Place to see Louise. 'You must eat or you'll make yourself ill.'

'I'm not hungry,' she protested. 'I feel sick all the time from sheer worry and I'm run off my feet at work. Yesterday was such a terrible blow, Daddy, I'm still reeling from the disappointment.'

As she talked, he listened attentively while making toast, getting a dish of butter and some home-made pâté out of the fridge, and placing them before her on

89

the kitchen table with a plate and knife and a glass of wine.

'When Victoria's finished supervising Louise's bath-time, we'll be having supper. You'll stay, won't you, Jo? I presume Freddie's working late again?'

She nodded wistfully. 'He thought the case would be over by now but yesterday the defendant suddenly produced another witness which has thrown everything into chaos. Freddie's really pissed off.'

'He's making his way, isn't he?'

'Yes, but I do miss being with him in the evenings, especially at the moment.'

'I'm sure, sweetheart,' Jeremy sympathised, his expression softening. He poured himself some wine and then lowered himself into the chair at the head of the table. His attractive face, usually so healthily cheerful, looked grey and drawn, as if he too was tired. 'So what happens next?'

'The police say they're going to step up their nationwide search. They're convinced Ma couldn't have left the country, although there was a wild suggestion at one moment that she might have been picked up by a private yacht off the south coast, but that still leaves her car. She'd have had to dump it somewhere and there's no trace of it.'

Jeremy considered this scenario. 'Bit far-fetched, don't you think?'

Joanna tightened her fingers around the stem of her glass. 'Maybe not entirely,' she said slowly.

'What do you mean?'

'DI Walsh came to see me this morning, at the office. He asked me if Mummy had a cocaine habit. Apparently a fashion model they interviewed admitted she used to get her supply through Arabella.'

Jeremy looked stunned. 'You're not serious?'

She shrugged, her black top making her shoulders look thinner than ever. 'I told him I was sure she never took the stuff herself. She does move in a groovy set though, Dad. I'm sure some of her friends and clients are into drugs. I just wondered if you'd heard anything?'

'To be honest, Jo, I'd be the last person to know.'

Joanna looked unhappy, hating to be disloyal to her mother and yet troubled by certain things. Why would the model DI Walsh interviewed have said that if it weren't true?

'The detective actually asked me if she was a dealer,' she continued.

'Presumably you denied it?'

'I felt I had to, for Ma's sake, but I don't know if it was the right thing to do.'

There was a long silence broken only by the sound of Louise giggling upstairs with Victoria.

Suddenly Joanna and her father locked eyes. Then he looked away, reaching for the bottle. 'Of course you'd know if she was getting it for other people,' he said robustly. 'Have some more wine, darling.'

Morning, Saturday 25 September

It was Saturday morning and Joanna was lying in bed, gazing out of the dormer window of their attic bedroom, aware she ought to get up but feeling too depressed to move. Fear seemed to hold her in its clutches permanently and her stomach was a knot of fierce dread. She also felt tired all the time.

Freddie had gone out to do the weekend shopping and she felt guilty that she hadn't lifted her head from the pillow and offered to go with him, but she still sought oblivion in slumber. Though she wondered why she bothered because her dreams were so bad these days.

At that moment the phone rang, jarring her with its warbling tones.

'Shit!' She opened her eyes and reached for it on the bedside table. 'Hello?'

'Jo? Is that you? Did I wake you?'

Joanna sat upright, an expression of disbelief on her face. 'Nina! Is that you? My God, what are you doing?'

'What are *you* doing, for heaven's sake?'

Joanna had originally met Nina Hammer at a friend's twenty-first birthday party which had been held in the London Dungeon. Nina, who hailed from Washington, was studying Fine Arts at Sotheby's at the time, and Joanna, still taking her Business, Administration and Computer Studies course, found they had a lot in common. They quickly became friends, spending a lot of time discussing art and going to all the galleries, and although Nina returned to the States at the end of her course, they'd kept in close touch.

'You've heard the news then?' Joanna asked, wide awake now.

'I only heard yesterday. I've been in India with my brother for the past month, touring around completely incommunicado. Then I get home last night and my dad tells me he's read in a newspaper that your mother's missing. Jesus, Jo, what happened?'

'I wish to God I knew. It's a total nightmare.'

'You've no idea where she is? What do the police think?'

'They've no idea either.'

'Oh, shit, that's terrible. I'm really sorry. Listen, I was thinking of taking a trip to London in a month or so, but shall I come now? Could you use a bit of support? You must be frantic with worry.' Her warm American accent and strong positive attitude reminded Joanna of all the fun they'd had. Nina was a character, large in build and large in heart. Generous, humorous, fun-loving, and always prepared to laugh at herself, she flung herself whole-heartedly into whatever needed to be done.

It was just the tonic Joanna needed.

'Oh my God, Nina, it would be great if you could come over,' she exclaimed. 'You could stay here. We've got a minuscule spare room but Freddie's mother uses it occasionally so it's not too bad.'

'Book me in!' Nina boomed cheerfully. 'Listen, I'll find out about flights and then call you back.'

'But what about your family? They must be wanting to spend time with you if you've been away?'

'Nah, they're cool. Your need is greater than theirs. I'll get right back to you, sugar.'

'Nina, you're a star.'

'I'm not, I'm the whole frigging galaxy,' she chuckled, 'so stand by for my arrival.'

Joanna was smiling as she replaced the receiver. Nina was like a shot in the arm. An instant remedy for depression. Energised, she hopped out of bed and was in the shower when Freddie got back, laden with heavy shopping bags hanging from each hand.

'I got all your favourite things,' he shouted from the kitchen as he dumped the bags on the floor. A minute later Joanna appeared, wrapped in a blue towel.

'Oh, I feel dreadful, Freddie,' she exclaimed as she watched him unpack smoked salmon and steaks, imported strawberries and peaches, and a couple of bottles of expensive-looking wine.

'What's wrong?' He grinned as he withdrew a package from one of the bags, saying: 'Catch!' as he tossed her a packet of chocolate digestive biscuits. She caught it and immediately burst into tears.

'Hey, what's this, babe?' he chided softly, putting his arms around her and hugging her close. 'Gone off chocolate biscuits?'

She gave a watery grin. 'I feel so *useless* and everyone is being so *kind*. I can't bear it.'

He rocked her gently, tucking her head under his chin. 'I know. I know.'

After a few moments she sniffed deeply before disengaging herself. 'Nina phoned while you were out. She's coming to England and I said she could stay here. That's all right, isn't it? You don't mind?'

'Of course I don't mind.' He liked Nina. She was a laugh and she'd be able to help him console Joanna as the situation worsened, which he was privately convinced it would.

Joanna sniffed again and then tore off a piece of kitchen roll and blew her nose. 'Have you anything that

94

needs to go into the deep freeze?'

He looked at her, perplexed. 'The deep . . .?'

'Because if you haven't, I'd like you to stop unpacking all these bags and come with me.' She took one of his hands and held it lovingly in both of hers. 'I can think of something that would be much more fun to do,' she added, lifting his hand and kissing his palm tenderly.

Early morning, Monday 27 September

It had been a peaceful weekend. Joanna couldn't say more than that. Quiet, peaceful and without incident. There'd been no news of Arabella. All police enquiries had drawn a blank. As a result, she and Freddie had taken the opportunity to stay close, eat, sleep and make love. Now it was early Monday morning and they were driving against the incoming traffic as they headed out of London to meet Nina at Heathrow.

Idly, Joanna reached for the car radio and started turning the tuning knob, looking for Classic FM. Shrill whistling, a snatch of pop music then raucous buzzing, hissing, more whistling, a female crooner singing 'I love my maaannnn . . .' A buzzing noise and then the voice of a male newscaster.

'. . . A man has been picked up this morning and is helping police with their enquiries into the disappearance of Arabella Webster, the fashion designer who vanished fifteen days ago. Hopes of finding her alive have been dwindling with each passing day . . .'

Every cell in Joanna's body froze and her descent into

hell began; it was deep and dark and filled with horror. Freddie swerved the car and brought it to a standstill on the hard shoulder of the motorway. He turned to look at Joanna. Her hand was clapped over her mouth and she was trembling violently.

Ripping off his seat belt he put his arms around her, one hand cradling the back of her head. 'You'll be all right, babe,' he kept whispering. 'Hang on to me, I'm here.' It was several minutes before she was able to speak.

'But . . . who?' she murmured hoarsely.

'I don't know but it doesn't necessarily mean anything. It's not like they've found her body. They're obviously questioning everyone who might have seen her or heard anything.'

'Oh, Freddie, I'm so frightened.' She swayed dizzily. Felt paralysed. Everything looked blurred. Leaning heavily against him, she was filled with exquisite terror because she knew in her bones what it meant. They were questioning the person they suspected of murdering her mother. She'd heard that phrase hundreds of times on the television and radio news programmes. 'A man is helping the police with their enquiries'.

But who . . .?

'Are you OK, babe?' he whispered urgently, seeing her head fall back, her skin bleached white. 'I think I have . . . yes.' He fished a small bottle of Evian out of the glove compartment and, unscrewing the top, handed it to her. 'Drink this.'

She nodded obediently, rallying with an effort. 'We'd

better get on. Nina's plane will be landing in a few minutes.'

'Are you sure you want to go on? She'd understand if you weren't there to meet her, seeing what's happened.'

Joanna shook her head. 'No, I want to meet her. I'm going to phone DI Walsh to ask what's going on. And why didn't he tell me they sus-suspected anyone?' Still shivering, she dug deeply into her bag for her mobile while Freddie started up the car again, easing himself into the traffic once more.

'Can I speak to Detective Inspector Walsh?' she asked when she got through to the police station.

'Hang on a minute, please.' There was a pause and then: 'I'm sorry, he's unavailable at the moment. Can I take a message?'

Joanna racked her brains for the name of Walsh's sidekick. 'Is his . . . um . . . his . . .' Suddenly it came back to her. 'Is DS Chambers there?'

Another pause. 'I'm sorry, but he's also unavailable.'

'Can you help me then?' she said desperately. 'My name is Joanna Knight and I'm Arabella Webster's daughter. I've just heard on the news that you're questioning someone in connection with my mother's disappearance and I wondered if . . .'

'I'm sorry, but we can't give out that sort of information on the phone, Miss. May I ask DI Walsh to give you a ring as soon as he can?'

'Oh! All right. But it is urgent.'

They were entering the outskirts of Heathrow, taking a left turn at the roundabout. In five minutes they'd be at the arrivals building.

'Why don't you ring your father?' Freddie suggested. 'He always watches GMTV before he leaves for work. They might have covered it more thoroughly than radio. The police probably made a dawn raid on where their suspect lives. That's how it's usually done and if the television company got wind of it, they'd have sent a film crew along.'

Joanna tapped in Jeremy's number. Victoria answered.

'Hello, dear girl. How are you?' she asked warmly.

'You haven't heard then? Is Daddy there?'

'He's taken Louise to the park with Caspar. What's happened?'

Joanna told her. Victoria sounded shocked. 'Oh, God, this is awful. Is there anything I can do?'

'Not at the moment, Victoria. Could you tell Daddy what's happened when he gets back? And can you make sure Louise doesn't find out? She still thinks Mummy's coming back . . . Oh, God, I'm sorry,' sobbed Joanna, breaking down again. 'I never thought it would come to this.'

'Oh, my dearest girl.' Victoria's voice was filled with compassion. 'We'll be here, any time you want us, day or night. And don't worry about Louise. We'll take good care of her.'

Nina came flying ebulliently through the arrivals swing doors, in a huge purple wool coat that drew attention to, rather than disguised, her size. She was pushing a trolley piled high with baggage.

'Hi-ya!' she yelled cheerfully, pushing her shoulder-length blonde hair behind her ears. A moment later

Joanna found herself being crushed against Nina's ample bosom. 'My, but you're skinny, Jo!' she exclaimed as she released her. Freddie was next in line to be hugged, and felt as if he was being greeted by an over-excited English sheep dog.

'Good to see you, Nina,' he said when he was able to say anything. 'Here, let me take your cases.'

Nina slipped her arm through Joanna's. 'So, how are you doing? You really have lost a helluva lot of weight, you know. Must have given it to me,' she chuckled. 'Are you eating anything these days?'

Joanna turned to her friend with anguished eyes.

'We've just had some terribly bad news, Nina. They've taken someone in for questioning.'

Nina stopped dead in her tracks, her expression horrified. 'You're kidding! *Jesus!* D'you know who they've picked up?'

'I've no idea.'

Nina stared at Joanna in concern, all traces of joviality erased. Then she glanced at Freddie. 'Holy shit! I'd no idea it was as desperate as this. What happens now?'

Freddie spoke. 'I'm driving you both back to the flat before I go to the office. Joanna's waiting for a call from the police and then hopefully we'll know more.'

They loaded Nina's luggage into the boot of Freddie's car and set off back to the centre of London. Joanna, sitting hunched in the seat beside him, was silent, her lips pressed tightly together. Shock, like a numbing paralysis, had taken hold of her mind, rendering her mute.

Freddie broke the silence. 'It's awfully good of you to come over like this, Nina,' he told her. 'I'm stuck in court every day and also having to work late most nights, which is a real bummer at the moment.'

Nina leaned forward from the back seat and patted Joanna's shoulder. 'Well, I'm here to stay for as long as you need me, and when you've had enough, just boot me out! Meanwhile, maybe I can shop and cook for the two of you,' she added lightly, eyeing Joanna's thin frame again, 'and feed you up, Madam! You'll become an X-ray woman if you're not careful.'

Joanna emerged from her stunned reverie and gave a tight little smile. 'It's so good to see you again, Nina. You've no idea . . .'

Her friend's round face creased once more into a broad smile, showing even white teeth. She looked affectionately at them both.

'It's the least I can do after the marvellous time you gave me when I was last here.'

When Joanna's mobile rang as they were driving over the Hammersmith flyover, they all stiffened immediately. Reaching for it with shaking hands, she switched it on.

'Hello?' Then her shoulders sagged with relief. 'Oh, Dad. I thought it might be the police. Have you heard anything more?'

'Nothing, love. There's only been the standard press release about "picking up a man for questioning", that's all. I tried to get something out of the police, but they refused to answer my questions. Walsh hasn't phoned you back, then?'

'No. Is it possible that it's just routine questioning? Or

does it mean they've found – Ma?' The last word was dragged out of her.

Jeremy didn't reply, not wanting to give her hope when he felt there was none. It was fifteen days since Arabella had vanished, and they'd taken a man in for questioning. To him that meant only one thing.

'I think we'll just have to wait and see, sweetheart,' he said lamely. 'You're not going to your office today, are you?'

'I must. We're absolutely drowning in work. The orders are pouring in since the show. But Nina's arrived which is a godsend.'

'Great. Give her my love.'

'Listen, Dad, whatever happens, make sure Louise doesn't find out . . .'

'I know,' he cut in. 'I'll make sure the television is disconnected and I'll hide the radio for the time being. Of course, if it *is* . . .'

Joanna interrupted him. 'We'll cross that bridge when we come to it,' she said, her voice harsh with pain. 'In the meanwhile, give Louise my love, tell her I'm frantically busy but I'll drop by with Nina this evening if I can.'

'See you then. And take care, my sweetheart.' Her father's deep rumbling voice was filled with anxiety. With a terrible sense of impending loss, Joanna whispered goodbye and switched off her phone.

As soon as they arrived back at Warwick Square, Freddie parked the car and then, grabbing his briefcase off the back seat, kissed Joanna tenderly on the lips.

'With any luck I'll be back around seven, babe,' he

101

said. 'And leave a message on my phone if you hear anything.'

She nodded silently.

Nina looked bemused. 'Why are you leaving the car here, Freddie? Why aren't you driving to work?'

'Parking problems, Nina. See you tonight.' He waved at them both as he strode off to catch the underground to Holborn.

'Great guy you've got there, Jo,' she commented robustly.

Joanna looked at the broad comforting lines of his retreating figure and smiled. 'I know.'

'Except . . .' Nina stared at the closed boot of the car. 'What is it?'

'Well, honey, I hope you've got an elevator in your building because he's forgotten to give us a hand with my luggage and didn't you say you're on the sixth floor?'

'Don't worry. There is a creaking old lift. We might have to make a couple of trips but we'll manage.'

'Whew! Cool!' Nina pretended to mop her brow. 'I may need to lose weight but I can think of more civilised ways of doing it.'

As soon as they'd deposited the suitcases in the spare room, Joanna hurried to the living room and switched on the television.

'Let's see if there's anything on the news channel.' She dropped on to the sofa and Nina sat down beside her. The weather forecast was showing, then the sports results followed the adverts. Joanna sat twisting her hands, hardly daring to breathe, rigid with tension. Up came the Sky logo, accompanied by the dramatic thrumming theme tune, and then a female announcer filled the screen, reading the headlines of the top stories from the autocue.

'A man is being held for questioning about the disappearance of fashion designer Arabella Webster.

'Pro-Indonesian militias are rampaging across East Timor in protest at the election results.

'Big business has failed to fill the coffers of the Tory Party . . .'

Joanna groaned, waiting impatiently for the rest of the headlines to finish. Then suddenly, shockingly, there was her mother's face, her lovely laughing face, talking to someone at a film première she'd gone to several months ago. It was the first time Joanna had seen her on film since she'd disappeared and the sight of her talking animatedly, arching her eyebrows in the way she did when she was listening intently, filled Joanna with the deepest sense of loss she'd felt so far.

'A man is helping police with their enquiries into the disappearance of fashion designer Arabella Webster, who vanished on the way to her showroom in Pimlico fifteen days ago . . .'

Joanna watched, gripped, as the picture changed to an exterior shot of Arabella Designs, filmed the day before.

'In spite of her description being circulated all over the country, there has been no trace of her since 8.30 on the morning of her disappearance. According to the police no money has been drawn from her bank account and her credit cards have not been used . . .'

They were now showing some film of her mother at Royal Ascot, wearing an outrageously feathered hat, moving with easy grace into the Enclosure and waving to a friend. It was almost more than Joanna could bear.

'So far the police have not released the name of the man being questioned.'

That was it. The announcer was going on to the next story.

'I'm going to ring the police again,' Joanna told Nina, reaching for the phone. 'I've got to find out who they're questioning. What's happened that I don't know about?'

'I suppose they've got to be careful,' Nina pointed out, 'because if they're questioning someone who happens to be innocent, and his name is revealed, he could sue for defamation of character.'

'But they could tell *me* what's going on.'

'I'll make us some coffee while you're doing that.'

'Thanks. The kitchen is on the right, past . . .'

Nina chuckled. 'Honey, in a three-room apartment I think I can find the kitchen.'

'Sure you don't need a compass?' They'd been famous for their back-chat when they'd been students and Joanna was glad that spark was still there between them, in spite of the present circumstances.

'Not even an oxygen mask.'

Joanna went through the whole rigmarole again of asking for DI Walsh or DS Chambers and explaining to the girl on the switchboard who she was and what it was about. The answers were the same, too. Sorry-they're-both-unavailable-at-the-moment-but-I'll-tell-them-you-called. Just that. Nothing more.

'Jesus, this is driving me crazy.' She wandered into the

kitchen, which was already filled with the aroma of coffee and toast.

'Sit down and eat this,' Nina commanded, plonking butter, marmalade and Bovril on to the table.

'What am I going to do?' Joanna said, flopping into a chair. 'Nobody will tell me what's going on.'

'They must have their reasons for keeping everything under wraps.'

'But who could this man be? I simply cannot think.'

Nina pursed her lips thoughtfully. 'A stalker? An ex-lover? A business rival?'

'Or someone connected to drugs,' Joanna said quietly.

'You're kidding!'

'The detective in charge asked me if Mummy was involved in the drug scene.'

'So you actually think . . .?' Nina looked incredulous.

'Nina, I no longer know. Ma didn't take drugs herself. That I'm a hundred percent sure of. But little things are coming back to me, like Ma having secret meetings in her office. I disturbed her once and she was furious. She was with a very rich client, and the safe was open. There were some packages on the desk. Little ones, you know? The client tried to cover them with her scarf, but she looked awfully guilty. So did Ma.'

'Have you looked in the safe since she disappeared?'

'Yes, there's nothing but cash. Wages mostly.'

At that moment they heard the phone ringing in the living room.

'Maybe that's Walsh!' Joanna gasped, running out of the room.

But it wasn't DI Walsh or DS Chambers, either.

Puzzled, Joanna found herself listening to Eric Webster's housekeeper, Mrs Holmes, whom Arabella had relied on heavily when she'd been married to him.

'. . . Sorry to bother you, Joanna, but you used to live here so you might know. We hardly ever open the french windows in the winter but the key's not in its usual place, and as I can't get hold of anyone else, I wondered if you knew where your mother used to keep it?' Mrs Holmes' tone was apologetic.

'What? What french window?' Joanna asked in bewilderment.

'The window that leads into the garden from the drawing room. Otherwise they're going to have to break the lock.'

Joanna felt hot and cold, her heart racing, her mind almost within reach of something of vital importance, but then it slipped away, beyond her grasp. But this shapeless terror was still there, hovering on the edge of her consciousness. To give herself time, she asked: '*Who* will have to break the lock? What are you talking about? Who wants to get into the garden?'

'The police, Joanna. They want to dig up the garden to look for . . .' Suddenly Mrs Holmes stopped. 'Didn't you know?'

'Know?' Black specks danced before her eyes. The room was disintegrating around her, her legs giving way as a wave of sick weakness swept over her. 'Know what?'

'They came to arrest the Professor this morning, Joanna. He's at the station now.'

Nina found Joanna on her knees, her arms wrapped

around herself. She was rocking backwards and for-
wards, moaning softly.

'Jo! For Christ's sake . . . what's happened?' She put
an arm around her friend's shoulders.

Suddenly Joanna struggled to her feet, pushing Nina
away with one hand, clapping the other over her
mouth. Her face gleamed with sweat. Then she rushed
to the bathroom, throwing up repeatedly as she knelt
crumpled over the loo. Nina, seizing a face flannel and
wringing it out in cold water, lowered herself on to the
bathroom stool and gently pressed it to Joanna's brow
and temples.

'Poor baby,' she kept murmuring softly. 'That must
have been one helluva phone call. D'you want to talk
about it?'

Joanna didn't speak, couldn't speak, but leaned
against the china basin, stricken and ravaged-looking as
she dabbed her mouth absently with the flannel.

When the phone rang again, she indicated to Nina to
answer it for her. It was Jeremy. He recognised Nina's
voice from three years ago and after saying he was glad
she'd come over to be with Joanna, asked if he could
speak to her.

'I'll tell her it's you, but she's very sick,' Nina told him.
'Have you heard what's happened?'

He sounded grim. 'Yes, they're questioning someone
about Arabella's disappearance. They're not saying who
but it sounds as if things are moving at last.'

'I think they've moved,' she told him succinctly. 'Hang
on a minute, here's Jo.'

Joanna, hunched forward like an old woman, gripping

her stomach as if in pain, came slowly into the room and took the phone from Nina.

'Dad?' She didn't even recognise her own voice.

'Sweetheart, it's probably just routine,' he began soothingly. 'The police can't leave a single stone unturned. I wouldn't worry about it if I were you . . .'

'Dad, they're digging up Eric's garden. They think he murdered Mummy and buried her there.'

Afternoon, Monday 27 September

DI Walsh looked at the sharp-featured man sitting opposite him with distaste. He hated intellectual snobs. Especially when they laced their educational superiority with a patronising arrogance. He glanced at DS Chambers who was sitting next to him, indicating with a brief nod that he should switch on the tape recorder.

'Interview with Eric Herbert Webster, in the presence of DI Walsh and DS Chambers, Monday the twenty-seventh of September at two-forty-three p.m.' He paused briefly, squared his shoulders and looked straight into Eric's mean little blue eyes. 'Name, please?'

'A stupid question when you know perfectly well what my name is.' The voice was as sharp as his features.

'Name, please. Sir.'

Eric gave a heavy sigh. 'Professor Eric Herbert Webster.'

'Address?'

'Ninety-one Milner Street, Chelsea, London South West Three,' he replied with pedantic sarcasm.

'Age?'

'Sixty-six – but why on earth is that of importance to you?' Eric folded his pale well-kept hands on the table between them and pursed his lips primly.

'Profession?'

'You make it sound as if I were a dentist or something!'

'Your profession, please.' Walsh was already having a problem keeping his irritation in check.

Eric stared back at him unblinkingly. 'Professor of History. Fellow of the Society of Antiquaries, Department of History, Cardiff University. Fellow of the Royal Historical Society. Doctor of Letters. Fellow of the British Academy, Federation of British Artists. Professor Emeritus, Marsham College, University of London, former Vice-Principal. Professor of Tudor History, and President of the Historical Association and the Society of Tudor Archaeology. Author of *Two Centuries of Tudor Monarchs. King James VI and I, A Study. James VI and I, Patron of the Arts. James VI and I, The Monarch and the Man*, and *A Study of Tudor Times* . . . Am I going too fast for you, Inspector? If I am, you'll find it all in *Who's Who.*'

Walsh continued to look steadily at Eric, but Chambers gazed fixedly at the floor. They had a right bastard here, he thought, wondering how long it would be before Walsh turned nasty.

His superior, however, with a flash of amusement in his eyes, asked coolly: 'What is your present marital status?'

Eric raised his chin, revealing the pristine whiteness of

his collar and the expensive navy blue silk of his tie. Although they'd arrived at his house at seven-thirty that morning, they'd found him already immaculately dressed in a bespoke cashmere suit and polished shoes.

'Divorced,' he snapped, 'as you very well know.'

'Your ex-wife's name is . . .?'

'Do I really have to participate in this childish . . .'

'Your ex-wife's name, please.'

'Arabella . . . Webster, alas. Do you also require to know what her CV says? I think you'd find that quite interesting.'

A slow flush began to creep up Walsh's neck and Chambers was aware of his breathing more deeply.

'Shall we cut out the sarcasm, sir?' he suggested coldly.

Eric nodded his balding head, smirking. 'That depends on how stupid your questions are and how much more of my time you intend wasting in this bizarre fashion.'

'Professor Webster, I suggest you treat this matter seriously,' Walsh warned. 'Mrs Webster vanished over two weeks ago and the last time she was seen was in your house. I want to know exactly what happened. Why did she call on you that morning?'

'Unfortunately we do have to keep in contact to make arrangements for me to see my daughter.'

'Was she in the habit of dropping in to see you at eight-thirty in the morning to make such plans?'

'She knows I start my day early.'

Walsh looked down at his notes. 'Surely her house-keeper, Melosa, made the arrangements most of the time?'

Eric tutted with impatience. 'Yes, sometimes. Does it matter?'

Walsh ignored the query. 'How often did you see your former wife? Were these meetings usually friendly – both of you wanting what was best for Louise?'

'Of course.'

'Always? Did you never argue about times and dates? Who was going to drop her off or collect her?'

'No.'

'So whenever you saw each other there was an atmosphere of co-operation? Of willingness to make the situation civilised and pleasant?'

'Absolutely.'

'Then why, Professor, did you have a violent disagreement with your ex-wife on the morning she disappeared?' Walsh challenged him.

'I'm not aware that there *was* any disagreement.'

'Then cast your memory back, Professor Webster, because we have a witness who saw you and your ex-wife through the open ground-floor window of your house.' Walsh consulted his notes briefly. 'We hear of a violent quarrel. Things being thrown. It was apparently a very bitter exchange.'

Eric's skin looked pale and sweaty. 'There is not a word of truth in any of that. I am an educated cultivated adult, not given to the tantrums of the lower classes.'

Chambers' head was raised swiftly and he stared at Eric in amazement. He didn't know people still aired such politically incorrect views.

But Walsh was almost smiling. 'Then how do you account for a statement made by this witness who swears he heard you shout: *If you do that, Arabella, I'll kill you?*'

'I'd say he had a very vivid imagination,' Eric scoffed.

'And why do you think this witness, who is one of your neighbours incidentally, would say a thing like that if it weren't true?' Walsh asked in an interested voice. 'Are you on such bad terms with your neighbours that one of them would invent something like this, out of revenge?'

'A lot of people are jealous of me,' said Eric stiffly.

Walsh stared at him speculatively. 'I wonder why?'

Chambers renewed his study of the floor. He'd been right. This interview was going to take a long time. Walsh was barely into his stride yet, and the Professor was going to be a very tough nut to crack.

Late afternoon, Monday 27 September

Joanna sipped the hot tea and a little colour began to return to her face. 'But why Eric?' she kept asking.

Nina, doing what she did best, which was looking after other people, had phoned Eleanor and reported Joanna was not well enough to go to work, and had then proceeded to sit with her friend, keeping her occupied as best as she could and making her relays of hot drinks and snacks.

'Was the divorce acrimonious?'

Joanna curled up on the sofa, feeling cold although it was a mild afternoon. 'Eric was humiliated at being dumped, when he was the one who wanted to do the dumping. Then there was the money. Ma wanted a lump sum so she could buy a flat, as well as maintenance for Louise, and herself.'

'Did she get it?'

'Yes, he was quite generous, actually. The trouble is, instead of buying the flat in Emperor's Gate with cash from the settlement, she instead arranged a large mortgage so she could use Eric's money to pay for other things.'

Nina raised her eyebrows and looked askance at this. 'And?'

'Then she asked him to pay off the mortgage.'

'Some smart lady, isn't she?' her friend commented. She'd never really liked Arabella, but she was Joanna's mother so that was that. There was something chilling about her under the charm. For one thing, Arabella's desperate desire for personal recognition completely overshadowed any concern she might feel for others. She had an overweening ambition. She also had a knack of making some people feel inferior to her, including Joanna who didn't even realise she was being manipulated because she so adored her mother. The really diabolical thing about Arabella, Nina reflected, was that she never *appeared* manipulative. People, including her two daughters, actually believed they were acting of their own free will in their dealings with her.

Joanna didn't yet fully realise it but what her mother really wanted was for Joanna to be her satellite, orbiting around her own starry presence, promoting and glorifying her until she became the most famous designer in the business. Totally without malice, because it had genuinely never struck her that Joanna might want a life of her own,

Arabella had believed that by persuading her to join the company, she was doing her a great favour.

Joanna spoke then, breaking into Nina's thoughts. 'I wonder what made the police suspect Eric?'

Nina considered this for a moment before answering. 'If he really was getting fed up with your mother's financial demands, then there's your motive, honey.'

At the police station the grilling was still going on, and Walsh was not letting go. If either of the men felt hungry or tired, neither of them was giving way. Chambers, still sitting beside the tape recorder, was longing for a pee. He moved carefully on the hard plastic chair, wondering when Walsh would bring this interview to a conclusion so they could all have a break.

Right now he was using the tactics of an angler, drawing in his catch, then letting it out a fraction, then gently easing it in once more, slowly, carefully, nearer and nearer.

'What was the reason for your divorce?' he was asking Eric, almost conversationally.

'Arabella had an infinite capacity for boredom.'

'You said *had*,' Walsh interrupted. 'Why are you talking about her in the past tense?'

'Because she has not been a part of my life since we divorced. When something ceases to *be*, it becomes *was*,' Eric retorted fastidiously.

'What was the sex like? Was she demanding?'

Eric flushed furiously. 'That's gross impertinence, and has nothing whatsoever to do with the present situation.'

114

'And what exactly *is* the present situation, Professor? Tell me. I'd be very interested to know.'

'The present situation is that you're wasting my valuable time, causing me great annoyance, and I want to know how long you're going to keep up this farce?'

'Professor, most people in your situation demand the presence of their solicitor. Tell me, why haven't you done that?'

'Because I've nothing to hide,' Eric replied arrogantly. 'My conscience is clear.'

Walsh looked pointedly at his wrist watch. 'That remains to be seen. I'm told the search of your house and the excavation of your garden won't be completed until tomorrow or even the next day. In the meantime you will remain here in police custody. That completes the interview held in the presence of DI Walsh and DS Chambers at five-fifty-eight p.m.'

An hour later DI Walsh returned Joanna's earlier calls.

'I'm sorry I couldn't get back to you sooner,' he said, his voice more gentle and considerate than on previous occasions. 'And I'm sorry,' he continued, 'that I didn't have a chance to warn you about what was going to happen.'

'Are you charging my stepfather with murder?' she asked hollowly.

'So far we haven't found any incriminating evidence and at the moment he is vehemently denying having anything to do with Mrs Webster's disappearance.'

'And his garden?' Joanna asked falteringly.

'How do you know about that, Miss Knight?' Walsh asked sharply.

'Mrs Holmes told me. I used to live there, you know. They couldn't find the key to get out to the garden . . .' Her voice trailed away.

'I see. I'm sorry you had to hear in that way. Nothing has been found so far. We had to stop working because of nightfall, but we'll resume first thing in the morning,' Walsh said.

'So you really believe he killed my mother?' she whispered.

'Let me just say at this point that he is our chief suspect, but without hard evidence we will not be able to charge him. It's that vital evidence we're looking for. We've managed to put together a picture of last Monday morning. The Professor's next-door neighbour came forward yesterday and made a statement. It appears that at around eight-thirty he saw, through an open window, Mrs Webster and the Professor engaged in a violent argument. He was actually threatening her. Our witness was then called away to answer his own phone and when he looked back later, there was no sign of either of them.'

'Why didn't he come forward sooner?'

'He left later that morning on a trip to Kenya. He's been on safari ever since and it was only when he returned home yesterday that he heard about your mother's disappearance.'

'Oh, my God! What about Mrs Holmes? Why hasn't she said anything?'

'Because she was still away on that day, having

been given a long weekend off. Tell me, Miss Knight, did your mother and stepfather have frequent quarrels?'

'Not frequent, but they did have the occasional fight. Like all married couples, I suppose.'

'Was it a volatile relationship? Did things often get thrown?'

'Sometimes,' she agreed cautiously. Arabella had a hot temper, and Eric had mastered the art of winding her up until she exploded with rage. 'Yes, I suppose it was rather volatile,' Joanna admitted.

'Have you any idea what he might have been referring to when he allegedly said: "If you do that, Arabella, I'll kill you"?'

She clutched the phone, the hairs on the back of her neck tingling. It was almost as if she could hear Eric's voice saying it.

'I don't know.'

'Could they have been fighting over custody of Louise?'

'That's the one thing they didn't fight about. It was agreed from the beginning that she would live with my mother but spend alternate weekends with her father, and also some time during the school holidays.'

'And your mother was happy to go along with that?'

'Quite happy. When she and my father divorced they had the same arrangement over me, and it worked very well.'

'Yes, I know. I've spoken to your father at some length.'

'So what happens now?' Joanna visualised the

117

autocratic Eric Webster, sharp-featured and angry-eyed, forced to remain in a holding cell. How would he cope without his extensive library, his doting housekeeper and his comfortable sybaritic lifestyle?

'According to Professor Webster, your mother slammed out of the house and drove away and that was the last time he saw her. But I'm convinced he's lying.'

'Oh, God.' Joanna felt her precarious composure shatter into a million shards. She started to shake. Walsh continued speaking. Through the pounding in her ears it sounded as if he was at the bottom of a swimming pool.

'We are currently searching all the garages in Clabon Mews in the hopes of finding Mrs Webster's car. We gather the Professor keeps his own car there, in a lock-up garage.'

'Yes,' she whispered, feeling as if she was drifting away, losing her grip on what was happening.

'If you can think of anything that might be helpful, just leave a message and I'll get right back to you,' Walsh concluded.

'And you'll let me know if . . .?' Joanna spoke with difficulty, barely able to breathe for the tightness in her chest.

'Yes. Of course.'

When she hung up, Joanna curled up in a foetal position and stayed like that for a long time. Long enough to persuade herself the police must have got it wrong. Long enough to slip into a state of semi-denial because she simply wasn't ready to face the truth.

Morning, Tuesday 28 September

Reality kicked back in with savage intensity the next morning when, after a bad night, she arrived at the office shortly after eight. The tabloids had found out it was Arabella's ex-husband who was being questioned and it was his garden that the police were digging up at this very moment.

The workroom was in an uproar with the younger girls weeping copiously. No one, on hearing the latest news, could cling to the hope that Arabella might still be found alive.

Rosie, looking stunned, carried on working like an automaton, her eyes blank and unseeing. Eleanor, at her desk, was whispering into her phone, bent double and shielding it with her hand. When Joanna looked at her she straightened up guiltily, her face stained an ugly red.

'I was just making an appointment with my gynae,' she said defiantly, although no one had asked. 'You shouldn't have bothered to come in. We can manage. Everything's under control. The girls in the workroom will soon calm down when I've talked to them.' Her black eyes locked intently with Joanna's. 'There's no need for you to be here.'

Joanna stood quite still in the middle of the top landing, staring at Eleanor through her open office door, as if trying to find the answer to a riddle that kept eluding her.

'I'm OK,' she said faintly. 'I have a lot to do.'

Jeremy had phoned her the previous evening and asked her how work was going, on top of all the stress

119

she was under. 'Are you managing all right without your mother?' he'd asked in concern.

'Eleanor's really got the bit between her teeth, Dad. She's upsetting Rosie and everyone in the workroom. I don't know what to do about her. I'm exhausted, and I don't have the experience to deal with everything.'

'Who's going to run the business on a day-to-day level, for the time being?' he'd asked.

Joanna knew what he really meant was: What's going to happen now Arabella's not coming back?

'That's the problem. I'm doing my best, but I haven't the experience. I can go on handling the PR, I suppose.'

Jeremy detected the reluctance in her voice, knowing, although she might not realise it herself and would not say so at this moment if she did, that she'd really like to go back to her original plan of going to art school. She'd never wanted to work for her mother. In his opinion, although some might say he was putting it too strongly, Arabella had used emotional blackmail to get Joanna to give up her chosen career. He also wondered who would design the next collection, if there was one.

'Have you talked to anyone about this?' he'd asked instead.

'Like who?'

'Arabella must have a good lawyer, and surely her backers want to know what's happening? It seems to me that a business manager should be appointed, one with experience of fashion houses.'

'Everyone's been very solicitous, ringing up and asking if there's anything they can do but . . . well, Ma's irreplaceable, isn't she? She *is* the company.'

'I know, sweetheart.'

'I don't know what's going to happen and I worry about the staff. More than twenty people depend on the company for their living.'

'Jo, that's not your responsibility. In the end you're a PR, not a dress designer. You've got your own life to lead.'

'Right now it seems as if Ma has *made* it my worry.'

As she sat at her desk now, those words came back to Joanna. Rosie was bringing all the workroom problems and grievances to her, not because she had the answers but because she was Arabella's daughter. There was a pile of work cluttering her desk. A long list of phone calls to make. Queries to answer. Fashion editors to talk to. And on top of all that Eleanor's neurotic sniping to deal with.

Afternoon, Tuesday 28 September

Joanna leaned back in her swivel chair, resting her head against the curved and padded back, her eyes closed.

God, Ma, how could you let this happen? she reflected in silent anguish and anger. I feel like I'm going crazy . . .

How *dare* you leave me like this? And Louise, too? The poor little thing is missing you terribly and I don't know what I'm going to do about her . . . Dad and Victoria can't look after her forever and . . . Oh, shit, it's all such a mess!

I simply can't do it all. I wish to God you'd never

made me be your PR. I wish I was at St Martin's . . .

I know it's not your fault. I know I shouldn't blame you and it's awful to feel so angry, but I'll never forgive you for leaving me like this. If you *knew* what I'm going through.

I can't eat. I hardly sleep. I feel ill . . .

She rose and stood looking out of the window, arms crossed in front of her, tears running down her cheeks, splashing on to her dark shirt.

I *hate* you right now, Ma.

'Designer Arabella Webster's ex-husband is still being questioned . . .'

Joanna, Freddie and Nina were watching the BBC nine o'clock news but nothing fresh was being reported, except that Eric now seemed to have acquired the services of a solicitor. A middle-aged distinguished-looking man with grey hair and wearing a pin-striped suit was shown in a clip of film, captioned *Howard Miller, Solicitor.*

'Professor Webster,' he proclaimed, as he stood on the steps of the police station, 'categorically denies any involvement whatsoever in the disappearance of Arabella Webster. He will continue to assist the police in any way he can.'

Then he strode off to a waiting car, refusing to answer the barrage of questions hurled at him by the press.

Freddie put his arm around Joanna's shoulders, and pulled her closer. Although she didn't say anything he could tell she was near to breaking point.

'They're going to have to charge Eric by tomorrow or release him,' he commented.

'They couldn't do that, could they?' she asked, shocked.

'Why can't they go on questioning him until he admits what he's done?' Nina demanded.

'They're not allowed to hold a suspect for longer than thirty-six hours, if they have no evidence against him.'

Joanna turned to look at him. 'Eric's not going to get away with it, is he?'

Freddie reached for her hand. 'I wish I could say of course he isn't, but the law's the law. If they have nothing to pin on him then they're forced to let him go. But it doesn't mean they couldn't re-arrest him if fresh evidence were to turn up.'

Joanna covered her eyes with her other hand. 'Jesus, is this ever going to end?'

Nina watched her anxiously. 'You must try not to torture yourself, Jo. You're going to get sick at this rate.' She exchanged worried looks with Freddie. 'Why don't you have a bath and get into bed, and I'll make you a hot drink? I still have the sleeping pills my doctor gave me for the flight. I'm going to give you one. What you need is a good night's sleep.'

Joanna shook her head. 'Thanks, Nina, but I never take pills. I'll be OK. I can't give in now. I've got to see this whole thing through to the end.'

'It'll be the end of you if you go on like this,' Nina said robustly. 'Freddie, make her go to bed. You won't be fit for anything, Jo, if you don't take care of yourself. Look how much weight you've lost. That skirt is hanging off you.'

'It was always too big for me,' Joanna replied, but she

was smiling weakly. 'OK, I'll get into bed, although it's absurdly early.'

'And have some hot milk and a sleeping pill?' Nina persisted.

'Of course she will,' Freddie said, rising and pulling Joanna gently to her feet. 'Come on, babe, I'll even wash your back if you're a good girl.'

It was like being a child again, having people fuss around her. Freddie even tucked in her side of the bed as she sat sipping the warm milk. And, like a child, Joanna found herself feeling comforted and reassured.

Within ten minutes she was fast asleep, the first time she had dropped off so quickly in two weeks.

Early morning, Wednesday 29 September

'It's a call for you, Joanna.'

She opened her eyes slowly, trying to remember what was happening. She'd been asleep for what seemed like an eternity. Now, confused, she wondered what her friend Nina was doing, standing over her with the phone. Shouldn't she be in Washington?

Suddenly, like a dark cloud descending and filling her horizon with pain and fear, everything came back to her.

'What time is it?'

'Half-past ten, sugar. There's a call for you. It's Detective Inspector Walsh.'

'*What?* Oh, God!' An arrow of pain shot through her heart. She grabbed the phone from Nina.

'Hello? What's happening? Has he confessed?' she

asked anxiously, the words tumbling nervously out of her.

'Unfortunately not,' the detective said flatly. 'We haven't been able to turn up a shred of evidence against him, and he's still maintaining Mrs Webster left his house after their argument.'

'But . . .'

'We've dug up every inch of his garden,' Walsh continued, 'and conducted a thorough search of his house, and there's nothing. Absolutely no evidence we can pin on him at all.'

The disappointment was overwhelming. It looked as if they were right back where they'd started. 'So you're letting him go?' Joanna asked, appalled.

'He remains our number one suspect but we may have a problem proving his guilt.' Walsh sounded dispirited. 'We had to release him at eight o'clock yesterday evening, owing to lack of evidence.'

'But you're still convinced he's guilty?'

'I'm certain of it. It's simply a question of trying to prove it. For all we know it may have been a contract killing which could make it more difficult.'

'I can't bear this,' she moaned softly.

'Miss Knight, you have my deepest sympathy. This is a terrible time for you and I'm only telling you all this because I want you to know we are doing everything we can. I don't have to tell you how seriously we are treating this case.'

So the nightmare wasn't coming to an end. Instead it was getting darker, more convoluted, more sinister. She tried breathing deeply to quell the rising panic.

'My stepfather hasn't got an alibi, has he?'

'We've discovered he kept an appointment with his publisher at ten o'clock that morning, looking perfectly calm and acting quite normally. But he doesn't have an alibi up to that time.

'As you know we've set up an incident room and we're putting extra manpower on to this case. Rest assured, Miss Knight, we're doing everything we can.'

'Hiya, kid. How are you doing?' Nina came quietly back into the bedroom a little while later and plumped herself on the side of the bed, making it sag lopsidedly. She put a mug of tea and a plate of buttered toast on the bedside table. 'It's kinda tough, eh?'

Joanna nodded, unable to speak. She was so stricken with grief she'd stayed in bed, unable to move.

Nina grasped her hand. 'Is there anything else I can get you?'

'It's just hit me that Ma really must be dead and I'll never see her again. I don't think I can bear it! I never got to say goodbye. The last time I saw her was on the Friday evening before the show. She was still working and I left without even saying good night.'

'Don't be so hard on yourself, Jo. Your ma would have understood.'

'But I miss her so . . .' Wracked with sobs, she buried her face in her hands.

Nina patted her shoulder. 'Have a good cry. It'll make you feel better. I don't believe in this English stiff upper lip thing. Let it all hang out, I say.'

'The trouble is, one minute I hate her and then

the next I don't know what I'm going to do without her.'

'That's quite normal, too. When my grandmother died my mother said she'd like to kill her, she was so angry with her for leaving them all.'

Joanna reached for the box of tissues on the floor by the side of her bed, and blew her nose.

'I'll die if that old bugger Eric gets away with it.'

'Are you really sure it's him?'

'I just know it is. So do the police. I knew he was sick of Mummy always asking for more money but I think she must have gone too far this time. He's always had a filthy temper.'

'You mean, he might have killed her accidentally? Pushed her over and she banged her head or something?'

'I'm not sure I know what I mean. I wish I'd tried to stop her going on at him, though. The trouble was,' Joanna added in a low voice, 'I was scared of facing up to her.'

'Most children find it tough squaring up to a parent.'

'No, there were times I was *really* scared of her. She was such a strong character – didn't like being criticised. She once flew at me and was really nasty because I told her she didn't suit pink.'

'I guess you were in awe of her because you were young. That's different from being scared.'

Joanna shook her head sadly. 'No, I was scared,' she insisted. 'I knew I could never be like her, and I knew she preferred beautiful women to plain ones. And she liked dynamic people while I was never able to stand up to her. She used to say I didn't know how to make the best of myself. And of course, compared to her, she was right.'

'Will you stop being negative about yourself?' Nina rebuked with friendly firmness. 'There's not a thing in the world wrong with you. All mothers are critical of their daughters. Look at mine! She tells people I'm so fat I look six months pregnant, and why can't I be a stick insect like her?'

Joanna managed a watery grin. 'What would I do without you, Nina?'

'Tell me, what was Eric's attitude when your mother told him she was leaving?'

Joanna's eyes kindled as she recalled the moment. She'd been in her bedroom at Milner Street, next to her mother's, when she'd overheard Arabella haranguing Eric, telling him she was leaving him. 'He stormed off,' she told Nina now, 'yelling at the top of his voice that he'd make sure she lived to regret it.'

Lunchtime, Wednesday 30 September

The showroom resembled a florist's. Dozens of blooms, some formally arranged, others artfully designed to look countrified, were being delivered every few minutes with touching notes of sympathy from scores of friends and acquaintances, clients, members of the media and even rival designers. It was as if Arabella's world had finally made up its mind, after eighteen days of speculation, that she was dead.

One of the juniors laid sheets around the outside edge of the floor where she placed the bouquets in ever-increasing heaps. Soon only a narrow pathway lay between the carpet of flowers.

A spray of white lilies from Arabella's favourite shoe manufacturer was placed in the window beside a simple black evening dress.

Sacks of mail were delivered too. There were over five hundred letters and cards of condolence, some addressed to Joanna personally, others to the rest of the staff in general.

'Eleanor, could you hire a couple of temps to deal with all these?' she asked distractedly. 'We'll have to answer them all individually. Isn't it wonderful that so many people loved my mother?'

Eleanor looked at her strangely but made no comment.

Five

A hysterical Melosa was on the phone while they were still having breakfast, jarring the morning calm with her shrill voice.

'We've been robbed!' she wailed. 'The mess . . . it is terrible. What shall I do? The flat . . . it is ruined!'

Joanna put down the mug of coffee she was holding. Freddie and Nina stopped munching cereal, able to hear Melosa's penetrating voice from where they sat at the kitchen table.

'When did this happen?'

'I dunno – I just got back now. You said I could have the weekend off to see my sister, you remember?' the housekeeper demanded accusingly.

'Yes, I remember.'

'It catastrophe!'

'Stay there, Melosa. I'll ring the police and then I'll come right over.'

She sobbed hysterically, 'I'm afraid to stay here.'

'Then wait downstairs in the main hall. And don't

131

touch anything. I'll be with you as soon as I can.' Joanna replaced the receiver and turned to the others. 'You got the gist of that?'

'I wonder if there's a connection?' Nina suggested.

Freddie shook his head, his mouth full. 'Probably not,' he said when he could speak. 'An empty flat at the weekend is an invitation to any robber.'

'I'd better get over there.' Joanna downed the rest of her coffee and dumped the mug in the sink. 'I'll phone DI Walsh on the way.' She shot back into the bedroom, gathered up her things and then rushed back to kiss Freddie.

''Bye,' he said. 'Let me know how you get on. I'll be in the office all day today.'

'Will you be going to work later on?' Nina asked.

'I expect so. 'Bye.'

Joanna hailed a passing cab and, once seated, tapped in DI Walsh's now familiar number. For once he was available.

'Yes, Miss Knight.' He sounded hopeful. 'Have you any news for me?'

'I have, but I don't think it has anything to do with my mother's disappearance,' she explained breathlessly. 'Her flat's been broken into. I've just had a call from her housekeeper who got back from the country a short while ago and discovered the break-in. I'm on my way there now.'

'We'll be right over.'

Joanna arrived at Emperor's Gate first. Arabella had insisted she should have a set of keys to the flat in case of emergency and so, letting herself in through the main street door, she almost stumbled into Melosa, who was cowering against the radiator in the communal hall. Her face was white and pasty-looking, her dark eyes even more melancholy than usual. She was still in her street clothes, clutching her handbag to her chest.

'Are you all right?' Joanna asked anxiously.

'It is terrible. First your mother, now this – what's going to become of us all?' Melosa wrung her hands in tearful despair.

Compared to what had been happening recently, a burglary was nothing, Joanna thought. Material things could easily be replaced. People were far more important than possessions. Leading the way, she hurried up the blue-carpeted stairs to the first floor with Melosa following nervously. The door to Arabella's apartment was open. Joanna entered the small square hall and then stopped dead in her tracks. The living-room and dining-room doors were wide open and she could see into the once perfect rooms.

'Oh, shit!' She stepped forward, hardly able to believe her eyes.

The place had been trashed. It looked as if a tornado had swept through each room, creating a turbulence that tossed everything up in the air so it crashed back down again. Broken glass and china paved the floors, a drift of white feathers from slashed cushions trembled upon the overturned furniture. Lamps lay on the floor in a tangle of flex, their shades at drunken angles. An oil painting had been ripped by a sharp instrument; a mirror shattered as if a heavy ornament had been thrown at it.

Walking on tiptoe over the crunching glass, Joanna stepped forward gingerly and looked into her mother's bedroom. If anything the destruction was worse there. It was a scene of madness. Clothes, some garments still on their hangers, had been torn to shreds with awesome violence. Most shocking of all, the word 'Whore' had been written in lipstick across a long looking glass.

'It's unbelievable,' Joanna said again in a horrified whisper. The burglary *was* connected with Arabella, after all. 'Whoever did this really hated her.'

DI Walsh said very much the same when he arrived a few minutes later with DS Chambers.

'It's an act of pure vengeance,' he remarked, looking at the damage which also extended to Arabella's en suite bathroom.

Further investigation, however, showed that the kitchen and Melosa's bedroom and bathroom were untouched.

'That proves it was directed at Mrs Webster personally,' he said. They went back into the hall and he looked at the staircase.

'What's up there?'

'Louise's bedroom, the spare room and a bathroom,' Joanna replied.

Walsh turned to Chambers. 'Have a look, will you? I bet they haven't been touched either.'

As Chambers mounted the stairs two at a time, Melosa burst into loud tears.

'I'm afraid . . . I can't stay. I have to go!' she sobbed, flapping her arms about. 'I don't want to get killed, too.'

Joanna put an arm around her shoulders. 'Of course

you can go, Melosa. You must return to your sister's. Why don't you pack a few things and I'll arrange for a car to take you back to Guildford?'

Walsh intervened, his voice gentle. 'I would like to ask you some questions first, Melosa. That is, if you feel well enough to talk to us for a few minutes?' he added courteously.

She became quieter, wiping her cheeks with the back of her small plump hands, her sobs reduced to gulping hiccups. 'I know nothing,' she kept saying.

Chambers came lumbering down the stairs again, his tread heavy in his thick-soled shoes. 'Everything's okay upstairs, sir.'

Walsh nodded. 'As I thought.' Then he turned to Melosa again. 'Can you tell us when you got back here today?'

'Before I ring Joanna,' she quavered.

'What time was that?'

She shrugged and Chambers started making notes.

'About eight-thirty,' Joanna interjected.

'I suppose,' Melosa agreed.

'And how long had you been away?'

She looked alarmed. 'J-Joanna, she say I can have the weekend off. It was all right for me to go.'

Joanna smiled at her reassuringly. 'Of course I said you could go away. The Inspector just wants to know which day you left here.'

'Friday afternoon, like you tell me. That all I know.'

'That's all right, Melosa,' Walsh said. 'So this place has been empty for two clear days. You obviously have your own set of keys?'

She nodded silently.

'Was the door open or closed when you arrived?'

'Locked. Like always.'

'So you had to unlock the main street door, and then this door, to get in?'

She nodded again.

'Can you tell us if anything is missing?'

The housekeeper shrugged expressively. 'How do I know? It is all mess.'

'Quite.' He shot Joanna a quick look. 'Would you be in a position to know if anything had been taken?'

She thought for a moment. 'If it were anything of importance, I'd probably know. I helped my mother move in. There should be some silver in the cupboard in the dining room, and there's a safe in her bedroom where she keeps her jewellery. As for the rest . . .' She glanced around sadly. 'To be honest, I'm not sure.'

A quick look in the dining room revealed the silver cupboard was still locked and hadn't been touched. Then they entered Arabella's wrecked bedroom again and found that the safe, at the back of her wardrobe and cleverly hidden behind what looked like a panelled wall, had not been tampered with either.

'I get the feeling that whoever did this was looking for something and, when they couldn't find it, they just tore the place to pieces,' Walsh observed. 'We'll get forensic to go over the whole place for fingerprints, but it's obviously an inside job and I suspect whoever did all this was careful not to leave any traces behind.'

Joanna's eyes widened. 'An inside job?' she repeated.

'No forced entry,' he replied briefly. 'Who else has keys

136

apart from you and the housekeeper?'

'Only my mother, as far as I know.' She frowned. 'If Melosa had hers, and mine are always kept in my handbag with my own keys . . . how can anyone else have a set?'

There was a silence Walsh didn't seem to want to break. Chambers looked at him. So did Joanna.

'Your mother may have given someone else a set,' he said at last, 'someone you don't know about. Alternatively hers may have been taken from her when she . . . disappeared.'

Walsh was silent, deep in thought, as he and Chambers gave Joanna a lift back to Pimlico Road. Melosa had been seen off, still trembling, and Joanna had given the detectives her set of Emperor's Gate keys for forensic to use while examining the flat.

'Do you think Eric could have trashed the place?' she asked tentatively.

Walsh's mouth tightened. 'Well, he couldn't have done it himself because we were keeping him under close surveillance. He hasn't left his house since he was released on Tuesday.'

'I didn't know you were watching him?'

'He's still our chief suspect. But I'm puzzled about this break-in . . . I don't see any motive for it. Especially from his point of view.'

'Perhaps he got someone else to do it?'

'Contract killers don't waste their time and risk being caught for merely wrecking a place. You remember I asked you some time ago if your mother was involved with drugs?'

She nodded uneasily.

Walsh shifted position in the front passenger seat so he could talk more easily to her over his shoulder.

'I'd say this break-in is the work of someone who is afraid there's incriminating evidence in her flat. They were obviously searching for something, and when they couldn't find what they were after, they went berserk and ripped the place to pieces.'

Joanna looked mystified. 'How do you know that?'

He gave her one of his rare smiles. 'You know the papers your mother kept in that Chinese chest drop-in file? The contents were clearly under the ornaments, lamps and what-have-you that were strewn around.'

Chambers drew up outside Arabella Designs. Several photographers were hanging around watchfully. As soon as they realised Joanna was in the back of the car they came forward, eager to get yet another shot of MISSING DESIGNER'S DISTRAUGHT DAUGHTER, for tomorrow's tabloids.

Both Walsh and Chambers got out to escort her across the pavement.

'Anything to tell us, love?' one asked.

'How do you feel about your stepfather being released?' demanded another.

'Miss Knight has nothing to say,' Walsh said firmly. As Joanna slipped inside he added quietly, 'We'll be in touch.'

Joanna phoned her father as soon as she got up to her office. Briefly she told him what had happened.

'What do the police think?'

She closed the door with her foot and talked in a low voice so she wouldn't be overheard.

'DI Walsh thinks someone was scared there was evidence lying around that might incriminate them for buying drugs. He's not sure and he admits he's speculating, but he believes that's why they ransacked her flat. Then trashed it out of frustration, because they couldn't find what they wanted. It's some sort of vengeance attack.'

'And nothing to do with Eric?'

'Nothing.'

'Listen, sweetheart, I wanted to talk to you about Louise . . .'

'Is she all right?'

'Absolutely fine, but it's becoming increasingly difficult to keep things from her. Eric hasn't phoned or been in touch. He's probably humiliated and scared in case Louise believes he *did* kill her mother, and I don't want to do anything without consulting you first, Jo. Are we to tell her Arabella has died and that her father has been accused of murder or what? We're keeping all the newspapers away from her at the moment, and not letting her watch television except under our supervision, but we can't keep the poor little thing in the dark forever.'

'I've been worrying about that, too. If we do tell her, she's going to be totally devastated, isn't she? It will mean, in effect, she'll have lost both parents. But how long can we keep it all from her? She's going to have to know sooner or later.'

'I think we should wait until we know more, Jo. It will be easier for her, in the long run, if she's presented with a *fait accompli* rather than have to go through the night-marish doubts you're having to face at the moment. If Eric *is* innocent, better she doesn't know until she's much older that he was ever accused of murdering her mother in the first place.'

'I agree, Dad.' Joanna felt sombre. At least Eric wasn't *her* father. What a terrible burden of knowledge Louise was going to carry around for the rest of her life if he was guilty.

'As a matter of fact,' Jeremy continued with a spark of his accustomed good humour, 'Victoria and I had a brainwave yesterday. You know Eric has always said he didn't want Louise living with him because, with all his lecture tours and general lifestyle, he couldn't provide a steady background for her. I'm due for some leave from *Metropolis*. Suppose we take Louise to Brittany for a little holiday? The weather won't be great but it's far enough away to avoid the daily battering of the press, and relatively cheap. She's not likely to overhear anything there. I'm sure Eric won't mind. What do you say?'

Joanna felt a swift wave of relief. 'Daddy, you're a star. That would be such a weight off my mind. I've been dreadfully worried about her. I know Eric can't cope. He never could really. Whatever happens I think she's going to have to live with Freddie and me, once the dust is settled, but I haven't even discussed this with him yet.'

'My darling girl, Victoria and I love having her here and we're only too happy to look after her for as long as you like. You've got enough on your plate at the moment. Look, leave it to us. We'll say we're going on a little holiday and invite her to come with us. How does that sound?'

'It sounds like you're the best father in the world.'

'Has she got her own passport?'

'Yes, she has but that might be a problem. It's at the flat. I'll have to ask the police to retrieve it from the debris and get it over to you.'

'Fine. I'll start making the arrangements and give Eric a ring soon.'

'Thanks, Dad. I'm really grateful.'

'It's no problem, darling. We're very fond of her.'

One of the temps hired by Eleanor had become Joanna's personal assistant, dealing with a lot of her calls as well as attending to the letters of condolence. She was called Alice, and was nineteen, eager and helpful. Squeezed into a corner of Joanna's office, at a hastily provided desk so the phones could be placed between them, she was also good company. She ran errands, brought back sandwiches for lunch and provided a sympathetic ear when it was required.

'I'm going to the bank now,' Joanna told her at lunchtime. 'I'll only be fifteen minutes.'

Eleanor was hovering on the landing just outside the door. 'Can I go for you?' she offered, having obviously overheard. 'Or would you like me to sign a company cheque?' she added helpfully.

'No, thanks. I'm cashing a personal cheque,' Joanna replied. 'Anyway, that wouldn't help, would it? Without Arabella's signature we can't cash cheques at the moment.'

Was it her imagination or did Eleanor turn deep red? 'Oh, that hasn't been fixed then?' she said quickly. 'I imagined accounts would have done something about that.'

Evening, Monday 4 October

Nina arrived to pick Joanna up so they could both go on to see Louise and have a drink with Victoria and Jeremy.

'Will you look at these dresses!' Nina exclaimed as she stood in the middle of the showroom, examining a rail of clothes. 'Why are all rich women thin? What size are these? Eight? Ten?' She sighed gustily. 'I'd need *four* stitched together before I could get into this style.'

Joanna grinned. 'Some are ten, but most are twelve. They're very well cut which is why they look as if they're for someone slim.'

'*Slim?* They look as if they're for nubile twelve year olds.' Nina shook her head, laughing. 'Nothing in an eighteen or twenty, I suppose? Not that I could afford it anyway.' She fingered the sleeve of a mulberry velvet jacket and looked wistful. 'I wish I took after my ma instead of my pa, who's like a pumpkin.'

Joanna slung her arm around her friend's shoulder. 'You're perfect as you are and I wouldn't want you to change a thing about yourself,' she said affectionately. 'Let's go. Dad's expecting us. Then we're meeting Freddie for dinner. Not that I feel I can eat a thing.'

In the taxi on the way to Portsea Place, Nina spoke. 'What's the latest? Was much stolen from your mother's flat?'

Joanna turned to look at her in genuine amazement. 'God, this morning seems like ages ago.' She shook her head as if feeling dizzy. 'My life is becoming unreal.'

By the time they arrived Nina was up to speed on what was happening. She looked at Joanna warningly. 'If it *is* to do with the drugs scene, shouldn't you be careful? You don't want them wreaking vengeance on you, too, sugar.'

'The police would have warned me if they'd thought I was in danger. I can still hardly believe my mother would be involved in something like this but I suppose it makes sense. She did know a lot of people who were part of the drugs scene. It just never occurred to me that she'd be a part of it, too.'

When they arrived Jeremy, with Louise beside him, opened the door. There were hugs and kisses all round, and then they trooped down to the kitchen where Victoria was feeding Caspar.

'We're going on holiday,' Louise informed them importantly, 'and Caspar's going on holiday, too.'

'Lucky old Caspar,' Joanna exclaimed. 'Where's he going?'

'Not far. Just to the house next door. The neighbours love him and they're going to look after him while we're away. But I wish we could take him with us,' Louise added sadly.

'But he would miss Hyde Park,' Joanna pointed out, cuddling her half-sister on her knee. 'I bet the neighbours will spoil him something rotten, too.'

Victoria was putting glasses on the table and Jeremy was opening a bottle of wine.

143

'Joanna, you need a holiday more than any of us,' Victoria observed anxiously, looking at Joanna's hollow cheeks and thin arms.

'Why don't you come with us?' Louise suggested, her face lighting up. 'And Freddie, too. And Nina,' she added politely.

Nine intervened diplomatically. 'I'm already on holiday and staying with Joanna,' she announced cheerfully. 'What are you taking away with you? Books? Games? A swimsuit? Louise, I'd love to see what you're planning to pack. I'm hopeless. I arrive with twenty-three pairs of shoes and no knickers. Could you give me some tips?'

Overcome with giggles, Louise offered to take her upstairs to see the things she'd already put in a case. At the door she paused to say to Joanna: 'A special man on a bike delivered my passport this afternoon from Mummy's flat.'

'My word, how smart.'

Nina, winking over her shoulder, followed Louise up the stairs, signalling she'd keep the child amused for a bit so they could talk.

'Louise didn't twig anything, did she?' Joanna asked worriedly.

Jeremy smiled. 'Absolutely not. She's so excited at going to Paramé she's not really concerned about anything else. Now she knows Caspar is going to be all right, that is.'

'Before I forget . . .' Joanna delved into her capacious handbag and withdrew a bulging envelope. 'Here's some cash to help with Louise's expenses.'

'My darling girl!' Jeremy exclaimed. 'Put that away at

once. We love looking after her.'

Victoria butted in. 'That's so sweet and thoughtful of you, Joanna, but honestly, it's a pleasure to have Louise with us. We couldn't possibly accept.'

Joanna placed the envelope in the middle of the table, propped up against a vase of scabious, their delicate shade of mauve echoing the lavender-coloured table cloth. 'I want you to have it,' she told them firmly. 'You've no idea how much it means to me to know Louise is safe and happy. Whatever you say, this trip is going to cost a bit and I insist you take it. It's Arabella's money, and it's the least she can do for Louise now she's no longer here.'

Victoria's eyes became over bright. Since she'd retired as a teacher they didn't have much money, and it was sensitive of Joanna to take that into consideration.

'That's very, very generous, dear girl. Thank you,' she said softly.

Jeremy laid his large hand on his daughter's shoulder. 'What can I say? Only you would think of being so thoughtful. Thank you, sweetheart.' He leaned over the table and kissed her on the cheek then sighed wearily. 'I just wish I could say this story will have a happy ending, but whatever happens, you can rely on us to look after Louise until things have sorted themselves out.'

Jeremy and Victoria were sitting down to one of her delicious lamb casseroles when the phone rang.

'Damn!' he said, giving his plate a regretful glance. 'Who the hell is that?' The phone was on the other side of the kitchen. He picked up the receiver and said briskly, 'Hello?'

'Is that you, Jeremy?'

It was a man's voice and there was something vaguely familiar about it. 'Yes,' he replied cautiously.

'This is Eric speaking.'

Jeremy shot Victoria a startled glance.

'Good evening, Eric.' It was impossible to keep his surprise out of his voice. 'What can I do for you?'

'I phoned Joanna just now but she's out and her boyfriend said I could get hold of her at your house. Can I speak to her?'

'She left here about ten minutes ago, to meet Freddie at a restaurant. They'll be home later.'

'The thing is, Jeremy, I'm extremely concerned about Louise. I haven't seen her since the weekend after Arabella disappeared. Freddie says she's with you and Victoria.'

Jeremy spoke with care. Eric sounded genuinely concerned and not nearly as crusty and arrogant as usual.

'That's right. She's been here ever since. Joanna felt it was better if she wasn't told anything – at least until there's something definite to tell her. We want to spare her the pain of wondering and waiting that Joanna herself is suffering now. Obviously the child is missing her mother and perhaps suspecting the worst, but you know what children are like. We keep her occupied, and we have a dog so we go for long runs together.'

'Does she know that I . . .?' Eric began stiffly.

'Absolutely not. Newspapers, radio and television

have been banned ever since. She has no idea what's been happening and we've been telling her you're extremely busy but will get in touch as soon as you can.'

'Thank you. But she'll have to know her mother's dead, sooner or later.'

'I know, but Joanna is adamant that she isn't told how serious things are yet. These are very difficult circumstances. If Louise were my child, I'd have told her from the start, but they're very close and I feel I must abide by Joanna's wishes.'

'Quite.'

Jeremy pulled a kitchen chair towards him so he could sit down. Victoria had put his dinner back in the oven to keep warm. As diplomatically as he could, stressing it was for Louise's sake, he told Eric they were planning to take her to Brittany for a couple of weeks. 'By then, we may have a clearer picture and Joanna can tell her everything. I was planning to phone and let you know.'

To his surprise, Eric didn't seem annoyed. In fact he said immediately, 'Thanks, old man. That's very good of you. You must allow me to send you a cheque to cover her expenses.'

'That's not necessary,' Jeremy said firmly.

'Would it be possible to have a word with Louise now?'

Suddenly Jeremy felt quite sorry for the poor sod. 'Actually, she's asleep, but why don't you phone back in the morning, Eric?'

'I'll do that. Thank you, Jeremy, and please extend my thanks to Victoria. I'm most grateful that Louise is in such good hands,' he added with typical formality.

'It's a pleasure to have her here. She's a dear little girl.'

'I know,' he said quietly.

Morning, Thursday 7 October

DI Walsh looked at Chambers quizzically. 'Well, *that's* a turn-up for the books,' he remarked dryly. 'You're telling me that fifteen days after Arabella Webster disappeared, someone went to Banham Locks in Kensington High Street and requested a new set of keys for her flat?'

'That's right, sir. There are two sets of locks on each door. The street door has a Banham lock and a Chubb lock, and so does the door to her flat. You can get the JMB Chubb keys anywhere, but not Banham.' Chambers consulted his notes. 'So that means whoever went in must have posed as Mrs Webster – only registered keyholders can request spares. And it looks like her signature too. And to get copies made they have to produce the original set.'

'I think we all know that,' Walsh replied with a touch of sarcasm. 'The thing is . . . it couldn't have been Mrs Webster herself because I'm certain she's dead, so who was it? They took a risk, didn't they? The assistant at Banham Locks obviously doesn't read the papers! And why did they want a second set if they already had originals?'

Chambers leaned forward eagerly. 'Whoever it was must be linked to her murder.'

'That doesn't necessarily follow.'

'You think the two incidents are unconnected, then?'

'It's too soon to be sure. Did Banham's give you a description of the person?'

'They couldn't, sir. They have people coming in and out all day long ordering new keys . . .'

'Well, that's not much good then, is it?' Walsh snapped.

Chambers looked defensive. 'But they do have a security camera in operation twenty-four hours a day, and they're getting back to us with the relevant video. Hopefully that will show us . . .'

'It will show us everyone who went in for keys that morning,' Walsh cut in irritably. 'We've got to do better than that. Someone has obviously forged her signature. I want you to go to Emperor's Gate to interview all the other tenants in the building, the neighbours, and anyone who might have been around to see who entered and left the building. If we can get a description that ties in with the Banham's video then we might be getting somewhere.'

'Yes, sir.' Feeling deflated, Chambers rose and left Walsh's office. As a youngster he'd longed to join the police force and experience the glamorous lifestyle portrayed in detective films and on TV. Now he knew that in reality it meant painstaking plodding through endless minutiae, day in, day out, with no glamour whatsoever, and he was beginning to feel he'd chosen the wrong profession.

Joanna held the phone to her ear and for a moment wondered if someone was playing a joke in terrible taste.

'I'm sorry,' she said coldly. 'Who are you?'

There was a pained silence before a man with a German accent spoke, slowly and patiently, repeating what he had said.

'This is Alberic Felke, of Felke, Dörre und Schauerhammer. From Hamburg, *ja*? You've heard of us? I tried to call Eleanor Andrews just now, but I'm told she's out. The young lady I spoke to suggested I talk to you, *ja*? You are, I believe, Arabella's daughter?'

'That's right,' Joanna replied, wondering where this was leading.

'That is good. And may I offer you our deepest sympathies in your loss? As you will be aware, I have been speaking with Miss Andrews about her suggestion that my company take over Arabella Designs, her proposal being that she will run the company in future now that she has found a talented young designer to replace Arabella, *ja*?'

'*Wait a minute!*' Joanna exploded. 'I'm afraid I don't know what on earth you're talking about. Eleanor is *not* in charge of this company and nor will she ever be. I don't know anything about a new designer and Eleanor had no right to go behind my back and make these suggestions.'

There was a lengthy pause. 'Is it true what you are saying?' Alberic demanded harshly at last.

'Yes, absolutely true, I promise you,' she said, appalled by this revelation. 'No one knows what's going to happen to the company – that's in the hands of our backers, really. And Eleanor Andrews is merely Arabella's personal assistant, nothing more. She has no authority whatsoever to make future plans.'

'We have given a lot of time to studying this proposal,' he said angrily. 'We obviously had to go through all the accounts, the costings, sales projections and targets . . .'

'And Eleanor provided you with all the relevant details?' Joanna asked, aghast. That would account for her secretive phone calls and stranger than usual behaviour recently.

'Absolutely.'

'I can only say I'm very sorry you've been led up the garden path . . .'

'Garden what?'

'I'm sorry she's misled you. Wasted your time. She had no such authority.' Joanna was doodling madly on her notepad, angular little boxes, interlinking, like traps.

'This is not good,' her caller said coldly.

'I'm afraid that's the situation,' she told him. 'You should never have been told otherwise and for that I apologise.'

'So be it,' he snapped. 'Thank you and good day.'

When Joanna hung up she realised her silk shirt was sticking to her back and her head was reeling. She felt alarmed, too. If Eleanor was capable of trying to seize control like this, what else was she capable of?

In the workroom the girls were busy; the sound of softly whirring machines, steam irons and gossip filled the air. Joanna rushed over to where Rosie stood at the cutting table, large shears flashing as they sliced through a length of plum-coloured dévoré.

'Can I have a quick word, please?' Joanna asked quietly. 'I wouldn't disturb you but it's urgent.'

Rosie nodded and followed her back down to her empty office.

'Do you know where Eleanor's gone?'

'She said something about having to go and see someone,' Rosie replied. 'I don't know how long she'll be.'

'The longer the better,' Joanna remarked, closing the door so they wouldn't be overheard. Then she told Rosie what had happened.

'She never!' the workroom manageress exclaimed, scandalised. 'What a flaming cheek!'

'I know. I'm going to have to warn Arabella's lawyer what she's tried to do.' Joanna's phone started ringing then. 'Now what?' she groaned, seizing it. It was DI Walsh.

'Miss Knight, is this a convenient moment to talk?' he asked without prevarication.

'Yes. What's happened?'

'Are you able to speak without being overheard? Is Eleanor Andrews around?'

'Eleanor? She's out at the moment. Why?'

'I'd like to see you right away, but it's important Miss Andrews doesn't get wind of our conversation. It would be better if we met somewhere locally.'

What the hell was going on? What was it with Eleanor that she seemed to be the centre of interest today? 'There's a café on the opposite side of the street, towards Buckingham Palace Road. We could meet there,' Joanna suggested.

'In ten minutes? Right. See you then.'

Swearing Rosie to secrecy about the phone call, and

telling Alice, who had just come in, that she was going shopping, Joanna slipped on her jacket and hurried out. Instinct warned her it would be better if she didn't risk bumping into Eleanor for fear her own face might give away the rage and indignation she felt.

The café was almost empty at this hour, the lull before the arrival of dozens of people from the nearby timber yard wanting their midday meal of anything that went with chips.

Joanna chose a table at the back, away from the front windows. Walsh and Chambers arrived a few minutes later.

'Thank you for coming,' Walsh said, once he'd ordered three cups of tea.

'What's happened?' Joanna asked, leaning forward attentively.

'Events have taken an unexpected turn which we want to monitor very carefully before taking any further action,' he began. 'But first, let me ask you something. Has anyone ever had access to your set of keys to your mother's flat?'

Joanna looked at him in surprise. 'No one,' she replied positively. 'I keep them in my handbag all the time.'

'During the day,' he persisted, 'do you ever leave your handbag lying around? Would anyone have had the opportunity to take something from it?'

'It's always on the floor by my desk.'

'Even when you go out of your office?'

'Of course. I wouldn't take it down to the showroom or up to the workroom with me, if that's what you mean.'

'I see.' Walsh nodded in satisfaction.

Chambers slurped his tea and looked longingly at the display of doughnuts on the counter, but said nothing.

Walsh spoke again. 'I believe the keys to your mother's flat were taken from your bag some time last week to be copied at Banham's where Mrs Webster's signature was forged in order to obtain them.'

'Yes?' Joanna wished he'd get to the point instead of building up the scenario, brick by brick.

He was not to be hurried. 'Your keys were then returned to your bag, so that you never knew they'd been taken, and the new keys used to obtain entry to Mrs Webster's flat.'

'Yes, but by whom?' she asked, exasperated. 'No one in the company would do such a thing.'

'But someone did,' he assured her. 'With the help of Banham's security video and a lucky encounter Chambers had with a road sweeper in Emperor's Gate, we are able to identify the intruder who smashed up the flat. It was Eleanor Andrews.'

Joanna hadn't expected that. She gaped at Walsh, feeling as if she was standing on an ice floe which was breaking up, great chunks of it drifting away while she was left wondering which bit to stand on next.

'Eleanor?' she croaked.

Walsh nodded. 'It's obvious she was looking for something and when she couldn't find it, she went berserk. That was my original appraisal of the break-in and ensuing damage, and it seems I was right.'

Joanna leaned back in the hard plastic chair and let out a sigh. She told them about the call she'd just had.

'Eleanor would have wanted everything she could lay her hands on to send to this company in Hamburg,' she agreed. 'I don't know why Arabella didn't keep her papers in a safe.'

Walsh raised his eyebrows. 'They probably weren't worth stealing – except to someone who wanted to secure control of the company,' he added. 'Something vital must have been missing, though, to send Eleanor Andrews over the edge like that.'

Joanna frowned, trying to recall the day she'd been searching for Arabella's personal papers and she'd looked in the drop-in file in the Chinese chest. Then her eyes cleared. 'I distinctly remember now that the file marked "contracts" was empty. I thought it was vaguely odd at the time but Arabella must have put those papers somewhere else.'

Walsh nodded slowly, a dawning respect for this young woman, who seemed to be growing stronger every day, showing in his eyes. 'We now have to consider the possibility of your mother's disappearance having something to do with Eleanor Andrews.'

Joanna stared at him, speechless. 'Not Eric?' she asked.

'We must keep our options open, but it's obvious to us now that Eleanor Andrews also had a motive: she wanted control of the company.'

'Oh, my God,' Joanna said slowly.

'As we may ultimately have a great deal more on her than mere breaking, entering and causing criminal damage, we want to put her under close surveillance. So I want *you* to pretend nothing's happened, and that

155

includes her dealings with this German company.'

'But I want her out of the company – now! Before she does any real damage.'

'She mustn't suspect we're on to her.'

'Can't I tell our lawyer, in confidence? Our existing backers ought to be warned, too. For all we know, Eleanor may be running about all over the place, trying to get the company taken over by a big firm who will guarantee to put her in charge.'

'We'll be watching her so closely she won't be able to buy a loaf of bread without our knowledge. Is it possible she's got allies in the workroom?'

'Rosie and the girls would never be disloyal,' Joanna protested, shocked by the suggestion.

Walsh looked cynical. 'People have a habit of mislaying their loyalty when their jobs are on the line, Miss Knight.'

'Please stop calling me that,' she snapped. 'My name's Joanna. And you're barking up the wrong tree if you think Rosie and the others could be seduced into working for anyone else.'

Walsh pursed his lips but did not argue further. 'For the next twenty-four hours, try to keep going perfectly normally,' he requested. 'Don't let Eleanor know you're aware of anything untoward. We'll be setting up a line tap on all your phones so we can listen in to every call she makes or receives. Now,' he drew a pad from his inner pocket, 'tell me everything you know about Eleanor Andrews . . .'

It didn't take long because there was not much to know. Age: 43. Address: Joanna scribbled it down together with Eleanor's home phone number at her flat in Baron's Court. 'She's been employed by us for the past twelve years.' Mother: living in Sevenoaks, where Eleanor sometimes stayed for the weekend. Father: deceased. Status: unmarried.

'Does she swing the other way, then?' Walsh asked casually.

'My boyfriend has suggested that,' Joanna admitted, 'but I don't think so. There was certainly never anything like that between Arabella and her.'

Chambers looked up from taking his own notes, his expression conveying interest for the first time. 'How can you be sure?'

A glint of amusement shone in Joanna's eyes. 'If you'd known my mother, you wouldn't even ask that question.'

'What about friends? Has Miss Andrews got any?'

Joanna took a sip of her now cold tea. 'None that I know of. I think she's a bit of a loner.'

Walsh rose briskly. 'Right. Leave everything to us and carry on as if nothing's wrong. Whatever you do, don't let her suspect a thing. Chambers, go and pay for the tea, will you?'

Night, Thursday 7 October

'I suppose you've been told, ever since you were a little girl, that you're beautiful? Yes, I thought so. You were certainly in the front of the queue when God was handing out looks, weren't you?

157

'I've never seen such amazing hair – it's the colour of
corn, just before it ripens. You look after it, too, don't you?
Soft as silk . . .

'Was your mother beautiful? Did you get your looks
from her? Or your father? It's a tragedy when a girl takes
after her father and he's big and bulky and as ugly as sin.
Well, no one could say that about you! I'm going to call
you Willow Wand. After all, you're tall and slender, golden
and graceful. Hey! I'm becoming quite poetical, aren't I?

'Seriously, though, I feel so lucky to have you here with
me. Now, when I wake up in the morning, I want to shout
for joy! Tell the world.

'You know how one has youthful fantasies? When I was
in my teens I used to day-dream a lot; imagine I was a
knight in shining armour and all that crap. Then of course
I'd have to rescue the beautiful princess from a fate worse
than death and carry her off to some wonderful secret
place.

'Funny, isn't it? Because that's what's happened now, in
real life. Well . . . almost.'

Dawn, Friday 8 October

Joanna awoke in terror, overwhelmed by apprehension
and fear. With her heart hammering in her chest and her
hands balled into tight fists, she turned in anguish to
Freddie but he was sleeping peacefully, unaware of her
torment. Taking long deep breaths to quell her alarm,
she realised this was the third time she'd been hit by a
panic attack in the middle of the night. Jumbled

thoughts ran through her mind, taunting her with terrifying visions of what might have become of her mother.
She turned on her side, anxious not to disturb Freddie,
but the silence of the night was filled with menace and
she felt like crying out: 'Help me! Somebody, help me.'

The panic had to be faced. Lying on her back,
thinking about it, only made it worse. Sliding out of
bed, she groped for her warm dressing gown and crept
out of the room.

In the kitchen she switched on the radio at low
volume, desperate to distract her mind with the down-to-
earth background of 'Up All Night' on Radio 5 Live.
Then she made herself a cup of camomile tea. Just when
she'd thought she was coping rather well, she realised she
wasn't coming to terms with the loss of her mother after
all. Arabella, whom she feared she'd never see again.
Arabella, indomitable and courageous, a woman who
had never let anyone dampen her dazzle.

For a moment Joanna buried her head in her crossed
arms on the table, trying to fight her way back to a state
of relative calm.

Six

DS Chambers looked glumly at DI Walsh as the latter sat behind his desk wearing an expectant expression.

'I haven't been able to turn up anything new on Eleanor Andrews, sir. We've checked out all Miss Knight told us and it's true. Andrews doesn't seem to have any friends or go anywhere in the evenings. I've drawn a blank with every line of enquiry.'

Walsh blinked, unconvinced. 'She must have some sort of life, Chambers. What does she do when she's in London at the weekend?'

Chambers consulted his notes. 'She goes shopping every Saturday morning, usually at Waitrose, where she buys a week's supply of food. Then she buys some newspapers at her local corner shop, and apparently, according to the people who live in other flats in the house, stays at home, reading and watching television.'

Walsh snorted impatiently. 'No one can lead *that* sad a life.'

'I gather she does. "Keeps herself to herself," as the

woman who lives below said. She doesn't go out in the evenings, either.'

'What about her banking? And her phone bills? Does she have accounts with any of the big stores? What about her past, before she went to work at Arabella Designs? Don't tell me she hasn't got a past either or you'll have me weeping.'

Not a flicker of humour showed in Chambers' expression. 'I'll see what I can do, sir,' he replied solemnly, 'but she doesn't seem to have much of a past or a present. And by the looks of it, not much of a future, either.'

'How much longer?' Joanna spoke in a low voice into her mobile. 'It really worries me having her here.' She was alone in her office, her door open so she could keep an eye on the landing. Alice had stepped out to get the *Evening Standard* while Eleanor was down in the showroom, acting as *vendeuse*, a role Arabella herself had always undertaken, believing that no one could sell her clothes as well as she could.

'I don't know yet,' DI Walsh replied. 'We're pulling out all the stops, but it's a bit like trying to read a blank sheet of paper. Eleanor Andrews hasn't given herself away once so far.'

'Which means . . .?'

'I'm afraid you're going to have to carry on working with her as if you know nothing.'

A few minutes later Eleanor came up the stairs, her arms filled with garments. She seemed to be running on empty, her voice high-pitched and shrill, her manner excitable.

'There's so much to do,' she babbled, hovering outside Joanna's office. 'Mrs Bartholomew has bought all these clothes. I'm just taking them up to the workroom because she wants some of the buttons changed and another buckle put on a belt . . .' Her voice trailed away as she charged up to the workroom.

When she came down again ten minutes later she shot into her own office and closed the door carefully behind her.

Joanna went on to the landing and crossed to the tiny kitchen on the other side. It was next to Eleanor's office. She stood in the doorway, listening. If someone passed her she'd pretend she'd gone for some water.

Eleanor's voice was low and mumbling at first, and Joanna couldn't make out what she was saying. Then it suddenly grew louder, the tone ferocious.

'But *when* will he phone me back?' she was demanding aggressively. 'I've left at least four messages but he never returns my calls.'

There was a pause and Joanna held her breath.

Eleanor's voice sounded desperate now.

'Tell Herr Felke that I have everything in place – a new designer and a whole new set-up. I urgently need the go-ahead from him.' Then she slammed down the receiver.

Joanna slipped back into her office, ready to explode with anger. So Eleanor was still in touch with this company in Hamburg? Joanna recognised the name at once. Felke. Alberic Felke, that's what he'd called himself. He was obviously avoiding taking calls from Eleanor.

Something in Joanna's head snapped. This was the

last straw. Eleanor's treachery was unforgivable. Her disloyalty to the company, after all these years; her willingness to sell Rosie and all the others, without their knowledge and behind their backs, was something she could no longer stand.

Walsh's instructions went completely out of Joanna's head. She pushed open the door to Eleanor's office.

'I want to talk to you now. In my office.'

Eleanor looked up, startled. 'I'm afraid it'll have to wait. I've got to check all these fabric delivery notes and . . .'

'*Now*, please, Eleanor.'

With her white face set in mutinous lines, Eleanor followed. Her hands, Joanna noticed, gave away her true state of mind. They were trembling violently.

'I can't imagine what you want to talk to me about,' she said with forced bravado. 'I have an awful lot to do.'

Standing behind her desk, Joanna looked at her coldly.

'You're been trying to get a German company to take over Arabella Designs, Eleanor. Don't deny it because they've spoken to me and told me of your plan to run the company. I gather you've also taken it upon yourself to find a new designer. Before Arabella's body has even been found!' For a split second she was afraid she was going to become emotional, partly from fury and partly from grief. Then indignation rose to the fore again and she could hardly contain herself.

'Get out, Eleanor! Get out now. I never want to see you again.'

An ugly flush suffused the older woman's face. She

became agitated. 'Now look, Joanna, you've got it all wrong . . . I only wanted . . .'

'What you wanted was to take over,' Joanna cut in hotly. 'Without consulting the backers or the staff.'

'But I wanted to spare you the worry,' Eleanor protested self-righteously. 'You've been through so much. I did it to save the company. Who's going to design now Arabella's gone? *You?* You should be grateful to me instead of accusing me of going behind your back. I was only trying to help.'

'That isn't how anyone else sees it,' Joanna retorted rashly, knowing she was not supposed to quote the view of their lawyer, knowing that Walsh was going to be furious with her.

'What do you mean?' Eleanor demanded.

'Disloyalty in an employee is . . .'

'I've never been disloyal! Arabella left me in charge of things when she was away, long before you came to work here.'

'In charge of the secretarial side,' Joanna flashed angrily, longing to blurt out that she knew it was Eleanor who had broken into her mother's flat but remembering that she wasn't supposed to know that either. 'My mother certainly never let you make policy decisions, and she'd have been horrified if she'd known you'd given some German investors all the details of this company.'

Eleanor's face looked bloodless. 'What do you know about this business? You're nothing but an inexperienced girl. A would-be art student. You pushed yourself forward in a disgraceful way at the show, ignoring the rest of us who had been working hard for months to make it a success. And then you had the cheek to waltz down the aisle as if you'd done it all!'

'I didn't want to . . .' Joanna began defensively but Eleanor was on a roll.

'. . . and what the *hell* do you think is going to happen to this company now, without Arabella?'

Joanna looked at her impassively. She suddenly felt totally calm, as if a switch had been flicked. 'That's up to our backers and advisers. I want *you* to leave, Eleanor. Immediately. I will arrange for the accountant to send you a cheque for whatever is due to you but I'd like you to clear your desk and go right away.' As she spoke she reached for the phone.

'You can't do this to me!' Eleanor wailed, raising her hands and clutching the hair on the crown of her head. 'I'm part of this place. I've given your mother everything I've got and I intend to keep her name alive. I have to keep this business going.'

'By taking over yourself?' Joanna looked at her incredulously. 'My mother was an incredibly talented woman – beautiful, clever, hard-working, a one-off. Loved by everyone. There'll never be another Arabella. I don't see, in the long run, how we can go on without her. She *was* the company.'

Eleanor's mouth worked furiously, her emotions shifting up a gear.

'It makes me sick the way you go on about Arabella as if she was a saint,' she blazed. 'She was a whore! A fascinating, bewitching, adorable, spellbinding WHORE. Her talent was limited, but she had more style in her little finger than anyone else. That's what made her so successful.

166

'For years I protected her reputation. She was a high-class hooker before she married Eric ... Did you know *that* about your saintly mother? She was even expelled from school when she was fifteen because no man, not even the school gardener, was safe! It's time you stopped deluding yourself, Joanna, and faced up to facts.'

Joanna stood, stunned. She felt the air escaping from her body so that at any moment she was sure she'd shrink, deflate, and end up on the floor like a perished balloon.

'That's ... that's a terrible pack of lies,' she gasped. 'She was a brilliant designer. A wonderful mother ...' She stopped as tears flooded down her cheeks.

'If you don't believe me ask your father! And Eric! They know what she was like. Your father tried to get custody of you when you were small and Eric finally turned against her when he introduced her to an old friend of his ... only to discover that the friend had wined and dined Arabella, who had finally weedled him into buying her a fur coat.'

Joanna leaned against the window frame behind her, as if she was being battered by incoming waves. 'My mother left Eric because he was a mean, boring old man. My father has never said a word against her. You're making all this up.'

'Get real, Joanna. Without me looking after her interests since she became well known, she'd have ended up in the gutter press, not the fashion press. Do you think royalty would have bought her clothes if they'd known about her past?'

Joanna resisted the desire to hit out and scream that it was lies, all lies. Instead she said scornfully: 'Then why did you stay with her if she was as awful as you say?'

'*Why?*' Eleanor looked at her blankly for a moment as if she didn't understand. When she spoke, her voice was rough with pain. 'Because I loved her. Because I hoped one day . . .' she turned away sharply, her thin face contorted with pain. 'I thought she'd need me. One day. When she grew old. When she could no longer bewitch every man who saw her. Then, when she disappeared . . . I thought if I can't have her, at least I can have her business, step into her shoes, make sure Arabella Designs lives on as if she's still here, even if someone else is designing the clothes. All I wanted was to keep her name alive.'

There was a silence in the brightly lit office that seemed to stretch for ever. A yawning chasm of nothingness, leading nowhere.

Joanna looked at this ungainly mannish woman with her bony features and tortured eyes, and actually felt sorry for her.

'Did she know . . . how you felt?' she asked awkwardly.

'Oh, she knew all right,' Eleanor said harshly. 'It amused her to taunt me with tales of all the men she'd slept with. She was cruel. When we were at school I told her how I felt and she laughed in my face. Said she'd rather bed my father. She used to flirt with all the fathers on Sports Day, and especially with mine, as if she wanted to punish me,' she added bitterly. 'Even recently she loved to describe what she did in bed with her men

168

friends, how large some men's penises were, and how much pleasure they gave her.'

Joanna turned away, feeling sick.

Without another word Eleanor walked out of the room and returned to her own office.

It was several minutes before Joanna had the strength to close her door so that she could be alone. Slumped at her desk with her hands covering her face, she was trying to blot out all Eleanor had said. I don't believe a word of it, she kept repeating like a mantra. Eleanor is a self-seeking bitch; she may even be jealous of me because I'm Arabella's daughter. Something that can't be taken away from me, Joanna reflected, no matter what.

'Are you all right, lovey?' she heard Rosie ask, as she put her head around the door.

Joanna looked up slowly. 'Yes, I'm OK.'

Rosie was agog with curiosity, longing to ask what had happened but not quite daring to. 'Eleanor's gone. Left about fifteen minutes ago without so much as a goodbye to any of us.'

'Good.'

'That's what I thought. I couldn't help overhearing you having a barney. Everything all right then, love?'

Joanna rubbed her face with her hands in a washing movement. 'Yes,' she said, picking up her bag and slinging the strap over her shoulder. 'I'm going out now, Rosie. I've got to clear my head. When Alice comes in, can you tell her I don't know when I'll be back?'

Early afternoon, Tuesday 12 October

DI Walsh summoned Chambers into his office as soon as the DS returned from his lunch break.

'I've received word from surveillance that Eleanor Andrews left work a little while ago, carrying a couple of bags of stuff; looked like personal things. She seemed very upset, too. Then she headed for Baron's Court. I think we should get over to her flat and charge her now. I want to know what she's up to, and as you haven't turned up anything significant, let's get on with it.'

Chambers, looking sulky at what he took to be criticism, said defensively, 'There wasn't anything to turn up, sir.'

Walsh rose briskly, buttoning his jacket. 'You may be right. Perhaps she hasn't got a life except for her obsession with Arabella Designs.'

This was the first time he'd ever worked on a case where there was no body and no evidence of any murder having taken place. Arabella Webster had seemingly vanished off the face of the earth as if she'd never existed. Frustration jabbed at him like hot pins. He *had* to find out what had happened to the missing woman. There'd been nothing he could pin on Eric. His one hope now was Eleanor. Once he got her to the police station he intended interrogating her until she cracked. For while she might not have killed Arabella herself, he was damn sure she knew who had.

Joanna walked slowly back from Pimlico Road to Warwick Square, a yearning for her own bolt hole, where she could rest and lick her wounds, paramount in her mind. She couldn't help hoping Nina was out. For all her well-meaning jollity and enthusiasm it was a tiny flat and Joanna craved some peace. She realised she was beginning to feel overwhelmed by her friend's home cooking and positive thinking, but then she felt guilty. Nina had put her own life on hold to fly over from the States and be supportive. Joanna ought to feel more grateful.

There was a scribbled note propped up against a jar of honey on the kitchen table. *'Dear Jo, Decided to go to Hampton Court and do the tourist bit! Supper's done and in the fridge and I'll be back around six. Tons of love, N.'*

Bliss. Utter bliss. Joanna made herself a cup of coffee, helping herself to some of Nina's homemade cookies, and went and lay down on the living-room sofa. She'd try and blot out Eleanor's hideous lies by watching mindless quiz programmes on television; maybe she'd doze a bit. At least she'd be alone.

The phone awoke her from a deep sleep an hour later. Groggily she reached for the receiver. It was DI Walsh calling.

'I thought I told you to carry on as usual in front of Eleanor Andrews,' he said heavily. 'I stressed, Joanna, that she was on no account to know we had evidence that proved she'd got into Arabella's flat.'

'I know, but . . .'

'I said repeatedly that secrecy was vital while we carried out further investigations.'

'Yes, but . . .'

'We were most anxious to take her unawares and

bring her in for questioning.'

'Wait a minute,' Joanna protested angrily. 'I never said anything about that. She's no idea I knew it was her. I sacked her because she'd gone behind my back to try and seize control of the company. I simply had to get her out because she was a disruptive element. Why can't you arrest her now?' she added hotly.

'That's just what we can't do,' he retorted testily.

'Why not?'

'She's done a bunk. Left her flat in a mini-cab with two suitcases, shortly before we arrived. She's not at her mother's place in Kent and none of her neighbours has any idea where she's gone.'

'Why are you giving *me* a hard time?' Joanna demanded. 'It's not my fault. You could have arrested her the minute you identified her as the intruder. Personally, I don't think she had anything to do with my mother's disappearance.'

'That remains to be seen,' Walsh said coldly, 'but if we are to proceed, I must ask you to do exactly as I say in future, otherwise you may hamper our work.'

Joanna felt deeply angry to be spoken to in this way. Arabella had now been missing for thirty days and Walsh was still no nearer to discovering what had happened to her than on day one. And now he had the cheek to blame *her* for Eleanor's having run off. A month ago she'd have been issuing a mewling apology and feeling dreadful. Now she felt more confident. 'I'm sorry Eleanor's given you the slip,' she retorted, 'but if you'd been concentrating all your energies on finding my mother, you might have found her killer at the same time.'

Seven

The padded jiffy bag lay on the kitchen table with the electricity bill, a Penhaligon's catalogue and a reminder for Joanna to make an appointment with her dental hygienist. Nina was standing at the sink, washing lettuce, and there was something highly spiced simmering on the hob.

'Hiya,' she greeted Joanna. 'How was your day?'

She grimaced as she perched on the high stool by the cluttered counter and ripped open the padded envelope. She peered inside, frowning, and pulled out a cassette. 'What's this?'

Nina glanced over at her. 'Is there a note?'

Joanna examined the envelope more closely. 'Not a thing. How strange. There isn't even a postmark.'

'It was on the hall table, so I brought it up with the rest of your mail.'

Joanna looked down at the tape and was filled with foreboding. There was something sinister about an anonymous cassette being dropped in by hand. 'I wonder what's on it?'

'There's only one way to find out, sugar.'

'I know.'

'So why don't you play it and put yourself out of your misery?' Nina chided.

Joanna led the way to the living room, and slipped the cassette into her hi-fi. Then she sat cross-legged on the floor and switched it on.

'Joanna darling, this is Mummy. I want you to know I'm all right . . .'

'What?' Joanna screamed, leaping up, her face ashen.

'. . . I can't tell you where I am because it involves someone else and at the moment I want to protect him from the media. Please tell the police I'm fine, darling . . .' Arabella's voice seemed to break at this point. Joanna looked wildly at Nina, who was staring open-mouthed at the cassette player.

'She's alive!' she said hoarsely.

'. . . I love you, darling, very, very much, and tell Louise I love her very, very much, too. Take care of yourself, sweetheart. 'Bye.' The tape went silent. Although they kept it running, nothing else had been recorded.

'Oh, my God! Oh, my God!' Joanna kept gasping. 'That *was* Mummy's voice, wasn't it? I'm not imagining it? But where is she? And who is she with?' She took out the cassette and held it in her hands, gazing at it almost reverently, as if it would bring Arabella nearer.

Nina sat there in shock, her mouth still open.

Clumsily, Joanna put the cassette back into the hi-fi and played it once again, holding her breath as she listened to Arabella's unmistakable warm tones. When the message ended she started weeping uncontrollably.

'I can't believe it,' she sobbed, trembling violently. 'I really thought she was dead. Oh, God, she's alive. ALIVE!'

Nina hugged her, her own cheeks awash with tears of relief. 'Who do you think she's with, Jo?'

Joanna shook her head, bewildered. 'I haven't the foggiest. And why didn't she phone me or e-mail the office?'

'She sounds happy and obviously cares about the man she's with. She's trying to protect him from the press.'

'But why did she go off, in secret, in the first place?' Joanna exploded, with the fury of a mother whose child has just escaped a bad accident. 'I can't believe she could do this to us all! Not for *anyone*. Christ! What are we supposed to do now?'

Joanna started pacing around the room. She glanced at her wrist watch. Pushed her hair behind her ears with both hands. 'Oh! I wish Freddie was back. And I must get hold of Daddy so he can tell Louise. God, this is so extraordinary – and just *wait* until I tell Detective Inspector Walsh! After the ticking off he gave me for sacking Eleanor, I'm dying to tell him he's got the whole thing wrong from the very beginning.' She stopped and looked at Nina as if she'd just had a revelation. 'Why hasn't he been looking for a missing person instead of a body, for God's sake?'

Nina raised her eyebrows. 'Well, this certainly puts Eric in the clear.'

Joanna looked confused for a moment. 'It changes everything,' she agreed. Freddie arrived at that moment and she ran into the hall and flung herself at him.

'Mummy's alive,' she said breathlessly. 'Come and listen. She's sent me a message on cassette.'

Freddie looked down at her, his expression both surprised and concerned. 'Are you sure, babe? I mean . . .' He paused. She looked so happy.

'Listen.' Joanna switched on the tape and once again the room was filled with the sound of Arabella's voice.

'That's certainly her,' he agreed. 'Have you told the police?'

'I haven't had time. What do you think?'

'It's a bit fishy, isn't it?' Freddie said cautiously. 'And what a bizarre way of telling you she's okay. I don't like the sound of it one bit, I'm afraid.'

Joanna looked crushed, sinking on to the sofa, her arms wrapped around herself as if she was in pain. 'No, Freddie, don't say that.'

'You don't think it's a hoax, do you?' Nina demanded shrilly.

'It can't be a hoax, it's definitely Mummy's voice,' Joanna protested.

'What's the postmark?' Freddie asked.

'That's just it – there isn't one. It's been delivered by hand,' Nina told him.

'Jo, don't handle either the tape or the envelope any more. Forensic will want to check for fingerprints.'

She gave him a despairing look. 'Oh, I was so sure . . .'

'Oh, sweetheart.' He took her hand and pulled her gently to her feet. Then, wrapping his arms around her, he held her close, his face buried in her neck. 'Let's take it a step at a time. Shall I phone the police for you?'

Joanna nodded, unable to speak. She'd been so sure this was good news. Now it looked as though she could be wrong.

'They're sending someone round to collect the tape,' Freddie told her when he'd spoken to DS Chambers. 'Walsh is off duty but Chambers will tell him what's happened in the morning.'

'Did he say anything? What was his reaction?'

Freddie shrugged. 'He was perplexed more than anything.'

'I bet he was!' Nina observed, digging deeply into a tub of ice cream she'd just fetched from the fridge. 'It's time that man got his act together.'

Joanna pulled herself to her feet with an effort. 'I must phone Daddy.'

'He can tell Louise her mother's okay now, can't he?' Nina observed.

'I don't think that's a good idea at all,' Freddie warned. 'As far as Louise is concerned we've got to be one hundred per cent certain. Chambers also said he'd drop back the keys to your mother's flat. They're finished there so we can get the insurance people in to assess the damage, and then we can clear up the mess.'

Night, Wednesday 13 October

'You've no idea how often I've dreamed of this moment – having you all to myself. I've longed for it for ages and ages. Of course, if you hadn't rejected me it could have happened much sooner . . .

'Do you regret that now? I'll always regret it. You shouldn't have done it, you know. I was so dreadfully hurt, I thought I'd never get over it.

'When you turned me away . . . Never mind, let's forget it now, shall we? Best forgotten. No good looking back.

'This is your life now, safe with me, isn't it? Away from it all. Just us together. All I ever wanted, really.

'And it's going to last, isn't it? Isn't it?'

Morning, Friday 15 October

DI Walsh contacted Joanna before she left for work to tell her they'd only found one set of fingerprints on the cassette and they were hers.

'There are some smudged prints on the jiffy bag, but they're very indistinct and probably belong to someone from your building, when they put it on the hall table.'

'Nothing else?' Joanna asked, disappointment sweeping through her.

'I'm afraid not. They've used an ordinary Sony cassette which you can buy anywhere. We're doing all we can but there's nothing even to indicate when this recording was made. I'm afraid it strikes me that if your mother has merely gone away with someone in the public eye whom she wants to protect, which is what her message seems to suggest, then they've gone to enormous trouble to ensure they're not traced.'

'What are you saying?' she asked dully.

'I have a feeling,' he said slowly, as if he didn't want to upset her, 'that this tape has been delivered to you to put us off the scent. It's quite likely it was recorded within days of her disappearance, over a month ago.'

Afternoon, Saturday 16 October

'What are we going to do with all this stuff?' Joanna asked in dismay. With Freddie's help, she and Nina had almost cleared the mess in her mother's living room. Broken china, glass and ornaments beyond repair were stuffed into boxes and put into heavy duty black plastic bags, designed for garden refuse. 'And we haven't even started in Ma's bedroom yet.'

'Christ, I hadn't thought of that,' Freddie replied.

'But I had,' Nina said robustly. 'I've arranged with the council to collect everything as long as we put it all out tomorrow evening.'

'Wonder woman!' murmured Joanna.

The once beautiful room looked sad and desolate now, bereft of the vibrant spirit of its owner. Torn between hoping Arabella would come back and a dreadful certainty she wouldn't, Joanna wondered vaguely what she'd do about the flat. Either way, none of them would want to live in it again. Melosa had also announced by letter that she wasn't returning to work: '*I to fritened!*' she'd scrawled on the lined paper. '*It bad place now.*'

It was indeed a bad place. Eleanor had desecrated it. They went into the bedroom. 'WHORE' leaped out from the mirror in the scarlet of Arabella's mouth. Savaged garments hung in ribbons as if clawed by attacking hounds. Shoes, bags, broken strings of pearls, lay scattered across the beige carpet like beached flotsam and jetsam.

Freddie's face was grim. 'Bin everything?' he asked, looking around.

Joanna was standing in the middle of the room, dry-eyed.

'Maybe you'd like to sort things out first?' Nina suggested. 'You and Louise are going to want some keepsakes, aren't you? Shall we start by just binning what's totally ruined? Then you can see what's left.' She stooped to pick up a taupe leather handbag. 'This is as good as new,' she remarked in a surprised voice. 'Hey, what's this?' she added, pulling out several letters.

Joanna took them, her lips pressed tightly together, and put them in her pocket. This was worse than anything she'd had to do so far. These were the things her mother had worn. Silk that had been warmed by her skin. Scarves that she'd worn around her neck. Clothes that still bore the lingering fragrance of her perfume.

Working swiftly and silently, they stuffed what had once been the contents of Arabella's stylish wardrobe into plastic bags which Freddie carried through into the hall. Nina placed the undamaged shoes and handbags back on the wardrobe shelves. Spoiled cosmetics and broken bottles of perfume were chucked away, along with costume jewellery which had obviously been stamped on. At last the floor and all the surfaces were cleared.

Joanna pulled back the curtains and opened the window to let in the fresh air. The flat had taken on an impersonal air, like a vacant hotel suite. From the living room came the sound of a hoover; Nina had insisted on cleaning the rooms before they left.

Freddie came back into the bedroom. He took Joanna's hand and held it tightly. 'All done, babe?'

She looked at him sadly and nodded, unable to speak. In her heart she knew that whatever happened, she'd never return here. It belonged to an era that once had been filled with light and laughter. Now all that was left was this cold, dark place.

Evening, Sunday 17 October

The handwriting was distinctive; small, strong but quirky, with tiny banners that flew across Ts and stabbed at full stops. A dart dipped in black ink, scratched imperiously on plain cream paper. A man's handwriting.

Joanna frowned, intrigued and puzzled. Who the hell had written these letters? While sorting through the papers they'd collected from her mother's flat, she'd discovered these notes from someone who signed himself 'R'. She presumed they were written to her mother, although there was no heading.

No address was given either, but at the top of each sheet was a printed drawing of a Jacobean-style manor house.

'What do you make of these?' she asked Freddie, who lay sprawled along the length of the sofa reading the *Sunday Telegraph*.

Taking them from her, his eyes swept over the pages

with the speed of someone experienced in reading documents.

'I'd say they were from a lover who'd been turned down,' he said immediately.

'He sounds very angry,' Joanna agreed, reaching for them again from where she sat cross-legged on the floor.

'Who does?' Nina asked, coming into the room at that moment, flushed pink from her bath and wearing a voluminous white towelling dressing gown.

'That's what I don't know. These are the letters you found among Mummy's things. Listen to this. *"You might have had the decency to listen to me."* And here: *"I still cannot understand why you asked me to leave. Do I mean nothing to you? Nothing at all?"* They're dated April the twenty-third, May the tenth and June the seventh.'

Freddie hauled himself into an upright position. 'You must show them to the police, Jo. They may be very important. They're obviously from someone with a grievance against your mother.'

'Artistic handwriting,' Nina observed. 'I bet he did the drawing of the house, too.'

'God, I wish I knew what this was all about,' Joanna burst out in frustration.

Morning, Monday 18 October

Joanna stopped off at the police station on the way to work the next morning. DI Walsh was already on duty.

'I was trying to get hold of you on the phone a few minutes ago,' he explained.

Immediately her pulse began to race, and she wondered why her heart hadn't learned the lesson that whatever Walsh had to say it was never good news. 'What did you want to see me about?'

'We picked up Eleanor Andrews last night. We're holding her for the time being but she'll be formally charged within the next few days.'

'Right.' Joanna managed to hide her disappointment. It was too much to hope that they'd have found Arabella. 'I've brought you three letters I found in my mother's flat when we were clearing up the mess. I felt you should see them.'

Walsh raised his eyebrows and took them from her. 'Right, we'll have a look at them.'

'They're obviously from someone with a grievance,' Joanna persisted. 'They could be vital to our finding out what's happened to her.'

A brief smile flitted across his face without reaching his eyes and she felt he was looking at her strangely.

'Thanks very much, Joanna.' He straightened up the papers on his desk. It was obvious he wanted to say something else but feared he'd be walking on eggshells if he did.

'Was there anything else?' she asked intuitively.

'Not really.' He looked vague. 'You've had your own flat for the last two or three years, haven't you? Never lived at Emperor's Gate with your mother? Not known that much about her private life?'

Joanna sat wishing he would stop acting like a doctor who knew you had a fatal illness but was afraid to say so. 'What are you getting at?'

'I was wondering if she'd had any boyfriends since her divorce from Professor Webster? A beautiful woman like your mother must have had many admirers, and she was – what? Forty? Pretty young by today's standards.'

'My mother led her life and I led mine,' Joanna said with more tartness than she'd meant to use. Eleanor's hateful accusations came flooding back into her mind. 'As far as I know she had no one special.'

'Just a thought,' he said carefully.

Evening, Friday 22 October

The moment Joanna saw another jiffy bag lying on the console table in the hall of Warwick Square, she knew what it contained. Her name and address had been typed on a sticky label this time and there was a postmark across the three first-class stamps. Although it was blurred, she could just make out the word 'Newport'.

The lift was stuck at the third floor. She couldn't wait. Hurling herself at the steep stairs, a relic of Victorian days when families had a large household staff, she ran up to her flat. She arrived panting and with aching legs, but deeply excited. If this was another message from Arabella, then she must still be alive.

Nina was out and Freddie hadn't returned yet. Joanna slid the tape into the hi-fi and switched on.

'Joanna, this is Mummy. Please don't worry about me, darling. I'm fine. I'm in a lovely place . . .'

Was her voice a bit strained this time? Did she sound as natural as she had on the previous tape? Joanna turned up the volume, concentrating on every nuance and change of tone, wondering if her mother could be reading from a prepared text.

'. . . *I'll sort everything out very soon, so do tell the police I'm OK and tell them to stop searching for me because I'm being beautifully looked after, and I don't want them interfering . . .'*

'YES!' Joanna heard herself yell, punching the air with her fist. Her mother had to be alive now, even if she did sound unlike her usual effervescent self.

'. . . *Take care of yourself and Louise. I love you, darling.'* There was a pause as if Arabella was finding it difficult to continue, then in a low choked voice she spoke again. *'Goodbye for now, darling. Mummy.'*

There was silence. The message had ended.

Joanna began to feel uneasy. Whatever the reason for her mother's disappearance, she was now convinced it was not of Arabella's own volition.

Grabbing the phone, she tapped in the number of the police station. The WPC on the switchboard informed her chirpily that Detective Inspector Walsh had gone off duty but would she care to speak to Detective Sergeant Chambers?

'Yes, please.'

There was a pause, a click, and the morose voice of Chambers on the line. 'Hello?'

'Yes, hi,' she said distractedly. 'This is Joanna Knight. I've just received another tape from my mother which I'm convinced means she's still alive, but I do think she's being held captive somewhere. I'll bring it over later tonight . . .'

'OK,' he said laconically. 'I hope you've held the cassette carefully? Forensic will have to examine it for prints.'

When she'd hung up, Joanna remained sitting on the floor; she hugged her knees, dropping her head on to them, deep in thought about Arabella.

I don't know what to believe any more, she reflected. Are you alive, Ma, or not? I can't believe, if you are still alive, that you're putting me through this torture . . .

I can't believe you're jeopardising all you've worked for, for the sake of some man. What the hell's going on, Ma? Don't you realise the mess you've left behind? Jesus, Eric's been suspected of murder! Louise is missing you . . . she's even had to be taken abroad to protect her from what's going on.

As for Eleanor! She's completely and utterly lost it. Ma, I simply can't believe you're letting this happen.

I'm so unhappy, so confused. I wish you'd come home. I wish you'd phone and tell me what's happening.

Freddie and Nina arrived back at the same time, he with his heavy case of legal documents he had to go through that evening, Nina with a carrier bag of food. As soon as they saw Joanna still crouched on the floor in front of the hi-fi, they knew something had happened.

She pressed the 'play' button. 'Listen to this.'

They listened, Freddie frowning and biting his bottom lip, Nina with her hands plunged into the pockets of her voluminous winter coat.

The recording came to an end. Joanna looked up at them. 'What do you think?'

'Have you told the police?' Freddie asked.

'Of course.' Joanna told him of Chambers' laidback response. 'I don't think they've done enough to try and find her. I think we've got to mount a nationwide search ourselves.'

'Atta girl!' Nina agreed robustly. 'Go for it. Let's make a plan of campaign.' As she was talking she picked up her shopping and headed for the kitchen. 'Anyone want a glass of wine?' she shouted.

'Yes, please!' Joanna curled up on the sofa, taking a notepad from her bag. 'Where do I start, Freddie?'

He dropped on to the other end of the sofa and gazed up at the slanting attic ceiling, deep in thought. 'Find a different photograph of Arabella – a casual, less glamorous one, and we'll get thousands of fly sheets printed. Then you want to find a company who will distribute them everywhere, from Land's End to John O'Groats. They need to be on billboards, attached to lamp-posts, and handed out in supermarkets around the country.'

Nina appeared with three glasses and a bottle. 'Don't forget to put an appeal in the *Big Issue*.'

Nodding, Joanna continued scribbling her list. 'I'll also get on to the Salvation Army first thing,' she observed, 'and the National Missing Person's Helpline.'

'The police will have done that already,' Freddie assured her.

'Well, I don't care, I'm going to talk to them again,' she said stubbornly. 'I'll also see if I can get myself on GMTV. Millions of people tune into breakfast tele-vision; it reaches an enormous audience. This second tape puts a whole new spin on things. From the beginning Walsh and that jerk he has as a sidekick have just been looking for a body.'

Freddie decided not to argue. Not to point out that apart from the one woman suffering from memory loss, they wouldn't have told her about the dozens of false sightings they'd have had to deal with.

Nina leaned her elbows on the arms of her chair. 'Do you think Eric could have had her kidnapped?'

Joanna only gave it a moment's consideration before shaking her head. 'Much though I loathe the man, I honestly don't think he had anything to do with Mummy's disappearance. Not now.'

Freddie raised his eyebrows and looked at her in surprise. 'What . . . in spite of the fact that a witness saw Arabella and him fighting a few minutes before she left his house, never to be seen again?'

'Oh, God, I don't know.'

'You know what I think?' Nina said slowly. They looked at her expectantly.

'I think you should go to a psychic. There was one on television the other day who specialises in finding missing people. She was terrific. They said the police often use her.'

Morning, Saturday 23 October

A woman with a kindly voice, who said she was called Heather, answered when Joanna phoned the National Missing Person's Helpline.

Joanna had started to tell her who she was and that she was ringing about Arabella Webster when Heather interrupted her, exclaiming sympathetically: 'I know all about this, my dear. We were contacted by the police back in September. The thirteenth, wasn't it, when your mother went missing? We've done everything we can and we're not giving up, but there's been no trace of her so far.'

'What can I do?' Joanna asked helplessly. 'I've had two messages from her so I'm sure she's alive.'

'Yes, the police have informed us about the cassettes, but of course no one knows when they were recorded. It sounds hopeful, dear, but my heart goes out to you. It's the not knowing that's the worst, isn't it? The waiting and wondering.'

'Exactly!' Joanna said, profoundly relieved to be talking to someone as experienced as this. 'What I don't understand is, how can someone completely disappear in a small island like Britain? It's not as if we're vast like America, or even Central Europe where people can skip frontiers.'

'I'm afraid a quarter of a million people go missing in this country every year,' Heather told her sadly.

'And how many are found?'

There was a momentary pause before she answered. 'It varies,' Heather replied vaguely.

'Would it help if you had a different picture of my mother? A more casual one which might strike a chord with people. I'm planning to have a new flyer printed in the hope it will jog people's memory.'

'That's a very good idea. We've already circulated the

original photograph but we would certainly like to have a different one. We'll send it to over a hundred regional newspapers, and I'll see if Carlton TV will put out another appeal.'

'Thank you,' Joanna said gratefully.

'The publicity department here do a "Missing Persons Report", and I'll have a word with Susie about that,' Heather continued. 'Of course, if your mother had been a young girl, we'd use a third party acting in secret who blends in with the scene, going to all the clubs and pubs in the area where she disappeared. That often produces results. They pick up snippets of information while they're mingling. In your mother's case it doesn't apply, though. She's too well known to go to public places without being spotted.'

'That's just it! With her distinctive face, I can't understand why she hasn't been found.'

Heather sighed. 'I know, my dear. I know. I hope you have some good news soon.'

Morning, Monday 25 October

Joanna awoke with a feeling of anxiety. She'd dreamed she was a child again, on holiday with her mother. They'd been on a beach and there was a stiff breeze whipping across the sea from the south-west, blowing gritty sand on to her wet bare legs so that they itched. Then Arabella had said it was time to go. They'd got into a car and it had seemed to float along winding lanes like a boat . . .

She turned on her side and wondered what had startled her into wakefulness. She tried to retrace the course of her dream. Her mother was driving . . . she'd said something like 'Look for the sign, Joanna' . . . they'd flown over a narrow bridge and then . . . That was it! The road sign had pointed to Newport, a town in the centre of the Isle of Wight. And the second tape she'd received was postmarked Newport.

They'd had a holiday there when she'd been small. Her only holiday alone with her mother and it had lasted a week. She'd usually been packed off somewhere with her nanny but, magically, Arabella had said she was taking Joanna to a charming hotel on the Isle of Wight where they had a swimming pool, play area and fabulous food.

Joanna phoned DI Walsh as soon as she arrived at Arabella Designs and told him the significance of Newport.

Maddeningly he was sceptical. 'It's highly unlikely it's Newport, Isle of Wight.' His tone was dismissive. 'It's my belief it's Newport in Gwent.'

'But how do you know that?' she retorted, rattled. 'My mother has never been to Wales as far as I know, but we *did* have a holiday on the Isle of Wight.'

'I'm afraid I think that's irrelevant. Right at the beginning we checked with the car ferries from Southampton and Portsmouth to the Isle of Wight, and there's not been any trace of your mother's car registration number on any of the ferries.'

'Have you checked the various car parks near the

ports? Perhaps she didn't take her car over. Perhaps she went on the hydro or the hover.'

'We've checked every car park, official and unofficial, throughout the country, Joanna,' he said, a touch severely. 'We're really doing everything we can, you know. At this moment the local constabulary are concentrating on searching the Newport and Gwent area, but I suspect whoever posted the jiffy bag deliberately went to Newport in order to put us off the scent, so we shall be widening our search throughout Wales.'

Afternoon, Monday 25 October

The room was small and square with only enough room for two hard chairs and a table. There was no window and stale body odour hung in the room like a solid mass: impenetrable, unbearable. Joanna had managed to get an appointment at short notice because there'd been a cancellation at the Spiritualists' Association of London, in Hornton Street, Kensington.

She tried to breathe through her mouth to bypass her olfactory system but it was no good. This dim box-like room, lit by only a single low-wattage bulb hanging from the high ceiling, stank of a thousand unwashed bodies, as far removed from the spirit world as she could imagine.

'Someone will be with you in a minute,' the receptionist had told her, after she'd paid the fifteen-pound fee with her credit card. Joanna wondered now if she could stick it out.

Suddenly a small wizened man with black hair and a sallow complexion came into the room, stopped as if someone had almost bumped into him and exclaimed; 'My word, you're in a hurry!'

Joanna looked around, wondering who he was talking to. Then he seated himself in the other chair, crossed corduroy-clad legs and smiled at her.

'Your grandfather's arrived,' he announced cheerily. 'He's standing just behind your left shoulder.'

Involuntarily Joanna turned round to look at the empty corner.

'There's a lot of confusion in your life at the moment, isn't there?' he observed, frowning. 'And I feel like having a little weep, because I can sense you're very unhappy.'

She looked into his eyes to see if he was genuine, but his glassy stare was fixed beyond her right shoulder, as if seeing some internal horizon.

'I'm trying to find my mother,' she said in a small voice, realising she sounded like a young child.

'I know you are. I know you are,' he repeated understandingly. 'Your grandfather's telling me he's looking after her. Making sure she's not hurt by recent events. You have to be patient, dear. Very patient. But you're a good person, aren't you? A lot of people think highly of you. I see lots of colour in your life. Fabrics . . . your mother's connected with clothes, isn't she?' He did not seem to need an answer, but nevertheless Joanna nodded.

'Where shall I look for her?' she asked, her own eyes brimming with emotion. 'Can you tell me where she is?'

The glazed eyes continued to stare blankly at the wall

behind her. 'I can see a forest glade. Bare branches and an overcast sky.' Then, for the first time, he looked directly into her eyes, and his expression was that of someone who had just woken up from a deep sleep. 'That's where you'll find her, dear. Good luck.'

He rose abruptly as if he didn't want to say any more and a moment later she was on her own again. She dashed into the corridor to go after him. 'Which forest glade?' she called urgently to his fast-retreating figure, but he didn't seem to hear and the next moment he'd shot into another cubicle-like room and shut the door firmly behind him.

Eight

The car sent by GMTV to take her to the studio arrived at seven-thirty. Joanna was already dressed in a pale grey flannel trouser suit, her hair newly washed, a dash of pink gloss on her lips.

Freddie, showered and with a towel slung around his hips, came to the door to see her off.

'Good luck, babe,' he said, smiling down at her.

'Oh, Freddie, I'm nervous! I've never been on TV before,' she said, clinging to him for a moment. He hugged her tightly. He was warm and damp and smelled of soap, and she pressed herself against him and he kissed her on the corner of her mouth. 'You'll be all right. Just be natural and forget about the cameras.'

Nina emerged sleepily from her room, hair tousled, eyes puffy. 'Shouldn't you be wearing make-up, Jo? You look very pale.'

'Thanks, Nina. That's all I need. I want to look like myself.' Joanna extricated herself regretfully from Freddie's arms. 'I must go. I'll ring you after I've done my bit.'

'Good luck. I'll be watching you,' Nina said, grinning. 'And I'll record it on video so you and Freddie can see it later.'

The driver switched on the engine of the waiting Honda as soon as he saw her come down the front steps. When she got into the car he greeted her as if he knew her very well.

'Good morning, Miss Knight. How are you? Have you had any news of your mother yet?'

Joanna looked at him in surprise, imagining he'd been told she was making an appeal on GMTV. 'Did they tell you Lorraine Kelly was interviewing me this morning?'

He smiled, amused. 'No, I recognised you from seeing your picture in the papers. You've had a hard time of it, though, haven't you? I was just saying to my missus only the other week, that daughter's a real looker, isn't she? Every bit as pretty as her mother.'

Joanna felt faintly disturbed and embarrassed. She'd never thought of herself as being recognisable and certainly hadn't thought of herself as pretty. Her mother was the star turn in the family so far as looks were concerned, and Louise was going to be the next beauty.

'I don't know about that,' she replied awkwardly.

He proceeded to chatter non-stop as they drove down Belgrave Road until they reached the Embankment, then across the Thames to Kennington, Lambeth, and past Waterloo Station until they came to the GMTV studios at Upper Ground. When he drew up at the side entrance, Joanna jumped out and hurried up the steps to be greeted by a charming receptionist who also seemed to recognise her immediately.

After she'd been asked to sign a release form, someone else appeared to escort her to the studio. Joanna was feeling more nervous by the moment and when she was ushered into a waiting area, and found herself surrounded by really famous show-biz celebrities, her heart started pounding uncomfortably.

A middle-aged woman dressed in a neat blue suit came forward, smiling. 'Can I get you some coffee or tea? Or is there anything else you'd like?' she asked in a hostessy voice.

'Coffee would be nice . . . no, tea, actually, please.' Joanna stammered, thinking coffee might make her feel more sick than she already did.

'And a croissant? Or a Danish?' The motherly manner was soothing.

'No, I'm fine, thank you,' Joanna replied sinking gratefully on to a chair, her legs weak with fright.

No sooner had she finished her cup of tea than someone else appeared, asking her to follow them to make-up.

'I don't normally . . . I want to look natural,' Joanna protested, almost trotting to keep up with her as she was led at breakneck speed down a corridor by a young woman in a boiler suit and trainers who was clutching a clipboard.

The make-up artist was putting the finishing touches to a royal commentator who was about to comment on Prince Charles' continued support of fox hunting. She smiled at Joanna, as if she too recognised her. Joanna smiled shyly back, not knowing what to say.

'Hello!' greeted the make-up artist when she'd

finished with the commentator. She put a plastic cape around Joanna's shoulders. Then, putting her face beside Joanna's, she stared at their reflections in the mirror, which was brightly lit by bulbs around the edges. Her eyes were critical and searching.

'We'll warm up your skin a bit,' she finally suggested as she fiddled with various pots and small sponges and different-sized brushes. 'The studio lights can be really draining. I'll just enhance your eyes with a little brown shadow . . .'

Joanna frowned in protest. 'I never wear anything but lip gloss.'

'Quite right, too. You've got lovely skin. But under the studio lights . . .' And off she went again, patting and stroking Joanna's face with soft beiges and pinks.

When she'd finished Joanna looked at herself in the mirror and had to admit the make-up was so subtle it didn't look like she had any cosmetics on at all. She just looked less tired.

Then it was back to the waiting area with such speed she thought the interview must be about to start.

'What time am I on?' she asked anxiously.

The young woman in the boiler suit consulted her clipboard. 'Six minutes past nine.'

It was still only eight-twenty. Joanna looked at her in astonishment but she was gone, sprinting off in another direction. Why was everyone in such a hurry when they had loads of time? she wondered.

The next forty minutes passed slowly. The waiting area gradually emptied as people were fetched and taken to the studio for their four-and-a-half minutes of fame.

At last, making her jump with fright, a man rushed up to Joanna. He wore earphones and seemed hung about with wires. He too carried a clipboard.

'Will you come this way?' he said breathlessly. He hurried her along another corridor, through one lot of swing doors then another, and suddenly she was in the brilliantly lit studio, with its sofas and chairs and coffee table set in front of a backdrop on which was painted a view of London buildings through a fake window. Cables snaked across the floor, and cameras were skittering around unnervingly by remote control, getting into different positions, closing in on Lorraine Kelly, who was finishing the previous spot.

As in a dream, Joanna let herself be led to the sofa, being warned not to trip on the cables. Then a mike, which was attached to a hidden contact down the side of the sofa, was clipped to the front of her suit with its thin black wire tucked inside her jacket.

The adverts were running. Lorraine leaned forward and explained they had two-and-a-half minutes before they were back live on air. She'd start off by asking Joanna to describe the latest developments since her mother's disappearance.

When the floor manager said 'Ten seconds,' Joanna's heart gave a huge lurch. Then he said: 'Five seconds,' as he held up his hand, fingers splayed. One by one the fingers pointed down, and then Joanna heard Lorraine launch confidently into a condensed précis of Arabella's disappearance.

'We have Joanna Knight, Arabella Webster's daughter, with us this morning.' Lorraine turned to her with a compassionate expression. 'Joanna, the past few weeks must have been terrible for you, but I understand you've recently heard from your mother? Can you tell us about that?'

Joanna heard herself talking about the tapes she'd received, and it was as if this interview was happening to another person. She forgot about the millions of viewers, the cameras swivelling around the studio on their own, the dazzling lights blazing down on them. In an assured voice and never taking her eyes from Lorraine's face, she outlined her plans to step up the search, adding that she was convinced her mother was still alive and being held against her will.

'And how are you managing to cope with all this worry? I gather you're having to help run her fashion business, too?' The interviewer's Scottish accent was lilting and soft.

'Yes, I am,' Joanna heard herself reply. 'All the people who work for us have been marvellous and we've . . . well, somehow we've got to keep going.'

Lorraine leaned closer. 'This must be awfully hard for you – all the waiting and wondering. Have you a message for your mother, just in case she's watching this?'

For a moment Joanna felt thrown, not having expected to make a direct appeal to Arabella. A camera only a few feet away was pointing in her direction. Then on a monitor she caught sight of herself and got another shock. She looked much better than she'd expected to.

Gazing directly into the lens, she spoke. 'If you're watching this, Ma, I want you to know we're doing our best to find you. If it's possible, *please* phone, fax or e-mail us to let us know where you are. We all miss you terribly.'

'Well, let's hope your mother's listening,' Lorraine said, 'and I wish you lots of luck in your search, Joanna. You're a very brave young lady and thank you for coming in this morning.'

Then she turned and looked directly into the camera. 'If anyone knows where Arabella Webster is, or can give any information that may lead to her being found, will they please get in touch with the National Missing Person's Helpline? We'll give you the number in a minute, or you can contact your local police station.'

The four-and-a-half minutes had passed in a blur so far as Joanna was concerned. Now she was having her mike unclipped from her jacket, and someone was guiding her out of the studio again, and she was being hurried down a corridor by the same girl in the boiler suit, being told she had done the interview 'beautifully', and that she'd 'looked-great-and-thank-you-for-coming'.

Another car was waiting for her. 'Where to, Miss?'

'Pimlico Road, please,' she replied, heady with relief that the interview was over. It hadn't been as scary as she'd feared, but nevertheless she didn't enjoy being in the public eye.

When Joanna arrived at work, she was greeted with congratulations because Alice had brought in a portable TV set and they'd all stood round it in the workroom, watching the programme.

Rosie patted her on the arm. 'Well done, love,' she said in her quiet way. 'Let's hope it does the trick.'

Freddie was surprised when his secretary told him, just after ten o'clock, that DI Walsh was on the phone and wanted to speak to him.

'What can I do for you?' he asked, after they'd formally greeted each other.

'I've been watching Joanna on television this morning,' Walsh replied, 'and she seems so certain her mother is still alive that I wondered if there was anything you could do to calm her down a bit?'

'In what way?' Freddie asked curiously. 'Are you saying you *don't* think Arabella is still alive?'

'Frankly, I think it's unlikely. We've had other cases when tapes or even letters started arriving from a missing person, made under duress before they were murdered and then mailed later, to try and get us to call off the search.'

'I've had my doubts about their relevance,' Freddie agreed. 'It was the arrival of the second one that really gave Joanna hope. But there *is* always that niggling feeling at the back of one's mind, knowing how capricious Arabella was, that they might actually be genuine. I mean, in the sense of having been recorded within the last week or so.'

'Yes, I understand.' Walsh paused, struggling to find the right words. 'Mr Foster, does Joanna actually *know* much about her mother? We have discovered by inter-viewing certain people in the fashion industry and a few of her friends that she had a . . . colourful, shall we say? . . . past. Before her marriage to Professor Webster she had quite a reputation. In fact, she was a high-class hooker. More recently, we've discovered she has been engaged in providing cocaine for certain people. All this makes it seem more likely that she has become the victim of someone who is out for revenge.'

'Do you consider Eleanor Andrews' trashing of her flat to be revenge?'

'While I believe that *was* a revenge attack, I'm thinking of something far more serious, something which goes much further back in Arabella's life. I believe there's someone out there who was desperate to get her.'

'Not Eric?' Freddie swivelled round in his leather chair so he could look out of the window at the terraced Georgian houses of Bedford Row. The trees were bare now, the sun without warmth. He knew what Walsh was getting at.

The detective continued, his tone now man-to-man: 'I've tried to get Joanna to talk more about her mother, give us a better picture of what she was like, but she's inclined to gloss over the details of her private life. She just says she was "too young to remember" or "away at boarding school" when I question her. I fear she may be in for a nasty shock when all the details come out, as they eventually will, and I wondered if you could . . . well... prepare her in some way?'

'Believe me I'd like to, but in the time we've known each other, I've begun to realise she's in complete denial,' Freddie said candidly. 'I think she really *can't* remember certain things. She's blocked them off. Her father told me a long time ago what Arabella was really like and how he tried to get custody of Joanna when she was six. She simply doesn't want to know.'

Walsh sighed loudly in frustration. 'It's going to be

awfully hard for her . . . Can't her father tell her the score?'

'Jeremy Knight is a lovely man. Warm, caring and very protective of Joanna. He doesn't want her hurt. Doesn't want her disillusioned about her mother. And now there's the younger sister, in the same boat. Both she and Joanna believing their mother is a saint in a couture dress,' Freddie commented flatly.

'And you don't think Eleanor Andrews said anything to her? Apparently they had a bust-up before Eleanor left.'

'If she did, Joanna hasn't said a word to me about it. I doubt she'd believe a word Eleanor said anyway. Just say she was just being bitchy.'

'Right. Sorry to have bothered you at your office, Mr Foster. I just wondered if you could prepare the ground, for her own sake more than anything.'

'I'll do what I can,' he agreed, 'but I can't promise I'll get anywhere.'

Evening, Friday 29 October

Freddie got home early that evening, having phoned Nina earlier in the day. 'Can I ask you the most enormous favour?' he said.

She grinned. If he hadn't been Joanna's boyfriend, she'd have made a dead set at him herself. She could picture him now, sitting in his elegant office in his dark suit, trying to look very formal and businesslike, but with a lazy smile and crinkly eyes that rather took away from the effect.

'Name your price?' she quipped.

'I have to talk to Joanna,' he said seriously. 'Walsh phoned me today. He wants me to warn her that Arabella wasn't perhaps the woman Jo thinks she was.'

'I know,' agreed Nina, shocking him.

'You *know*?'

'Jeremy told me a few things the other day. He thinks Arabella's come to a sticky end, and privately I get the feeling he isn't too surprised. I asked him why he didn't tell Joanna straight up? After all, she is twenty-two. But he's desperate to spare her feelings.'

'I know,' Freddie said hollowly. 'Now I've got to do it.'

'It sucks, doesn't it? Listen, Freddie, no probs. I've been desperate to see *Phantom of the Opera* ever since I came over. I'll see if I can get in – there are usually a few returns. If not, I'll take in another show and let you guys have the place to yourselves.'

'Is that really all right, Nina?'

'Absolutely no sweat.'

Alone in the flat now, which had been left clean and tidy by Nina, who had also put some salad, a plate of ham and a bowl of fruit on the kitchen table, he took off his city suit and had a shower. Tiredness clung to him like a heavy cloak, pressing down on him, weakening his arms and legs. The last few weeks had been relentless, his workload seemingly neverending. What he needed was a break, but until this Arabella business got sorted out, that was off the agenda. Changed into jeans and a shirt, he switched on the news and collapsed on the sofa. He was almost dreading Joanna's return.

She came back a few minutes later, looking pinched

and weary. 'You're early, Freddie,' she observed with a faint smile. Then she looked round. 'Where's Nina?'

He dropped the newspaper on the floor by his side. 'Gone to see *Phantom*,' he replied, stretching his arms above his head. 'She's left supper out for us, though.'

'Thank God for Nina,' Joanna said fervently. 'I'm just going to take off my things. I'm absolutely knackered. Want a drink?'

'Yes, let's have some wine,' he replied, thinking that was actually quite a good idea.

'How were things today?' he shouted, as he heard her opening and shutting a wardrobe. He realised he was trying to sound conversational, and it made him feel awkward. Usually he didn't have to sound anything with Joanna. They just relaxed in each other's company, talked when they wanted to, were silent when they didn't.

'Pretty hellish,' he heard her shout back. 'At least the TV thing went all right this morning. Now we've just got to wait for the results.'

'Do you think you'll get any?'

There was silence. Then suddenly she shot back into the room, looking cross. 'What do you mean – will we get any? If Ma isn't able to get another message to us herself, someone may know where she is. My appeal will hopefully have jogged someone's memory: of seeing her somewhere, hearing rumours she's in the area. Anything that will give us a tip-off.'

Freddie looked at her levelly. 'Babe, it's been over a month now.'

'So?' She'd put on jeans and was pulling a white sweatshirt over her head. Suddenly her bare feet with nails painted pale pink looked awfully vulnerable.

'I don't want you to be disappointed,' he said tenderly. 'I don't think you know what you've got yourself into. I don't think you know what you're up against when it comes to Arabella.'

Joanna stood in the middle of the living room, looking at him as if he was about to betray her.

'Rubbish!' she scoffed, tossing her head. 'You don't know what you're talking about.' He saw the flicker of fear in her dark eyes.

'Jo . . .' Purposely, he wasn't going to refer to Arabella as her mother. 'Jo, she was mixed up in more than you realise. There were things in her life that may have caught up with her.'

'What do you mean? How can you talk like that?' she flashed.

Freddie sat upright to deal better with what he saw as the impending crisis.

'Because I know,' he said quietly. 'I know, babe. There are things in her past that could be directly connected to what's happened to her now. Your father told me, right at the beginning, that he feared it would all come out. She was a hooker, Jo. A drug dealer. I told him he should tell you himself, but he kept putting it off. Hoping it would never be necessary. I think you should be prepared.'

Joanna looked stunned. 'I don't believe you! How can you say such terrible things? You know nothing about her. The only past Ma had was working her fingers to the bone making clothes so she could look after me and give me a decent childhood. Even when she married Eric and we had money, she still worked to give Louise and me everything we needed. I'll never forgive you for talking about her like this,' she wept.

'Would I lie to you?'

She stopped crying and looked at him in confusion. 'You're supposed to be being supportive, Freddie. I thought you cared about Ma, too? The last thing I need is this.'

'Would your father lie to me?'

'He was probably drunk . . . angry at her for leaving him all those years ago . . . I don't know.'

'Please, babe, don't get so upset. Arabella was a fascinating, talented woman, but she wasn't perfect. That's all I'm saying.'

'I won't listen to any more of this,' she shouted. 'Shut up, Freddie! I love my mother. She's always been wonderful to me and I won't have another word said against her.'

Freddie jumped to his feet, energised by anger. 'That's it,' he said angrily. 'I've had enough. I'm trying to prepare you for the worst, for your own sake, but if you refuse to listen then there's nothing more I can say. I've been working twelve hours a day for weeks now, and I'm totally whacked. I simply can't take any more. If you're going to bury your head in the sand then you'll just have to get on with it.' He strode out of the room, snatching his car keys off the hall table as he headed for the front door.

'Where are you going?' she yelled.

'Out.'

'Well, fuck off then!'

The door slammed and she could hear him running down the endless flights of stairs to the street door. For a few moments she was too shocked to move. They'd never quarrelled in all the time they'd known each other and Joanna was stunned to discover he could say such cruel things, just when she needed him most.

Slowly at first uncontrollable weeping took hold. She slumped on to the sofa, feeling she was going to disintegrate under the onslaught of her own salty tears, like the sandcastles she'd made as a child which had dissolved under the incoming tide.

'Oh, Mummy . . .' she sobbed. 'Mummy . . . why did you have to go? I need you . . .

'When I was small you loved me and looked after me and I miss all that now . . . Do you remember the birthday and Christmas presents you used to give me? Extravagant, wonderful presents – party frocks and pale blue shoes, and that beautiful dolls' house I badly wanted? You always made Christmas so special, with a big tree and candles everywhere. We were happy then, weren't we? Just you and me before you married Eric . . .

'I know there were nannies but they didn't count. They were a nuisance when they wouldn't let me get into bed with you in the mornings: they always said you had to have your beauty sleep and I remember saying you were beautiful enough, why did you need more sleep?

'I used to love watching you getting dressed to go out in the evenings. I remember you once had a deep purple floaty dress and the shoulders were all studded with diamanté. How I wished my school friends could have seen you! I was so proud you were my mother. None of the other children had mothers who looked like you . . .

'Oh, Ma, what am I going to do without you?'

Nina let herself quietly into the flat, expecting the bedroom door to be shut and Joanna and Freddie tucked up for the night, but although there was silence the lights in the living room were on. She stepped through the doorway and saw Joanna curled up on the sofa in a foetal position. Then she noticed the bedroom door was open and the room in darkness.

'Joanna?' she whispered anxiously.

She awoke with a start and looked up at Nina fearfully for a moment, then she remembered what had happened. 'Oh, shit! What time is it?' she asked, sitting up.

'After eleven, honey. Are you all right?'

Joanna rubbed the heels of her hands into her eyes. 'I feel terrible. Freddie and I had a monumental fight and he stalked off. I cannot *believe* . . .'

Nina stiffened. 'What were you fighting about?' she asked carefully.

Joanna looked up. She sounded devastated. 'He's somehow got it into his head that Ma was . . . Oh, Jesus, he said the most dreadful things! He said she'd been a hooker . . . can you imagine? My mother a hooker? I'm so angry I don't know what to do with myself. She might be a bit involved with drugs. Not taking them, but getting them for some of her clients. I might believe that, but nothing else.'

'So then what happened?' her friend said carefully.

'He pissed off in a rage. Said he was trying to tell me

for my own good. What help does he think that's going to be? I'm stressed enough as it is. The last thing I need is a pack of lies,' Joanna added hotly.

Nina studied the carpet, her face grave for once.

'Jo,' she said at last, 'Freddie would never do anything to hurt you. You've got so many people in your life who love you and want to help you through this nightmare and he is the leader of the pack. You can't really imagine he'd make it all up, can you?'

'But it's not true,' Joanna wailed, her eyes brimming.

Nina said nothing. She just sat there, looking at her quietly, letting the moments tick past, hoping they'd bring some sort of enlightenment for Joanna.

'Why do you think I went out this evening, Jo?'

'Because . . .' Joanna frowned. 'What are you saying?'

'Freddie wanted to talk to you alone and he knew it was going to be very difficult. He loves you more than anything, you know. You must hang on to that, honey. The whole point of his talking to you was to spare you pain in the long run. To get you to realise that there were . . . complications in Arabella's past which may be connected to her disappearance.'

Joanna sat absolutely still. 'Who told him to talk to me? If it's true, who told him?' She looked up suddenly, eyes flashing. 'Eleanor? Was it her?'

'No,' Nina said in surprise. 'Why should it be her?'

'Because she said those things about Ma, too.' Joanna's voice was so quiet it was almost inaudible.

'You never said.'

'I couldn't. It was too awful.'

'It wasn't Eleanor. It was DI Walsh. But Freddie had

211

also been told by your father what had been going on, and why he'd been desperate to try and get custody of you.' Nina rose from the armchair and came and sat on the sofa beside Joanna. 'Of course you loved your mother, and there's no reason why you should stop loving her just because she had feet of clay. But all of us who care for you, Jo, want you to be able to cope, want you to be prepared, so that it's not too much of a shock when it's blazoned all over the front pages of the tabloids, which it probably will be in due course.'

Joanna closed her eyes. Still she did not move.

Nina put her arm around her shoulders. 'It'll take time,' she said gently.

'Then,' Joanna said as if she hadn't heard, 'she wasn't really the person I knew at all, was she?'

Nina hesitated. 'You knew her all right, Jo, you just didn't know *all* of her. No child does know everything about its parents. Only the part that's presented to them.'

'Oh, my God.' Joanna covered her face with her hands and sat like that for several minutes. The lovely illusion had been destroyed. There was now the unmistakable ring of truth in what Eleanor had said. And because she hadn't told anyone, Freddie had been forced to warn her, too.

Nina patted her shoulder. 'Are you all right, honey?'

She nodded.

'Can I get you anything? A warm drink, perhaps?'

'No, thanks.'

'You'll be OK, you know.'

Joanna looked at Nina, her expression calm. 'I expect so.'

'I'll be off to bed then. You try and get some sleep, Jo.'

'Yes. And thanks, Nina.'

She was getting undressed when she heard Freddie's key in the lock. A moment later he was standing in the bedroom doorway, looking at her.

'OK, babe?' His blue eyes looked tired but his expression was tender. 'Sorry I lost it earlier.'

'No, Freddie. I'm sorry. I'm so ashamed I accused you of being cruel . . .' She was in his arms, being pulled close and held tight, and she had her arms around his neck and her face buried in his shoulder, and he was cupping the back of her head in the palm of his hand, like a baby.

'It's all right,' he kept whispering. 'I was clumsy in the way I told you. I'm sorry, Jo. I'm really sorry.'

'Don't be,' she gulped, looking up into his face. 'I had to know . . . in fact, I sort of *did* know, but I wouldn't admit it even to myself. I realise now I was in complete denial. It was because I loved her so . . .' She broke down again, unable to continue.

Freddie guided her to the bed, half lifted her on to it and then lay beside her, still fully clothed but not wanting to let go of her, because he realised with a sense of shock that this was the moment in which she'd finally grown up.

Nine

Afternoon, Monday 1 November

Alice put her head round the door. 'Your father phoned when you were out, Joanna. He asked if you could ring him back.'

'Was he phoning from Brittany?'

'No. He said he came back early this morning.'

There was no answer when she phoned Portsea Place, so Joanna tapped in Jeremy's direct line at his office. He answered immediately.

'I didn't know you were coming back so soon,' she exclaimed, after they'd greeted each other.

'Darling, I've got a job to do and I've already been away for over ten days. There's a pile of work in front of me in spite of the fact we did the advertising for Christmas four months ago.'

'Christmas!' she said aghast. 'I can't begin to think about Christmas for at least another six weeks. How's Louise?'

'Thanks to your generosity, sweetheart, Victoria and she are staying on for another week or so. I suppose there's no more news? Eric agreed with me before we went away that Louise should be kept in the dark a bit longer, until we know the score.'

There was a pause before she replied, 'Dad, I want to talk to you about that. What are you doing this evening?'

'Nothing, love. Why don't you let me take you out to dinner at that nice place round the corner from you?'

'That would be great.'

'We can catch up then. Shall I collect you from the shop? Or would you rather I picked you up from Warwick Square?'

Joanna thought quickly. She wanted to speak to him on her own. 'The shop, Dad. Shortly after seven?'

'What's up, Jo?' Jeremy asked as they set off for Mimmo D'Ischia in Elizabeth Street. It was only a couple of weeks or so since he'd seen her but he was shocked by the change in her. He couldn't quite put his finger on it, but it was as if she'd aged without growing any older. She was very thin, of course. She must have lost nearly two stone since Arabella's disappearance, and her face was pale, the skin tightly drawn over her cheek bones; but there was something else. A look in her eyes. A sadness around her mouth, and yet . . . she seemed more quietly confident, as if she now knew where she was going.

'Freddie okay?' he asked casually, hoping she hadn't suggested he join them for dinner.

Joanna smiled warmly, her eyes lighting up. 'Freddie's fine, Dad. Starting another big case which means he's working all hours, but he's great.'

They walked on in silence. Was he missing something? He'd never felt this strange distance between them before, as if they'd grown apart. How could you grow apart from your own daughter in such a short time?

Jeremy waited until they'd ordered and the wine had been poured.

'So what gives, Jo?' he asked quietly.

She looked at him across the table, her hands with fingers interlaced in front of her. 'I wish you'd told me, Dad.'

'What?' He drew his brows together. 'Told you what?'

'About Ma. Freddie had to tell me in the end, and it was awful for him. I wouldn't believe him at first because I didn't want to, but then I realised Eleanor had said exactly the same things when I'd asked her to leave. Even Nina knew. I felt such a naïve fool apart from anything else.'

Jeremy's face was puckered with distress. 'Oh, Christ, Jo. I didn't want to upset you. Don't think too badly of her. She was very young when we split up. She liked nice things.' He gave a great sigh. 'If none of this had happened, you'd never have needed to know.'

'But it has happened and Detective Walsh told Freddie that when Arabella's found it's bound to come out,' she said sadly.

'So Walsh knows everything?'

'Apparently he's got a whole dossier on Ma. I suppose he would as it's his job to try and find out what's happened to her.'

'And he thinks she's still alive?' Jeremy asked incredulously.

'I'm not sure about him, but *I* think she is.' Joanna took a sip of her wine. 'I think she's being held against her will by someone who signs himself "R" and lives in an old house somewhere in the country. Finding out about Ma's past hasn't changed a thing. I wouldn't have gone on GMTV the other morning if I hadn't believed she's somewhere out there, waiting for us to rescue her.'

After he'd dropped Joanna off at her flat, Jeremy took the taxi on to Portsea Place. He was shaken and upset that she'd found out about Arabella, and wondered if even now Joanna realised it wasn't just that her mother had been a hooker; it wasn't just that she'd been happy to supply drugs to people who could afford them – it was her whole life that had been ruthlessly self-seeking. She'd been greedy, wanting it all for herself. Treading on people if they stood in her way. Grabbing for herself every passing pleasure. And then, just when he'd thought Joanna had escaped the manipulative queen bee in her honey pot, Arabella had insisted the girl should work for her instead of going to art school. Cleverly, of course, she'd used emotional blackmail to get her way, and in spite of his asking Joanna repeatedly if she was doing the right thing, Arabella had won. She not only had a grown-up daughter at her side day and night, she had a personal slave to blow her trumpet for her.

Jeremy wished he didn't still feel so bitter; Victoria had more than made up for his first marriage and he had personally suffered very little in the end. But he felt bitter because of what Arabella had done . . . and was doing . . . to their daughter. And he worried greatly about Louise's future.

Morning, Tuesday 2 November

'There was a call for you,' Alice told Joanna when she arrived at work. 'He wouldn't leave a name but said he'd call back later.'

'Thanks.' Joanna went through the mail, most of which was landing on her desk these days, ever since Eleanor's departure. There was a letter from the bank who wanted to know what the future prospects for Arabella Designs were. She added it to the pending tray.

'He's on the line again for you,' Alice said a few minutes later. 'Shall I get you a coffee?'

Joanna nodded. She picked up the receiver and spoke in her professional voice.

'Good morning, Joanna Knight speaking. Can I help you?'

The voice was strange, rasping and wheezy. 'Leave Arabella Webster alone. If you don't, you could die! This is not a hoax. Get real, Joanna. Stop trying to find her.'

There was a click. Her caller had gone.

'Holy shit!' she exclaimed, instantly punching in 1471. A moment later the recorded voice of a BT operator said: 'You received a call at 9.24 a.m. The caller withheld their number.'

'Fuck!'

Alice came hurtling back into the room looking startled. 'What's wrong? What's happened?'

'I've just had a threatening call. And he'd blocked the line so I can't trace it,' Joanna said, rattled.

Alice's eyes were startled pools of blue. 'That man? The one who called before?'

'Yup.' Joanna was ringing the police station. Walsh had arrived at his desk minutes before and she told him what had happened.

'It may still be a hoax, even if he said it wasn't,' the detective said, as if he didn't take the call too seriously. 'Nasty for you, I admit,' he added. 'Next time, get your secretary to say you're out. Tell her to get his name and number, and you can bet anything you like he'll refuse.'

'I just thought you ought to know.' Joanna felt let down. The call had scared her and he wasn't going to do anything about it.

'While you're on the line, Joanna,' Walsh continued, 'I'm afraid our enquiries in the Gwent area have proved negative. That postmark, as I feared, was probably a red herring.'

'What about the drawing of the house on the writing paper?'

'We will continue with our enquiries, Joanna. We're not going to leave a stone unturned.'

'You may already be too late,' she said in a small frightened voice. 'That call I had . . . the man meant business. And now I'm frightened I've made things worse by going on television.'

'I told you, it was almost definitely a hoax. You've no idea how many cranks try and get in on the act in a case like this. We've had dozens of calls saying they've seen your mother, talked to her, been on a bus with her . . .

and every one has turned out to be a sick hoax. I'd forget it completely if I were you.

'The other thing I wanted to tell you is that we have a complete confession from Eleanor Andrews.'

'You do? So she's been charged? When will her case come up?'

'That's hard to say, Joanna. I'm afraid Miss Andrews is suffering from a bad nervous breakdown. She's in the psychiatric wing of Sevenoaks Hospital, near where her mother lives.'

At lunchtime Nina came into the salon, looking flustered. She was flying back to the States the next day as her mother wasn't well, apparently. She'd grumbled on the phone about Nina's being away from home so long. 'So I gotta go!' she told them sadly.

'See what I've found, though,' she gabbled breathlessly. She was clutching a book. 'I bought this to take home to my mother because she loves anything about Olde England. Stately homes and tourist attractions and all that sort of thing.' She opened the book and laid it flat on the desk before Joanna. 'And just look at that.'

Under the heading 'Roxwell Manor' there was a photograph of an old grey-stone house, with deep-set lead-paned windows and a gabled roof. The chimneys were Tudor and to either side of the wide steps leading up to the heavy oak door were ferocious-looking wolves, carved in stone.

'My God!' Joanna gasped in excitement. 'That's it – the house on the headed paper!' She stared at the picture for several moments before trying to read the accompanying description, the words dancing before her eyes. 'What does it say? Where is it?'

Nina leaned over her shoulder and started reading aloud.

' "Roxwell Manor, Roxwell, Somerset. A most beautiful and fascinating historical house, containing twelve hundred years of history. Open to the public . . ." de-da, de-da. It gives all the details. Now listen to this, Jo. "Parts of the house go back to the days of Alfred the Great; it also contains a series of exhibitions of historic interest, including collections of Victorian dolls and toys, Jacobean pewter, costumes from the reign of Charles I, and fine seventeenth-century needlework. There is also a gift shop and tearoom. In the summer guests can enjoy walking in the surrounding grounds where rare shrubs grow in profusion." There! What do you make of that?' Nina demanded triumphantly.

'It must mean the man who wrote to Mummy actually lives or works there, mustn't it?' Joanna's eyes widened. 'She couldn't be there now, could she?' she added in a tremulous voice. 'Listen, I had a horrible anonymous call this morning. The man said if we didn't leave Arabella alone, I'd die. I wonder if this could be his house?'

'You're *kidding*?' Nina gasped in horror. 'What does that detective friend of yours say?'

Joanna shrugged. 'Not much.' She stared at the photograph, as if hypnotised by it. 'I want to go there,' she said slowly. 'I want to go and find out exactly what's happening.'

Nina stuck out her bottom lip thoughtfully. Suddenly

she exclaimed: 'I know! I'll phone and say I'm an American tourist who wants to visit. Then I can ask all sorts of questions.'

'That would be perfect. They'd never connect us,' Joanna agreed. 'Ask all the usual questions about opening hours, how much it costs to get in, and if there's a discount for coach parties. Anything to put them off the scent, but everything you can think of to get information out of them.'

'I'll ask, casually, who lives there? Like, is it a family home? Try and get a name out of them, too.' Nina grabbed the phone on Joanna's desk.

'I can't bear to listen,' she said, rising suddenly. 'It's too nerve-wracking.' She hurried out of her office, telling Alice, who was making more coffee, that Nina wasn't to be disturbed.

Up in the workroom she talked to Rosie but it was hard to concentrate. All she could think about was that drawing of the old manor house at the top of the letter, and the matching photograph in the book. What could the connection be with Arabella? Was the museum-cum-house a cover for drug running? Or was 'R' merely a spurned lover Arabella had gone to pacify?

'Jo . . .?'

She started, hearing Nina call her.

'I'm coming,' she shouted back, dashing out of the workroom and back down the stairs to her office. 'What happened? How did you get on?'

'It was very interesting,' her friend said, 'but I'm not sure how helpful it is. A man answered the phone and seemed quite chatty. He said they get a lot of Americans visiting the house. He also said they hire out some of the big rooms for private functions . . .'

'Yes? So what?'

'It's open to the public next weekend. In the winter they're only open at weekends. It's four pounds a head . . .'

Joanna was exploding with impatience. 'Nina, get to the point!'

'The house is owned by a Mr and Mrs Gilbert. It was left to her by her uncle nearly thirty years ago. They open the place to raise money towards the running costs.'

'Gilbert?' Joanna repeated, frowning thoughtfully. 'It doesn't ring a bell.'

'No, but the next bit might.'

'Why, what did he say?'

'I said to him something like, "So you're the owner, are you, Mr Gilbert?" '

'And?'

'He laughed and said: "No, I'm the son, Ryan. I help run the place." '

Evening, Tuesday 2 November

'I don't like it, Arabella. I feel they're getting closer. I thought we were so safe, thought they'd never find us, but now I'm not so sure . . .

'This is the best part of the day, isn't it? It's so quiet and still you can almost hear the worms turn. I'm glad it's warm enough to be out here . . . listen to the breeze! It's

very gentle, isn't it, now the leaves have almost all gone?

'Before you came here to be with me, I used to plan our evenings, dream of all the things we'd talk about and how we'd read to each other. I haven't read to you for ages, have I? I saw a lovely book of poems in a shop the other day . . . only a paperback, you know, with a rather lurid modern cover but I opened it at random and a line caught my eye. Something about "A veil of innocence descends" and I thought of you.

'Funny, isn't it, how things remind you of people? Oh, Arabella, Arabella, are you innocent? You can't be, can you? But how guilty are you? That's the real question.'

Evening, Wednesday 3 November

'Dad, I'm *not* going to tell the police my suspicions about this man Ryan at Roxwell Manor,' Joanna protested. 'That second anonymous call last night really freaked me out but Detective Walsh doesn't want to know. He says it's a hoax and to pay no attention. If I tell him I want to visit this house, he'll only start talking about wild goose chases.'

The phone had rung at nearly midnight, making Joanna fear someone had been in an accident or some other disaster. She'd answered because the phone was on her side of the bed. The voice she heard was raw with malice, each word an assault on her.

'You're going to *die* if you go on searching. Leave her alone! Don't you understand? She's with me now. She doesn't want anything more to do with you. D'you hear me?'

'Who is that?' Joanna shouted furiously. Freddie had sprung up in bed, eyes dazed with sleep but his body automatically alert. He reached for the phone. 'Give it here,' he muttered hoarsely but Joanna held on to it.

'Damn you to hell, you bitch!' a man's voice exclaimed viciously, and so loudly Freddie could hear it. Then there was a click and silence.

'He's done it again,' Joanna said, shaken. 'God! He sounds evil.'

They tried to trace the call but once again it had been blocked. After that sleep eluded them for hours although they were both exhausted. 'Bastard!' Freddie kept muttering under his breath as he struggled to find a comfortable position.

Jeremy, having supper with them now, echoed these sentiments. 'If this caller is as lunatic as he sounds, you must tell the police, Jo,' he remonstrated. 'If you think he's the person who wrote to Arabella and is now trying to prevent you from searching for her, what's stopping you?'

'I told DI Walsh about him after I'd had the first threatening call, but he pooh-poohed the whole thing. I don't think this man's a hoaxer, though. I think he knows where Mummy is and is determined to stop us finding her. I want to go to Roxwell Manor this weekend, when it's open to the public. I want to meet this man, Ryan Gilbert. We can't leave things as they are.'

With an expression of incredulity, Jeremy turned to Freddie. 'What do you make of all this?' he said.

Freddie pulled a face and tipped back in his chair,

digging his hands deep into his trouser pockets. 'I obviously don't want Jo to put herself in danger, but although I think she ought to tell the police, I can understand her point about not wanting to. Especially as Walsh has been so scathing about these anonymous calls. We're absolutely certain the person who wrote those letters to Arabella is also the man making these threatening calls, and that they emanate from this place Roxwell Manor. But whether he's a nutcase, a stalker who's obsessed with Arabella, or whether she is actually at Roxwell Manor is another question. He may be only fantasising about her, and wanting to keep the police away so that he can keep his fantasy intact? D'you see what I mean? It may all be in his head, and anyone turning up to look for her will shatter his fantasy. He knows it, and that's why he's trying to scare Joanna off.'

They sat in silence digesting this theory, Jeremy sipping his wine and Joanna suddenly missing Nina's presence in their midst because she'd flown back home to the States.

'I think,' said Freddie, almost as if he was addressing a courtroom, 'that it would be a mistake to call off our search. But I think Joanna should announce to the press that it *has* been called off. And if Walsh doesn't like that when it appears in print, it will be too late to do anything about it and we can always deny all knowledge of it.'

'Then what?' Jeremy demanded.

Freddie looked at Joanna and reached for her hand. As he spoke he smiled at her and she gave him a look of deep gratitude. 'Against my better judgement, I'm ready to go with Joanna to Roxwell on Saturday. We're going to tour the house and investigate the place.' He shrugged, letting go of Joanna's hand and reaching for his wine glass. 'We may find something or we may not. If this chap Ryan is suffering from delusions and imagines Arabella is there with him, then I'm sure we'll get an angle on the situation. I think, after our tour, we should ask around the village, find out if anything odd has been going on there. We might pick up something. On the other hand, we might not.'

Jeremy's lips tightened. His usually genial expression had been replaced by one of intense anxiety. 'I don't like it,' he muttered. 'You could be dealing with a psychopath who has a fixation on Arabella, but he may not actually *know* her. People in the public eye do have stalkers, you know, who believe they're on intimate terms with the person they're obsessed with when often they've never even met them.'

'What about the tapes Ma sent? She's with someone.'

Jeremy said patiently, 'But we don't know for sure that she recorded them at this house. She may have absolutely no connection to it or to this man called Ryan.'

'And the letters I found signed "R"?' Joanna persisted. 'They surely link her with that house?'

'They could just as easily have been sent by an unknown stalker, couldn't they? They were highly ambiguous. What was it he said? Something like, "You might have had the decency to listen to me"? Typical stalker's language. Don't you agree, Freddie?'

'In all fairness this may be a wild goose chase,' he confirmed wearily. 'We could be dealing with a sicko or a hoaxer, but either way I don't think we should leave a stone unturned if Joanna is ever to find peace of mind. She's got to discover what's happened to Arabella before she can get on with the rest of her life.'

Night, Wednesday 3 November

'Since I learned about you, I've sometimes felt like a splat of semen that had got shot off in the wrong place. I am a no one. A casual fertilisation that was never supposed to happen. I cry then. Cry into my pillow until it is wet. I am just an entity floating in space. Unattached. Not belonging . . .

'Connie and Tom said I'd been born on May Day, but how could they be sure?

'I'm sorry, I didn't mean to break down . . . It's just, I've missed so much of my life. As if I wasn't really there to enjoy it. There's nothing like your own flesh and blood, is there? Anything else is a sort of sham. A kind of make-believe, pretending you belong in a family when you don't . . .

'Don't get me wrong – Connie and Tom have been very good to me. They were kind at the beginning, but they didn't understand. You understand, though, don't you, Arabella? You must sometimes have had that feeling of not belonging . . .'

Ten

Dawn, Saturday 6 November

London was waking up to a wet but sluggishly mild morning as Joanna and Freddie left the flat and crossed the square to reach his car. It was just after six-thirty.

'We've got over two hundred and fifty miles to do,' Freddie pointed out when Joanna sleepily asked why they had to leave so early. 'Hopefully we'll have a clear run if we leave now.'

She'd hardly slept at all and hadn't felt well enough to have any breakfast. Freddie had helped himself to cereal, toast and marmalade. Wearing jeans, trainers and a black puffa over a polo neck sweater, she got into the passenger seat and belted herself in. Apprehension was making her feel sick. It was going to be a long day, made worse by the fact that she had no idea what it was going to hold.

'All set, babe?' he asked as he switched on the engine.

'Yes.' She gave him a little smile and snuggled down deeper into her seat.

'Can you get the map out of the glove compartment?

231

I'm not sure which motorway we should take.'

'We don't need a map until the last few miles, I've already looked up the route. We take the M4 all the way to Bristol and then the M5 to Taunton.'

The car glided smoothly through the quiet residential streets around Victoria and then headed south-west. 'We might as well find out what's happening in the world,' said Freddie, switching on the radio. 'And we can catch the weather forecast, too.'

The roads glistened with rain and the tyres made a swishing sound as they skimmed through the puddles. The windscreen wipers danced a jig, clearing a space to see through the glass bejewelled with raindrops, which picked up the colour of the traffic lights. Soon the car's heaters fanned warm air around their feet.

'What time will we arrive?'

'Around nine-thirty, I'd say.'

'Roxwell Manor doesn't open until ten o'clock.'

'Then we'll stop for a cup of coffee.'

'Government set to pass bill on immigration . . .' blared the radio. Joanna turned down the volume.

'Shit, I'm tired! Would you mind if I took a nap, Freddie?' This thing was really getting to her. For weeks now it had been like a black cloud hovering over her. Now she sensed a crisis point drawing closer.

'You do that, babe,' he said encouragingly and switched the radio to Classic FM. Cocooned in the warm intimacy of the car, with soft music playing in the background, Joanna slept as they headed into a pale watery dawn. Gradually the suburbs gave way to fields and forests, the bare branches etched against a grey sky, the land stripping itself of leaves and vegetation in readiness to lie fallow until next spring. Joanna continued to sleep. Her head rolled slightly to one side so that Freddie could see her face when he glanced across at her.

By seven-forty-five low banks of mist shrouded the countryside. Turnings for Reading, Newbury, Hungerford, Swindon, Chippenham and Bath seemed to float past the windows, like ghostly signposts to outer space.

Joanna awoke suddenly, just as a sign for Bristol flashed past. 'This is where we join another motorway,' she said, alert now. Wind blowing in from the Bristol Channel had replaced the mist with a bracing chill and she opened her window to breathe in the air which was sharp and heavy with salt.

Joining the M5 they by-passed Bristol, and then with directions from Joanna as she pored over the map, Freddie followed the signs to Weston-Super-Mare, Bridgwater and Taunton. Joanna's stomach muscles tightened. Taunton was the nearest big town to Roxwell. In less than thirty minutes they'd be there.

'Where do we go now?' Freddie asked, as they came off Exit 26 on the far side of Taunton.

Joanna tried to keep her voice steady. 'We have to join the A38 for a few miles until we come to a place called Wellington.'

He was also trying to appear calm. 'Then what?'

'We go on to Langford Budville, Milverton, then cross the A361 and the next village is Roxwell,' she said hollowly.

Freddie changed gear as the road climbed steeply and

bent to the right. 'It's pretty countryside,' he remarked as if to defuse the tension. 'And we're in good time.'

Joanna glanced at the dashboard clock. It was nine-twenty-five.

The road sloped steeply. A canopy of bare branches arched in a lacy pattern overhead. Freddie drove slowly until the ground levelled out and there was a sharp turning to the left. Ahead of them, nestling in a hollow of the valley, lay the village of Roxwell.

It was a charming, rambling place, a typically English village virtually unchanged since the nineteenth century, with its scattering of small grey-stone houses, roofs tiled in weathered shades of pink, a Norman church, and a few old-fashioned shops. It was remarkable only for its ordinariness.

'Look.' Freddie pointed to a signpost sticking out of a grass verge by the side of the road. It said: ROXWELL MANOR.

He put his arm around Joanna's shoulders. 'What do you want to do first, babe?' he asked gently. 'Do a recce of the joint or go straight in?'

She paused, biting her lip. This place had now assumed enormous importance in her search for Arabella. She couldn't explain it but in a terrifying way it was like finding something she'd lost, though now that she'd discovered it she wasn't sure she wanted it. 'Will it be open yet?'

Freddie edged the car forward. 'No, it's not quite ten, yet. Let's have a look at the entrance and see what's going on.'

'Good idea.'

He drove very slowly up a narrow road in the direction in which the signpost was pointing. At the end they came to a five-bar gate which stood open. Beyond it lay a stony piece of waste ground signed 'Car Park'. There were already three cars lined up on one side, their occupants waiting for the house to open.

'We don't want to look too obvious,' Freddie said. 'Why don't we wait until there are a few more people? Have you brought a head scarf or something? In case you're recognised.'

'Yes.' She reached into her bag and took out a dark blue silk square, tying it on the point of her chin. 'I've got dark glasses, too.'

'I think that *would* be drawing attention to yourself in the depths of Somerset on a dull morning,' Freddie rejoined, smiling. 'Let's stop and have a look at this.'

By the gate was a large notice board headed 'ROXWELL MANOR', in rather amateurish writing. Artfully arranged upon it were photographs of the interior and exterior of the house, which included what looked like an attractive tearoom leading out to a lawn on which was arranged Victorian wrought-iron garden furniture. Of more interest were the interior shots: a Jacobean panelled hall, a low-ceilinged bedroom with a carved four-poster, a stone-flagged kitchen equipped with fifteenth-century artefacts, and a narrow uncarpeted staircase, the wood polished with age and wear.

'It's a nice house,' Joanna admitted grudgingly.

'And it looks to be very well maintained,' Freddie agreed, peering at a picture of a table set with ancient pewter dishes and tankards. 'I'd say everything in it was authentic, too.'

ENTRY £4.00, CHILDREN & PENSIONERS HALF PRICE had been painted on another notice board, and below it: LICENSED BAR. TEA AND LIGHT REFRESHMENTS AVAILABLE.

Freddie raised his eyebrows. 'Value for money, I'd say.'

Joanna dug her hands into the pockets of her puffa and shivered. 'You're right. We want to wait until there's a bit of a crowd so we can blend in. Why don't we drive back into the village? We could have some coffee there and ask about Roxwell Manor, find out as much as we can about the place before we go in.'

'Good idea. Always prepare your case thoroughly before you go into court,' he agreed, patting her hand.

In the village they parked the car off the main road and then walked around, finding an olde worlde inn called the King's Arms which looked dark but cosy inside, a village shop packed to the ceiling with every conceivable requirement, several gift and antique shops, obviously aimed at attracting the tourists who visited the Manor, and a collection of picturesque cottages and tiny gardens as self-conscious of their prettiness as if they were on permanent stand-by to be photographed.

In Daisy's Tearoom they sat at one of the small gingham-clothed tables and ordered coffee and hot buttered toast from a young girl with curly red hair and the flat, round, blue-eyed face of a rag doll.

'Nice place you've got here,' Freddie remarked casually when they'd ordered. 'Do you live in the village?'

The girl nodded briefly and made as if to move away.

'I bet you have a brisk trade from tourists visiting the old Manor?'

'They've got their own café,' the girl retorted sullenly. Then she turned on her heel and marched off to the kitchen.

'She's not giving away anything, is she?' Joanna observed.

Freddie shrugged. 'She's probably bored witless. I don't suppose, even in the height of summer, there's much going on here.'

When they'd had their coffee and toast, they drove slowly back through the village and then once more up the lane leading to the Manor.

The car park had filled up in the last thirty minutes and a straggle of visitors were now wending their way through a gap in the high hedge that bordered the car park to the north.

Joanna and Freddie parked the car and joined a group of middle-aged couples, well wrapped up in anoraks and raincoats.

When they stepped through the gap they found themselves at the top of a long winding drive that was steep and slippery with loose stones and gravel, and only eight feet wide. Joanna took Freddie's hand, head scarf pulled well forward as they trooped behind the others. The over-grown hedges to either side obliterated any view that might lie to left or right and created a curious tunnel effect.

The drive curved sharply to the right and there at the bottom, to their left, stood Roxwell Manor.

Joanna was by now familiar with the front elevation

but from the side the building looked larger, sturdier, and not nearly so attractive. The stone walls were a darker shade of grey, too, and as they walked round to the front, they saw a dilapidated roof, grubby darkened windows with rotting sills and a general air of neglect.

Shocked, they looked around the garden in front of the house. It seemed to have been abandoned long ago to the elements, the changing seasons and the ravages of nature. In what had clearly once been a formal design, there were now empty flowerbeds, dead shrubs, sacks of rubbish and piles of logs, stacked against an ornamental archway. A small gate leading to a lower terrace swung from a broken hinge. Flagstones around the bottom of the entrance steps were cracked or broken, weeds sprouting between them.

'Did you ever?' Joanna heard a woman remark to her husband.

'It's terrible to see a place like this so run down,' he agreed.

'Are you sure it's open to the public?' someone else in the group asked.

Joanna and Freddie exchanged looks. 'Come over here,' he said, leading her to the circular stone pond set in the middle of the drive in front of the house. He'd noticed that in the pictures on the notice board it had been blooming with water lilies and filled with dozens of large goldfish. Now it was empty, drained of all life and vegetation. The wind stirred a few withered leaves near the centre.

'I wonder what the hell's going on?' Joanna whispered.

'How can they be open to the public when the place is such a shambles? Shall we look around the garden before we go in?'

'I think we should go round the house first. There may not be many more tourists today, so let's join them while we can.'

They walked between the large stone beasts set to either side of the steps, and when they arrived at the brass-studded oak door, found themselves in a small stuffy lobby.

A short, thick-set man, grey-bearded and in his late-fifties, stood selling tickets. His once brightly patterned Fair Isle sweater was stained and dirty. An overpowering stench of whisky and stale sweat emanated from him, causing Joanna to take an involuntary step back as he came near her.

'That'll be eight pounds, please,' he said, extending an unwashed hand.

As she heard his voice an icy prickling sensation swept through her, almost taking her breath away.

'Is there a brochure about the house I can buy?' she heard Freddie ask. The man took a ten-pound note from him and fished in a carved wooden box for two pound coins.

'Help yourself to a leaflet from the hall table,' he replied, giving Freddie his change with one hand and with the other waving in the direction of a dark-panelled room which led off the lobby. 'That'll tell you all about the Manor.'

Joanna listened closely to his voice, leaning slightly towards him, holding her breath against the stench that rose like a miasma, straining to catch every tone and nuance.

'And where should we start the tour?' Freddie asked, seeing other people wandering around at random.

'After you've seen the hall go on through to the morning room and then come back and go up those stairs. There are exhibits in every room. At the top of the house is the doll and toy museum. Then come back down and I'll show you where to go next.'

She *had* heard that voice before. That rasping, wheezing, poisonous voice, threatening her down the phone.

Forcing herself to remain expressionless, Joanna followed Freddie into the hall, but while he headed for the central table to pick up a leaflet, she walked to the window on legs weakened by fear and sank down on to the wide oak window seat.

Wandering over to her, Freddie read aloud: ' ". . . Jacobean panelling in the hall is complemented by furniture from the same period, suggesting people and life rather than a fossilised exhibit." ' He looked askance at Joanna. 'Not much life about this place so far,' he remarked sotto voce. Then he saw her expression. 'What's the matter?'

'His voice,' she whispered urgently. 'He's the man who made the threatening calls.'

'Are you sure?'

'Absolutely. I'd recognise that wheezy tone anywhere.'

'That's Ryan?' Freddie looked incredulous. 'The man who wrote those letters to Arabella?'

'Hush! Keep your voice down.'

'I'd expected him to be much younger.'

'So had I.'

The hall was empty now. 'We'd better move on or it will look odd. Are you all right, Jo?'

She nodded, tight-lipped, and stood up. The door on the far side of the hall led to the morning room, which was also panelled but contained several high-backed carved chairs and a chest against one wall. In the middle there was another round table on which stood a battered pewter candlestick and an inkwell with a quill sticking out of it. The deep stone grate was empty. It was obvious no one had lived in these rooms for years. They were sadly deserted and lacking in any human warmth.

'I've known museums which feel more lived in,' Joanna whispered as they turned back into the hall.

From the sound of clomping feet above their heads, the other visitors had obviously gone ahead of them. For a moment she stood very still, concentrating on her surroundings, as if trying to divine the essence of the place. Freddie, poking around, opened one of the wooden window shutters, for there were no curtains, and said in a stage whisper: 'Come and look at this.'

Behind the shutter was a gaping hole, the plaster crumbling and rotten, the stonework of the outer wall visible.

'The place is falling down,' he told her. 'Look at the deep cracks in the ceiling. Smell the damp in this room.'

'But it is a very old house, Freddie. There are bound to be cracks everywhere.'

'This is more than just antiquity.' He closed the shutter with care. 'Age needn't have anything to do with

241

a building's condition. Look at Windsor Castle, built in 1179. Or Leeds Castle, going back to 1272. Buildings were built to last then. They can be preserved and maintained. Costs a lot of money, though. It's obvious that Ryan, if he does own this place, is broke. They couldn't charge more than four pounds a head to get in here if they tried. You only have to look at the grounds to realise the whole place is suffering from total neglect. The interesting question is, why? It's listed as a historic building, they must get grants. They're open to the public . . .'

'That book Nina bought came out several years ago,' Joanna cut in.

'Well, there you go. I'd hazard a guess that what money they've got has gone down the throat of that old drunk who let us in.'

'Ryan Gilbert,' Joanna said thoughtfully. 'How does he fit in to all this? He told Nina on the phone that his mother had inherited the place from an uncle. Perhaps there was no money to go with it but the will said she mustn't sell it.'

Freddie looked puzzled. 'She must be quite old if that's her son. Perhaps he's waiting for her to pop off so he can sell up then.'

As they crossed the hall again to go towards the staircase, Joanna caught a movement out of the corner of her eye. She spun round, wondering what she'd seen.

'What is it?'

'Something moved,' she whispered. 'That wall . . . it seemed to . . .'

Freddie peered closer into a room made dim by small

dirty windows. Then he stroked the panelling. 'A secret door,' he said softly.

'A secret door!' Joanna repeated. And the implication reverberated through her head. They exchanged looks. She knew now, without a shadow of a doubt, that they'd come to the right place.

But what in God's name was Arabella doing here?

Early morning, Saturday 6 November

'I knew you'd never forget me. Never. How could you? Knowing that was a great comfort, you know. Sometimes I'd pretend you'd taken me back to your home and it would be a lovely sunny house . . . not like this dump . . . and you'd kiss me and hold me tight . . . Oh, Christ! CHRIST! How I wish that had happened.

'I'm sorry . . . I didn't mean to get upset but I can't help thinking how different things would have been . . .

'Where's my hankie? I did have a hankie . . . Oh, here it is.

'When I first saw you, I thought my heart would stop. It was the strangest feeling, you know, but I felt we belonged right away. That we'd always been meant to be together. And when you looked at me with those blue eyes of yours . . . Christ, I thought I'd die! I've never seen eyes like yours on anyone else . . .

'But then you rejected me! I almost did *die in that moment, you know. You almost killed me there and then.*

'Thank God we can put all that behind us now. Thank God we're together at last . . .'

Late morning, Saturday 6 November

The higher Joanna and Freddie climbed, the more dilapidated Roxwell Manor became. Rotting floors, mouldering plaster and decaying window frames were disguised by thin drapes and threadbare rugs. In some places, pieces of plywood painted dark brown had been roughly nailed over offending areas, to look like panelling. But Freddie's eyes were sharp. What he had first suspected was true. The place was falling down and unless skilful restorers were brought in soon, the interior, if not the stone walls, would soon become dangerously unstable.

On the first floor various rooms led off each other, each a 'museum' according to the glossy leaflet they'd picked up. This had obviously been printed a long time ago because the photographs showed rooms resplendent with polished furniture and pristine brocade drapes, and even portraits framed in gilt.

In one room, Freddie noticed, Jacobean pewter platters, goblets, jugs and candlesticks would have made an impressive collection had they not been displayed on dusty shelves and threaded with cobwebs. In another room magnificent examples of handmade lace and needlework were marred by being displayed in disintegrating show cases with cracked glass under which lay dead bluebottles and flies.

Most impressive was a collection of original historical costumes, but the effect was spoiled by their being exhibited on battered shop dummies, which looked as if they'd been rescued from a skip.

Joanna took little of it in as she went from room to room, watching, waiting, almost holding her breath as if she expected Arabella to step through a doorway at any moment.

'It must have been a lovely house once,' Freddie observed, putting his arm round her waist, feeling her tension which was almost palpable. He led her gently into another room, dark and dingy, with a heavily carved four-poster bed, a chest, and a wooden rocking cradle.

Joanna consulted her leaflet. In the photograph the bed was covered with a red brocade counterpane, there were rich rugs on the floor and velvet drapes at the window, and a bowl of flowers stood on the chest. The room in the picture looked bright and airy and infinitely desirable. She looked up and glanced around her again. The bedding was now lumpy-looking and the counterpane grubby. The floor was bare. Several of the leaded glass window panes were cracked, letting in little blasts of cold air.

She shook her head, oppressed by a fearful premonition.

'Something dreadful has happened in this place,' she murmured.

They climbed the final narrow flight of winding stairs to the top floor, the 'Museum of Childhood'. Here there was no furniture at all, but glass showcases all round the walls of the three rooms. Imprisoned behind the dirty glass were hundreds of dolls of all sizes and make, some Victorian with exquisite but dirty wax faces, others made of china with blue glass eyes which seemed to follow Joanna round the room. All were dressed in clothes appropriate to their era, but the fabrics were dirty, moth-eaten, and in some cases perished with age.

Arranged on the floor and on shelves in the showcases was also a variety of toys: nineteenth-century miniature prams, a dolls' house, tops, hoops, music boxes, rocking horses, teddy bears, boxes of marbles and battered train sets ... a cornucopia from bygone days and long-forgotten nurseries. Now cast aside, their amusement value long gone.

And what had happened to the owners of all this childhood memorabilia? Joanna wondered. The little boys who had taken their teddies to bed? The little girls who'd spent hours dressing their dolls?

She felt like weeping for the children who had played with these toys but now were probably no more. And she felt like weeping for the dolls that had been left behind.

She turned to Freddie and said in a quavering voice, 'This is the unhappiest house I've ever been in.'

As they came down the main stairs again, they saw the bearded man taking money from a bunch of new arrivals.

'Let's go straight past him and out into the garden,' Freddie whispered.

Joanna nodded. He had his back to them and did not notice as they slipped past.

Freddie took a deep breath when they were in the drive, as if anxious to fill his lungs with clean air. 'Well, they've never heard of the Trade Descriptions Act, have they?' he remarked, trying to lighten Joanna's mood of quiet desperation.

He dug his hands into the pockets of his Barbour. 'Have you noticed something, Jo? Only the rooms in the front part of the house are open to the public.' He strode ahead of her, past the derelict goldfish pond. 'The house goes back quite a long way. You can see the depth clearly from this angle.'

They walked across the muddy grass to where they could get a better look at the building. Half as much again of the Manor appeared to be kept private, and although he hadn't mentioned it for fear of scaring Joanna, Freddie had noticed secret panels and doors in several of the rooms they'd been in, which obviously led to the back of the house.

'Let's go this way,' she suggested. 'It says tearoom on that sign.' They walked along a narrow path, overgrown with weeds, past a hodge-podge of rundown out-houses and barns and abandoned gardening tools. It brought them round to the back of the building with a clearer view of obvious Victorian additions to the original Jacobean structure.

'We may be able to see through the windows into the back rooms,' Joanna said hopefully.

'Most have the curtains drawn, though,' Freddie pointed out as they drew nearer.

'Isn't that a bit odd? Who keeps their curtains drawn in the middle of the day? I don't like it, Freddie. What the hell's going on in there?'

'We're really too far away to see. We need to get nearer. The tearoom's at the far end. Let's see if it's open. The leaflet says they've got a licensed bar. I don't know about you but I could do with a stiff drink.'

Joanna followed him past a long-defunct aviary which bore a rotting notice saying 'Birds of Paradise', and several out-houses filled with junk including old lawn mowers, garden tools, broken tiles, rolls of chicken wire, bits of timber and rusting pots of paint.

'Nobody's done anything around here for years,' Freddie exclaimed. 'How can they open a place like this to the public?'

The tearoom, obviously attached during the fifties to the rear of the house at one end, was a one-storey extension with floor-to-ceiling windows on three sides overlooking a sadly neglected lawn. The doors were open, but there was no one inside.

'Let's go in,' Joanna whispered. 'Look, there's a hatch on the far side with a sign above it saying "BAR".'

Winding their way through empty metal tables and chairs, arranged as if two hundred people might be expected, they moved across the tearoom, their feet echoing hollowly on the tiled floor.

The hatch was large, with a counter on both sides. Through it they could see a large ramshackle kitchen: messy, shabby and with a mishmash of old pots and pans, colanders and dishes, stacked up on work tops. The central table, large and solid, was cluttered with empty whisky bottles, beer cans, dirty glasses, plastic bags marked Tesco, and a stack of what looked like bills. On one side there was a handbag which lay wide open as if it had recently been pillaged for its last penny.

Joanna drew back from peering into the room at the sound of approaching footsteps. From the light quick tread she knew it was a woman.

Noon, Saturday 6 November

Jeremy phoned L'Hotel Fôret every day to make sure Victoria and Louise were all right. He'd been so disturbed by the thought of Joanna receiving anonymous death threats that he'd feared Louise might become another target. After all, she was Arabella's daughter, too, though she was not actively trying to find her mother.

'She's fine,' Victoria assured him when he got through. 'I'm keeping an eye on her, of course, not letting her out of my sight, but I honestly don't think she's in any danger.' She was standing in the lobby of the old-fashioned hotel and could see Louise in the public lounge, doing the lessons Victoria set for her every day.

Jeremy sighed heavily. 'I'm sure you're right, but if this man isn't a hoaxer, he's bloody dangerous. I'm worried sick about Joanna. She and Freddie have gone down to see the house in Somerset I told you about. She's sure Arabella is being kept there against her will.'

'And what do you think, darling?'

'I think she could be walking into a trap,' he said bleakly. 'I tried to stop her going but she wouldn't listen. At least Freddie has his head screwed on, but I'm still worried about Jo.'

'You don't think Arabella's already dead?' whispered Victoria, looking through the open door and waving reassuringly to Louise.

'If she is,' Jeremy pointed out, 'why is this nut case trying to stop Joanna looking for her? I have to agree with Jo that he's making it sound as if Arabella is still alive. But if she's dead, I'm perfectly certain her body won't be found at Roxwell Manor. That would be altogether too obvious.'

'Oh, dear,' Victoria sighed sympathetically, 'you sound awfully down, darling. I think we should come back to London so we can all be together. And I think it's time Louise was told what's been happening.'

'I agree. Joanna knows all about her mother's past now and told me the other night she wished she'd known before. She blamed me for not telling her all about Arabella when she first disappeared.'

'Louise certainly doesn't need to know what her mother was really like, but Joanna should tell her she fears something has happened to her. Mind you, I'm sure she guesses. She's stopped asking when Arabella is returning. In fact, she hardly mentions her these days.'

As she spoke, Victoria could see the child trying to work out some arithmetic she'd been given. She looked so small and innocent, her blonde head bent over her exercise book and little fingers curled around a pencil. For a moment Victoria wished with all her heart that Louise was hers. Not even to Jeremy had she voiced the thought that Arabella didn't deserve to have such an adorable child. But what if Arabella never returned . . .?

'Phone me as soon as you hear from Joanna,' she said hurriedly. 'I'm anxious to hear what happened.'

Noon, Saturday 6 November

The footsteps had quickened their pace as they drew nearer, as if someone was hurrying along a corridor with a stone-flagged floor. Joanna held her breath, her hands gripping the ledge of the counter on her side, her eyes straining to see who would appear.

Suddenly a tall, very thin woman in her fifties shot through a door to the left and came hurrying over to them with an apologetic air. The shape of her face reminded Joanna of a keyhole: long and narrow and secretive. Her thin brown hair was cut short and almost transparent white skin did nothing to alleviate the gauntness of her appearance. She laid bony hands on her side of the counter and leaned towards them.

'Can I get you anything?' she asked. Joanna had the curious sensation of thinking the woman looked dead behind the eyes. She was totally expressionless, neither warm nor cold, friendly nor hostile.

Freddie stepped forward and turned to look at Joanna.

'What would you like, Jo?'

'Gin and tonic, please,' she said automatically, still staring.

'Two gin and tonics, please. And two bags of crisps.'

'Thank you. Ice and lemon?'

'Yes, please.'

The woman withdrew and went over to a fifties-style fridge out of which she took a tray of ice cubes, giving them the opportunity to study the kitchen once more. Joanna was searching to see if there was anything she might recognise as Arabella's. The open handbag certainly wasn't hers. It was made of cheap fake leather. Her mother was very particular about her handbags which were always made of crocodile or snakeskin. But was there a wallet or a silk scarf lying amongst the jumble of domestic detritus that lay scattered around? All she saw were the seedy signs of poverty.

The woman was returning with their drinks.

'And here are your crisps,' she said, adding them to the tray. 'I can make you some fresh sandwiches, if you like?'

Freddie thought: Not in that filthy kitchen you won't. Aloud he said: 'Not right now, thanks. Maybe later. How much is that, please?'

As he counted out the right change with slow care, he remarked casually, 'Stunning old house you have here. Are you the owner?'

'Yes, I am. Thank you. I'm glad you enjoyed going round it,' she replied politely.

'Have you always lived here?'

'For nearly thirty years now.'

She's not going to unbend, Joanna thought, watching that still blank face.

'My word!' Freddie's eyes widened. 'What a responsibility. All those years of history in your care. Was it handed down to you by your family?'

The woman took the money, and without looking at it slipped it into the pocket of her droopy brown cardigan. 'My uncle left it to me.'

'Really?' Freddie was sounding enthusiastic now, trying to coax her into relaxing, hoping she'd open up a bit. 'I hope he left you a fortune to go with the house?' he added jocularly.

The woman's eyes didn't even blink. 'No, he didn't,' she replied shortly.

He decided to push it further. 'And you haven't

thought of selling? I'm sure you'd get a really good price for such a historic building . . .' He paused, sensing she was cracking. Her eyes, which had been like grey glass marbles, suddenly swam with unshed tears.

'There's no question of selling.'

'I do beg your pardon!' he exclaimed, as if horrified by his own gauche behaviour. 'Mrs . . .'

'Gilbert. Mrs Gilbert.'

'Mrs Gilbert, I'm so sorry, I was just thinking what a burden this place must be for you,' he said earnestly.

She'd withdrawn again, absorbing the tears into herself, switching off as if she'd pressed a button in her head.

'We decided to open the house to the public.'

'You . . . and your husband?' Freddie asked silkily.

'Yes. My husband . . . and my son.'

Freddie feigned a beaming smile. 'You have a son! How nice. But wouldn't he prefer to live in town perhaps?'

Mrs Gilbert seemed to close in on herself completely, as if she nursed some inner pain. It was several seconds before she spoke and then she said hurriedly, 'He's the one who doesn't want us to sell. Now, are you sure you wouldn't like some sandwiches? Or perhaps a salad?'

'She was the oddest, saddest woman I've ever met,' Joanna told Freddie as they sat huddled in the car an hour later.

'She looks scared to death of something,' Freddie agreed. 'It's as if all the stuffing has been knocked out of her. I think she knows what's going on and is so terrified

253

of whatever it is, she's retreated behind a psychological barrier where no one can get at her.'

'But what *is* going on?' Joanna groaned in frustration.

'The house stinks, that's for sure. The old guy on the door is a lush and probably hasn't had a shower for a year. But what else? There wasn't a single thing to give us a clue that Arabella has ever been near the property. All we've got to go on is that it's definitely the old man who made those threatening calls to you. And as you recognised his voice, one can only assume he wrote those letters to your mother, signing them R. And that he's the chap who told Nina his name was Ryan.' Freddie leaned back in his seat and closed his eyes.

Joanna sat hunched in the passenger seat, her hands clasped tightly together in her lap. She'd taken off her scarf and he looked at her profile. She seemed far away, lost in her own thoughts.

'So what do you want to do, babe?'

She came out of her reverie, her eyes troubled. 'I can't help it, Freddie. I know it may sound crazy but I'm still convinced my mother's here. I can sort of sense it.'

He frowned, privately unconvinced. To him, Roxwell Manor was only a crumbling ruin, inhabited by dysfunctional people. The situation was unsavoury, sad, and Freddie hated seeing what had once been a beautiful house fall into a state of decay, but otherwise it wasn't so unusual. The only thing to link Arabella to this place was the behaviour of a drunken middle-aged man who was obviously fixated on her. And having

seen Ryan face to face, even that didn't seem so odd
now.

'What are you thinking about?' Joanna asked.

'I'm trying to get two and two to make four,' Freddie
said reflectively, 'but I keep making it three . . . or five. I
mean, think about it, Jo. What on earth could Arabella
have in common with that old soak?'

Joanna was wondering the same thing, but the longer
she searched for the mother she knew, the more she
realised a total stranger was emerging. Like a diamond,
the glittering surface was revealing dark cracks and fatal
flaws upon closer examination.

'Yes, but . . .' she began obstinately '. . . what about
the fact that the second tape was posted in Newport?
Gwent is only . . . what? Eighty miles away? Far
enough to confuse, perhaps, and not near enough to be
automatically associated with this place, either, but
easy enough to drive to. There's something else,
Freddie,' she continued, brightening. 'It's only a small
point, but that woman was surely too young to be
Ryan's mother.'

Freddie shrugged. 'Nina said he'd told her he was the
Gilberts' son; he may well be Mr Gilbert's son, but I
suspect that woman is his stepmother.'

Joanna sank back, deflated. 'Yes, you're right. His
father's probably too old to help around the place.'

'What a goddam' awful life,' Freddie remarked. 'Just
imagine being stuck in that depressing dump with an
elderly man and an alcoholic stepson. No wonder that
poor woman looked as if she'd been hit on the back of
the head with a mallet.'

'So what are we going to do?'

He knew what he wanted to do, but one look at Joanna's face told him she wasn't ready to give up yet. Her eyes were deeply troubled and her mouth turned down sadly at the corners.

'I'm sure Mum's in that house,' she said forlornly. With bowed head she looked down at Freddie's hand which was resting on her thigh, and a hot tear splashed on to his knuckles.

'Oh, babe.' He pulled her close and she clung to him, sobbing.

'I do still love her, you know . . . in spite of everything,' she wept.

'I know . . . I know. Listen, I have an idea. The problem is we haven't been able to get a proper look at the private rooms of the house. We were never going to find Arabella in the ones open to the public, were we, Jo?'

She sat up again, blowing her nose. 'True.'

'We need to go back when it's dark, to see if we can't see something through those back windows. There are bound to be chinks in the curtains and if they have the lights on . . .'

'You mean it?' Her face had lit up. 'D'you think we could?'

'I think it's the only thing to do,' he said flatly. 'Actually, we should try and get into the house, if we can.'

She looked stunned. 'Suppose we got caught?'

He smiled for the first time. 'I think we can probably look after ourselves.' He fished the car keys out of his pocket. 'I have a suggestion to make. It's not going to get dark for another six hours, and if we really want the coast to be clear, we should come back at about seven o'clock this evening. So why don't we book into a hotel, eat, have a rest and maybe a kip, and then come back later?'

Eleven

Afternoon, Saturday 6 November

'They've come to take you away! I know they have. But I won't let them. You're going to stay with me – you are, aren't you? You're not going to let them take you back, are you?

'You can't, Arabella. We were going to be together forever. We were going to be happy. You can't let them spoil all our plans, all our dreams, not now.

'I couldn't bear it if we were parted now. Not after all I've been through. Not after all the lonely years without you. That would be terrible . . . so terrible it would kill me.

'You won't go, will you? Promise me? Promise me you'll never leave?

'I'm so scared. I was so afraid they'd find out you were here. And I think they have. Oh, God, I think they have . . .

'I can't help crying! I can't help it. I'm so frightened that everything will be spoilt. Please . . . please don't go.'

Late afternoon, Saturday 6 November

Jeremy sounded anxious. 'So where are you, Jo?'

'We're staying at the Rising Sun, just outside

259

Taunton,' she replied, mobile in one hand, can of Coca-Cola in the other as she lowered herself on to the double bed in the small room. 'It's not far from Roxwell but we're inconspicuous on the edge of a big town so that's why we chose it. Freddie's gone off to buy some torches. As soon as it's dark, we're going back.'

Her father gave a soft groan of frustration and anxiety. 'Sweetheart, I really don't think you should. Not without telling the local police first. Have you any idea what you're letting yourself in for? How do you know you weren't recognised this morning?'

'I'm absolutely certain we weren't. I've got to find out what's going on for myself, and I don't want some local bobby blundering in there, giving away our suspicions and screwing everything up. I'm certain the man who made the threatening calls *is* Ryan Gilbert, although he's not what I expected, but who else can he be? I recognised the voice. And I believe Mrs Gilbert, whom we presume must be his stepmother, knows what's going on. She's an utterly cowed and sort of blanked out creature.'

'And if you do find . . . signs of Arabella?' Jeremy couldn't bring himself to put into words what he feared they'd find.

'Once we've got some evidence that they're keeping her there, we'll call the police.'

He was thankful there weren't television telephones in operation yet for he found himself screwing up his face and shaking his head like an animal in pain.

'Jo, please don't do this,' he begged. 'It's utter madness. How can Freddie let you?'

'It was his idea, Dad. We're only going to see if we can

glimpse something through the back windows. It'll be dark. No one will see us.'

There was silence on the line and she knew Jeremy was frightened for her. 'We'll be fine,' she added.

'You will let me know what's happening?'

'Of course, Daddy.'

'Even if it's four in the morning, Jo. Ring me as soon as you're out of that place.'

Touched, she said: 'Don't worry. I'm going to be with Freddie. We'll be fine.'

Early evening, Saturday 6 November

Jeremy had spent an agonising hour pondering what to do. Pacing restlessly around the rooms of Portsea Place, followed by Caspar who watched him, hopeful of being taken for a walk, he couldn't decide whether to ring the police or not. In his opinion DI Walsh should be made aware of what was happening. He'd been in charge of the case since the beginning. He'd have discovered by now, if he'd done his job properly, that Arabella had not been all she'd seemed.

For someone who was so fastidious about her designs and her personal appearance, it appalled him to think of the spiritual squalor that lay beneath the glossy surface.

What sort of a place could Roxwell Manor be?

Jeremy couldn't stand the uncertainty any longer. On impulse he looked up the number of Belgravia police station where DI Walsh was based. Jeremy felt compelled to tell him what Joanna was doing. He simply could not let his only child run the risk of being destroyed by her mother's past.

'I'm afraid Detective Walsh is off duty this weekend,' the girl on the switchboard informed him a moment later. 'Can I take a message? He'll be in on Monday morning.'

'Can you get a message to him? Or else someone in his department? It's in connection with the disappearance of Arabella Webster and it's very urgent.'

There was a pause and he could hear her tapping into a computer. 'Detective Sergeant Chambers is also out of town until Monday, I'm afraid, but I'll see what I can do. I might be able to page one of them. Can I take down your details, please?'

Evening, Saturday 6 November

Waiting by the bedroom window for the return of Freddie, Joanna watched as darkness fell over Taunton with the swiftness of a black-out curtain descending on a stage set. Distant buildings and nearby picturesque cottages became visible only for a rectangle of light in a window here, or the outline of a wall in the headlights of a passing car there. She'd forgotten that she'd always hated the countryside at night. The silence seemed threatening, the stillness oppressive. No one walked the streets. The town seemed almost deserted. She felt like the last soul in the world, abandoned and alone, and all she could think about was her mother, with a mixture of dread and excited anticipation.

'I wonder if we'll really find you tonight, Ma?' she reflected. 'Oh, God, I hope we do. I don't think I can stand this waiting much longer. What's it been? Nearly eight weeks. Eight weeks on Monday. The longest two months in my life . . .

'I've missed you, no doubt about that, but have you missed me? It's going to be different in future, isn't it? I know I'm going to feel awkward, especially at first.

'In many ways it'll be like meeting a stranger; not for you, of course, but for me. I realise now I never really knew you at all. You're a totally different person from the one I thought you were.

'How could I have lived with you on and off until I was eighteen – spent most of my childhood with you, my mother – and not known what you were like?

'I wonder if it'll be the same between us once I get used to . . . you know . . . the idea of you being different. Poor Freddie, having to be the one to tell me. I was so angry with him!

'I simply couldn't believe . . . I know one thing, I could never do what you did if I had a child. How could you go out every night like that? And there was I, thinking you were going to lots of lovely parties and being so proud of you . . .

'It *is* going to be difficult, seeing you again, coming to terms, trying to understand . . . but, oh God, I want to find you so much. You *are* my mother, after all.'

'Talking to yourself, babe? True sign of madness.'

Joanna spun round, startled to find Freddie standing in the doorway, smiling at her.

263

'God, you gave me a fright,' she said. 'I was miles away.' She moved from the window and went and sat on the bed.

'I got a couple of torches,' he announced, dropping on to the bed beside her. 'I reckon we should push off in a few minutes.'

She clutched his hand nervously. 'OK.'

'You all right?'

'I'm fine.'

He pulled her close, their bodies fitting together perfectly, the familiarity sweet and comforting with no words needed. After a few minutes he said: 'Shall we get on with it?'

Joanna raised herself on to one elbow. 'The sooner the better,' she murmured. Then it will be over, one way or another, she thought.

Freddie drove through the village of Roxwell and parked the car off the main road, on a wide path that led into some woods. From here passing vehicles could not spot it; neither would the inhabitants of the Manor.

Its front façade was just visible through the trees, stone walls ghostly-looking in a shaft of moonlight that broke momentarily through the clouds.

In any case it looked empty. No one would have guessed anyone lived there, and no one would have imagined that earlier in the day tourists had gone round it. There were no lights on in the front rooms and the place looked forbiddingly shuttered and closed.

'Which way shall we go?' Joanna said.

Freddie craned his neck, refreshing his memory of the

lie of the land. 'We can go across that field, which will lead us to the front garden, but that will mean negotiating a couple of hedges and maybe a ditch or two, so I suggest we go the way we went this morning.'

'What? By the proper entrance? Along that drive?'

'It's the best bet, Jo. We know the way now. There shouldn't be any nasty surprises. If we try and get into the grounds any other way, we might end up in trouble. Come on.'

In silence they left the woods, walked along the road and up the lane leading to the Manor, and then approached the five-bar gate which was now shut. The car park, as they'd expected, was deserted.

'Are you ready?'

'Yes.' Joanna clambered up and swung her long jeans-clad legs over the top before dropping down the other side. Freddie followed.

The darkness seemed dense and solid, like walking in a coal tunnel, but Joanna remembered the entrance to the drive was slightly to the right, sheltered by high bushes to either side.

A light suddenly flashed around her feet, making her stop, her heart throbbing painfully. Freddie bumped into her. He was pointing his torch at the stony uneven ground to see where they were walking.

'For God's sake!' she whispered. 'Turn that thing off. You nearly gave me a heart attack. They might see us.'

'The hedge will screen us from here.'

Suddenly the pitch darkness seemed to dissolve as the sky was lit by the glow of moonlight, and there in front of them was the gap in the hedge and the drive.

It had been tricky to negotiate in broad daylight, with its potholes and loose stones, deep ruts and a gradient of one in four. By night it was treacherous. Falling steeply away, and closed in on either side by the high hedges it was like entering a ravine.

They took it slowly, step by cautious step, not daring to use the torches in case they were spotted from the upper windows at the side of the house.

Joanna stumbled suddenly, skidding on a scattering of loose gravel and nearly falling.

'Shit!' she swore under her breath.

'For God's sake, be careful,' Freddie warned. 'If one of us twists an ankle we're fucked.' He switched on the torch for a moment, shielding the glare with his hand. They took a quick glance at the next couple of metres before he turned it off. 'Not much further to go.'

A few minutes later the house rose up sharply in front of them, looming in the darkness like a great menacing fortress, even more hostile than it had looked earlier in the day.

'Let's skirt round the front of the garden, staying close to the bushes,' Freddie breathed in her ear.

As Joanna followed, she prayed the house wasn't equipped with security spotlights that were triggered by walking through a laser beam or they'd be exposed in a blaze of illumination like rabbits caught in a headlight.

They were halfway across now and the empty stone pond lay between them and the house. A sudden breeze came whipping through the bare branches of the surrounding trees with a roaring sound like the incoming tide.

Joanna held her breath, looking up at the windows, wondering what secrets those rooms held. The house stared back, remote and unfriendly.

'Come on,' she heard Freddie whisper as he headed for the far side. Once there she knew they'd find themselves amid overgrown shrubberies, divided by narrow pathways, ancient trees, brokendown stone walls and archways, and beyond that heaps of discarded rubbish.

A dog barking in the far distance sent a thrill of panic through Joanna. The headlights of a car speeding along the nearby main road brought Freddie to a standstill. They stood, holding their breath. The noisiest thing they could hear was the thumping of their own hearts.

Then it was quiet again.

They moved on, working their way round to the back of the house, slowly and carefully, using the torch only when faced with an obstacle in their path, which included lumps of masonry, a broken chimneypot and scattered logs.

At last, under cover of a shrubbery, they faced the rear of Roxwell Manor and for the first time saw evidence of life.

Four uncurtained windows showed rooms which were lit by naked central bulbs. Three were on the ground floor and the other on the first floor. They couldn't see into the upper room, but the lower ones showed another side of the kitchen they'd seen earlier, next to it a narrow hallway with stairs leading to the floor above, and beyond that a sitting-room.

Crouching low, they edged forward to the nearest window and peered in. The sitting-room was small and dingy, furnished with a shabby three-piece suite, some other battered pieces of furniture and a flickering television set in the corner. In the grate logs smouldered in a bed of grey ash that had spread on to the hearth. On a table dirty glasses, a half-empty whisky bottle and an unfinished plateful of baked beans added to the squalid air of the room. There was no one inside it.

Joanna and Freddie exchanged glances and crept along to the next window. The narrow uncarpeted hall and staircase seemed even darker than the sitting-room for the walls were painted the same shade of grey as the stone-flagged floor and the stairs were made of dark wood. There were several empty beer crates propped against one wall.

A dull sense of disappointment made Joanna's heart start to ache. If there was no one in the kitchen either, what were they going to do? And where were Mrs Gilbert and her husband? Perhaps he was an invalid and bedridden? Perhaps his was the lit room on the first floor? Maybe he never came downstairs and that was why his son took the money on the door and his wife served the refreshments.

This theory was confirmed when they reached the third window. In the middle of the room at the kitchen table Ryan stood opening a bottle of beer. His face was even more florid than when he'd collected their money that morning. His matted grey beard and stained jersey made Joanna shudder. And *this* was the man who'd written to her mother? Who'd abused Joanna herself on the phone? Who was somehow involved with the dazzling Arabella?

Sitting at the table, Mrs Gilbert was pouring tea from a large brown pot into a patterned mug. Then she picked up a paperback and started reading. It reminded Joanna of watching the first moments of a play, waiting for the dialogue to start and the drama to unfold. Then suddenly it did.

A young man of around twenty-three or four came bounding into the room through the door from the hallway. He moved with the fluid grace of the young, unlike the older man whose joints seemed stiff and limbs heavy and awkward in comparison.

Mrs Gilbert looked up, her face pinched and shoulders hunched. She said something to the young man and Joanna strained forward, desperate to hear, but Freddie grabbed her arm and pulled her back. She gave a little shake of her head without taking her eyes off the group around the kitchen table and leaned forward again.

What was going on? What were they talking about? She was entirely focused on what was happening now, her face pressed dangerously close to the glass. If one of them were to glance in the direction of the window they'd see her.

Ryan Gilbert was saying something, his glass halfway to his mouth, and Mrs Gilbert shrank back, as if he was going to hit her. Then the young man strolled over to a dresser on the far side, took a mug off one of the shelves and, returning to the table, poured himself some tea. He was arguing with the older man. Small dark eyes flashed dangerously in his white face, his prominent cheekbones and hollow cheeks strongly defined by the single light shining down on them. His black moustache and goatee beard were closely trimmed around his mouth in the style of a pop star, his hair unkempt and spiky-looking.

Gesticulating wildly, he raised pale clenched fists as if about to strike the older man.

But Ryan Gilbert could hold his own. Obviously fuelled by alcohol, he struck the young man a blow to the shoulder, sending him staggering back. Ryan's voice rose then fell in anger and Joanna could only catch part of what he was shouting but she heard; '. . . fucking trouble from the beginning . . .', '. . . going to fucking happen?' Then: 'Sodding stupid to . . .'

Joanna could see that Mrs Gilbert had started to shake violently, the book dropping out of her hands as she watched the men quarrelling, her face a study in pure terror.

Then the young man slammed down his mug, spilling the tea. He turned on them both with renewed fury but his voice was low. Frustrated, Joanna tried desperately to catch what he was saying. His words were a continuous rumble, incomprehensible and garbled. Then, as she watched, his white face became blotchy with colour and, suddenly and unexpectedly, tears began to stream down his cheeks.

A moment later he turned and marched out of the kitchen by a door which led to the public tearoom on the far side. Her eyes followed his disappearing figure, wondering where he was going. And at that moment she was able to hear, quite clearly, what the older man was shouting.

'RYAN! Come back . . . Running away isn't going to fucking solve anything!'

At that moment Mrs Gilbert looked round as if she sensed someone looking in at them. Freddie grabbed Joanna and pulled her sharply away from the window, dragging her to a nearby rhododendron under which, losing their balance, they sprawled with legs entangled on the damp soil.

They heard a door bang and footsteps running away into the distance. Then silence.

Freddie lay full-length on his back, looking up at the leathery leaves of the dense shrub.

'Jesus!' he breathed. 'What the hell was all that about?'

Joanna, lying beside him, rubbing her knee where she'd banged it, didn't answer at first. Then she said slowly, 'If *that's* Ryan, who is the older man? And why did *he* make the threatening calls?'

On the main road, by the side of the wood, several cars were now parked. There was movement among the trees. Freddie's car was being examined, the number plate in particular.

The men stood in a group, listening to instructions from their leader. Voices were muted, movements silent, the villagers unaware of their presence. Then there was a signal.

It was time to go.

The door leading into the tearoom was swinging open.

'I want to get into the house,' Joanna whispered.

'Are you crazy?' Freddie protested. 'We can't just go in.'

But Joanna was up on her feet, hurrying in a crouched

271

position towards the tearoom, following the path they'd taken that morning. Freddie went charging ahead of her, pausing at the open door to listen.

'I'm worried in case Ryan is lurking around,' he whispered.

Joanna peered past him into the tearoom. It was in darkness. 'We did hear him run off.'

'D'you want to risk it, then?'

'Yes.'

They went in and started moving gingerly among the tables and chairs, fearful of bumping into them. The hatch was closed now and the only light came from the partly open door to the kitchen where they could hear Mrs Gilbert and the older man talking.

Hardly daring to breathe, Joanna and Freddie stood in the shadows behind the door, listening to snatches of their conversation.

'. . . but what can we do?' It was Mrs Gilbert's anxious voice.

'Buggered if I know. I wish to God we'd never . . .'

Mrs Gilbert was whining now. 'I've done my best, Tom. It's not my fault. None of it. When we got married . . .' Her voice caught on a sob.

'Don't start that all over again, Connie,' Tom Gilbert was saying in a warning tone. 'I'm sick to death of the whole business. This place. You. Ryan. Sick to fucking death! Now I'm going to go and watch *Coronation Street*.'

Joanna heard the clinking of glass, as if he was carrying several bottles of beer, and then shambling footsteps as he left the kitchen by the door on the far side. She knew exactly what he'd do. He'd cross the hallway and enter the room beyond, where she'd seen the television set.

Almost immediately they heard the sound of something being scraped on the stone-flagged floor and guessed it was Connie Gilbert, rising to follow her husband.

'Wait here,' Freddie whispered in Joanna's ear. 'Don't move. I'll be right back.'

She waited, peering cautiously around the door. Saw Mrs Gilbert's backview as she went to the far doorway. There was a faint click as she switched off the lights, plunging the kitchen into darkness. Then Joanna heard her call out, 'Has it started?' Her footsteps receded, a door was banged shut and then there was silence.

Grey speckles danced before Joanna's eyes as she clung to the door lintel, suddenly feeling sick and giddy. Without the light from the kitchen, the tearoom had vanished into pitch darkness, too, making her feel disorientated. She didn't dare move. Didn't know where Freddie had gone. Forcing herself to breathe deeply, she stood and prayed he'd come back before Ryan did.

Night, Saturday 6 November

'Jesus CHRIST! This is what I was so afraid of . . . they've come to get you. They're going to take you away and I'll never be with you again.

'Of course I'm crying . . . I feel desperate! I'm drowning in the pain from my heart. I can't believe this is actually

happening. It's my worst nightmare come true.

'*Don't you realise that I'm going to miss you even more than I missed you before? Since we've been together you've become a part of my life. The most important part.*

'*Having to part with you is going to kill me. I don't think I can bear it. I really don't . . .*

'*Please, Mum. Please don't leave me again . . .*'

Night, Saturday 6 November

Pressed up against the wall, Joanna froze as she saw the flicker of a torch weaving its way across the tearoom towards her.

She didn't know what to do. There was no place to run. Then it was switched off and she heard Freddie's whispered voice.

'I went out and looked through the windows again. They're in the sitting-room watching television and they've closed the door. Now's our chance.'

'OK.' Joanna was so relieved it wasn't Ryan who had come back, she felt momentarily weak.

'Let's go across the kitchen and into the hall,' Freddie whispered, leading the way. Briefly he flashed the torch so they could negotiate the big table in the middle of the room. Joanna's clothes were sticking to her with sweat and her heart was roaring in her ears.

They made it across the room to the hallway where they could hear the television blaring behind the closed door of the sitting-room. The Gilberts were on the other side of that door, only yards away now.

'This way,' Freddie breathed, indicating the stairs on their right. 'Ready?'

Joanna nodded. She put her foot cautiously on the first tread and there was a creaking sound. It was an old wooden staircase and probably every tread would squeak or groan under their weight.

Petrified, she stood motionless, eyes glued to the sitting-room door, waiting for it to burst open, waiting to be confronted by Tom's drunken figure.

Nothing happened.

Freddie, gesticulating, indicated that the outside edges of the treads should be walked on.

Taking a deep breath, Joanna climbed the steps two at a time, slowly and carefully testing her weight and keeping as close to the wall as she could, balancing herself by holding on to the banister on the other side. She didn't pause until she'd got to the top. Her ascent had been soundless.

Freddie followed a moment later, using the same method, but halfway up he paused, frozen, as they heard a noise from behind the closed sitting-room door. Then Tom Gilbert's voice.

'Did you hear anything?'

The television was turned down. If he opened the door the light in the hallway would reveal Freddie's presence.

On the top landing Joanna closed her eyes and prayed. She could hear a murmur of voices. Then the television was turned up again and she let out a long breath of relief.

In seconds Freddie was by her side. She clung to him

275

for a moment, wishing they'd never embarked on this crazy scheme; never come to this house with its pervasive atmosphere of menace.

Then she noticed a strip of light from under a closed door on the far side of the landing. It came from the room on the first floor that they'd observed from the garden.

She started to tremble, scared witless of she knew not what. Only knowing that she was at the heart of the sudden sense of danger and dread that was engulfing her. She grabbed Freddie's hand, pulling him back as he crept towards the door.

'It's OK,' he whispered. 'They've gone back to watching the box.'

'I don't want to . . .' Panic swarmed through her, her body prickling as if ants were crawling all over her skin. She could hardly breathe. 'I can't!'

'We must.' He moved forward and stood close to the door, listening intently. Joanna stood by his side.

Then he turned the handle very slowly and quietly. The door opened a fraction. He pushed it open further and stepped into the room. Joanna followed.

For a moment they stared, then Joanna only managed to stifle a scream by clamping her hand over her mouth.

'Jesus Christ,' she heard Freddie mutter under his breath.

With tears of shock streaming down her cheeks, she tried to suppress her emotions, but this was the last thing she'd expected. It was better and yet it was worse than anything she'd imagined. And far more horrifying.

Every wall in the bleak little room was plastered with

pictures of Arabella. They'd been cut out of magazines and newspapers and stuck on all four walls and the ceiling too, many of them endless photocopies of the pictures that had been printed in the press recently. Sections of her face had been cut out and enlarged enormously, so that hundreds of huge eyes stared back at them, again and again and again. And dozens of mouths, lips voluptuous and glossy, smiled endlessly around the room.

'Oh . . . my . . . God!' whispered Joanna, stepping further into the room, glancing at the grubby unmade bed in one corner, the battered armchair and small table in the middle, cluttered with dirty mugs and crushed Cola tins.

Clothes were scattered all over the floor. There were no curtains at the window and the room was freezing.

She felt Freddie tugging her hand, trying to draw her attention to something, and then she saw what he was looking at and felt as if she'd been punched in the chest.

There were wide white ribbons suspended from the flex of the central naked bulb, but they'd been shredded and hung limply, torn and tattered. Tied to the end of one of them something glinted.

It was a wide gold ring, fashioned in tiny blocks so that it resembled miniature brickwork. For the last two years Arabella had worn it in lieu of a wedding ring.

The men climbed the five-bar gate and then fanned out on silent feet. Their cars were still where they'd left them, standing on the road by the side of the wood. Nearby, two other men stood by Freddie's car, on the alert, ready for action.

Down below a door banged. Footsteps were clumping over the stone floor of the kitchen as Joanna and Freddie turned to look at each other. The young man was back. Ryan was back. *Arabella's murderer was back.* There was no doubt in their minds now. If she was here, it would only be her dead body they'd find.

'Quick,' Freddie urged, pushing Joanna into the passage outside. They could hear Ryan in the hallway below, opening the sitting-room door so that the sound of the television wafted up to them.

Then he was shouting angrily. Joanna couldn't make out what he was saying but she knew they had to get out of this place, and get out quickly before they were discovered.

Tom Gilbert was bellowing back, his voice deeper and stronger than Ryan's, and she caught the words, 'I've done every fucking thing I can to keep . . .' before the sitting-room door was slammed shut again and they heard Ryan's footsteps walk along the hallway beneath them, as if he was going through to the front of the house.

They listened. The house was quiet again.

'Shall we hide in there?' Joanna whispered, pointing to a door on the opposite side of the passage from Ryan's room.

Freddie shook his head. After a moment he said, 'We'll go out the way we came.' He tiptoed ahead of her towards the top of the stairs, beckoning her to follow. 'As

278

fast as you can . . . NOW!' he whispered.

It happened so quickly Joanna stood petrified, watching helplessly, as Ryan suddenly appeared in front of her, blocking her off as he leaped through a secret panel in the passage wall they hadn't known was there.

He took a running jump at Freddie, who turned as if to save himself by catching the banister with his left hand. But Ryan was right behind him, kicking his arm, his shoulder, his lower back, with savage venom.

Suddenly, Freddie lost his balance, crashed forward, and thundered down the wooden stairs head first.

There was a terrible silence as he lay there, inert, before Joanna started screaming.

'How did you think you'd get away with it, coming here and spying on me like that?' Ryan asked slyly. He was sitting in the shabby chair, studying Joanna with his small dark eyes as she lay on his bed, her wrists bound behind her back, her ankles tied together tightly.

He'd turned on her seconds after he was sure Freddie wasn't going to come back up the stairs, and with astonishing strength for one so puny-looking had grabbed her by the wrists. Although she'd kicked with all her strength, he'd managed to drag her back into his room, slamming the door behind him with his foot before temporarily stunning her by throwing her on to the bed in such a way that she banged her head on the wall.

She looked at him with loathing, but most of all with anger. She'd got to the empty stage beyond shock. If she could understand . . . and she was beginning to think she could . . . what had been between Arabella and this crazed young man, then she would be facing the ultimate moment of truth.

Ryan's tone was creepily conversational as he went over to his bedroom door and locked it. 'I saw you from the garden. Having a good snoop, weren't you?' he said over his shoulder.

Then he looked around the room at the dozens of pictures of Arabella. His face glowed with an obsessional light.

'Beautiful, isn't she? Absolutely gorgeous,' he said, coming back and sitting down again. 'Pity you don't take after her, but she was a one off, wasn't she? I never get tired of looking at her. She's with me when I wake up in the morning and she's with me when I go to sleep at night. That was all I ever wanted, you know. To be with her all the time.'

With a curious sense of detachment Joanna felt as if she was watching a poisonous snake that could lash out at her any moment. He even seemed to have a snake's markings in the lines of the widow's peak of his black hairline, his goatee beard and thin moustache, trimmed in neat lines down each side of his narrow mouth.

'You can't begrudge me having her now,' he continued, sounding disgruntled. 'After all, you had her for all of your life, didn't you? Had her for every birthday and every Christmas. But then, you were privileged, weren't you? You had it all,' he added bitterly.

Still she said nothing. She was beyond words, in a strange limbo outside the limits of emotion.

'She rejected me when I went to see her in London,

you know,' he said angrily. 'Told me I was a fucking embarrassment. That I wouldn't fit in with her lifestyle. Told me she didn't want people to know I even existed.'

Suddenly his face crumpled and he clenched his fists to either side of his head. '*Her own son!* And she didn't want anything to do with me,' he roared in a paroxysm of rage and grief.

Instinctively, Joanna drew up her knees so that she lay hunched up on her side, aware she was in danger. He had the strength to strangle her and none of the sanity that would prevent him from such an action.

'She had me when she was fifteen – did you know that? Fifteen. And what makes me *sick* is that she'd have kept me with her if only she'd been older and married. Like she kept you. Like she kept Louise. That's not fair, is it? Arabella got her timing wrong and I've had to suffer ever since.'

He'd risen again and was standing with his back to Joanna, thumping the walls with his fists, hitting out at Arabella's face – her lips, her eyes, her delicate cheekbones – until he suddenly crumpled and slithered down to his knees, sobbing with mad grief.

Joanna closed her eyes, unable to watch this deeply disturbing spectacle. Then he got up and stumbled towards her, his hands spread before him as if they were covered in dirt.

'And now I've lost her again,' he mourned. 'You shouldn't have come here. We were happy until you came.' He wiped his eyes with the backs of his hands. 'Now you've spoiled everything.'

'Arabella's my mother, too,' she said, her numbed

feelings making her bold, making her feel she had nothing to lose now.

He ignored her as if she hadn't spoken. 'We had long chats. I read poetry to her. We listened to music on my CD player. And now it's all over.'

'Where is she?'

'She'll leave me now you've come for her.'

'Can't we share her, Ryan?'

He flashed her a look of unspeakable hatred, his eyes burning bright, then stood looking down at her with an arrogant expression.

'Easy for you to say that. She was there when you needed her. She loved you. She loved your sister. I know all about her. When I found out she was my mother, because Tom told me who she was, and that she and her mother had dumped me on them when I was ten days old, I looked her up on her website. I found out everything: where she lived, where she worked, what she'd done with her life . . . a life of which I'd been no part. Yet I probably know more about her than you do.'

I doubt that, thought Joanna. And if you had, maybe you wouldn't have worshipped her as much. Aloud she said, 'Please take me to her, Ryan. She might want to stay with you, but shall we find out?'

'Don't try to trick me like that, you bitch!' he suddenly screamed. 'I know what you're after! You want a confession, don't you? I'm not going to let you have her back, d'you hear me? She's never going back with you.'

Joanna lay there looking up at him, her shoulders and wrists hurting, her back aching, her whole life skewed into a direction she had not anticipated. And she wondered what he was going to do to her now.

Jeremy's anxiety was becoming unbearable. It was nine o'clock, and although Joanna hadn't said when she'd phone back, he couldn't shake off a gut feeling that something was terribly wrong.

He'd tried to get hold of her on her mobile, but not surprisingly, he reflected, she'd switched it off.

Then he dialled 192, to find out the number of the Rising Sun in Taunton.

'I'd like to speak to Joanna Knight, please,' he said when the proprietor answered.

'I think she's out, but I'll go and see.'

While Jeremy waited, he heard chattering and laughter in the background, obviously coming from the bar. It was a jolly sound, and he allowed himself to hope that Joanna and Freddie had decided against returning to Roxwell Manor and were enjoying a convivial drink with this happy-sounding crowd.

A moment later his hopes were dashed.

'She's not in I'm afraid, sir,' the landlord was saying. 'She and the young gentleman went out some time ago. Shall I leave a message for her?'

'Will you ask her to phone her father as soon as she returns?' Jeremy said, his heart sinking. His unease was transmitting itself to Caspar, who was sitting at his feet and looking up at him with anxious eyes. Then he gave a little whimper and pawed at Jeremy's trouser leg.

'All right, old boy,' he said absent-mindedly, scratching the little terrier behind the ears. He wished he could rid himself of this gnawing fear that Joanna was in danger.

From the very beginning he'd been against her hare-brained idea of looking for Arabella. And although he knew it was awful to think like this, he'd long since come to the conclusion that Arabella wasn't worth it. She'd always put herself before the feelings of her children, and it was only because they had such trusting and loving characters that they'd continued to adore her.

At last, unable to bear the wait any longer, he phoned the police station again. Another operator answered so he had to explain who he was and why he was ringing all over again.

'I left messages for Detective Inspector Walsh and Detective Sergeant Chambers several hours ago,' Jeremy continued. 'Do you know if they received them?'

'Will you wait a moment, sir, while I check?'

It seemed like a very long wait. Jeremy poured himself another glass of wine and realised with a sense of shock that he'd drunk a whole bottle in the past couple of hours.

'Are you there, sir?' asked the police operator, coming back on the line.

'Yes.'

'We haven't been able to contact either Detective Inspector Walsh or Detective Sergeant Chambers, but I've spoken to someone else in their division and they'll try and contact them as soon as possible, sir.'

'Oh, my God, that may be too late,' he shouted in frustration. 'Can't you get on to the local police in Taunton? Tell them my daughter and her boyfriend are at Roxwell Manor and may be in terrible danger?'

There was a long silence and Jeremy wondered if he'd

been cut off. 'Are you still there?' he bellowed.

'Yes, sir. I'll see what I can do.'

Ryan had come over to the bed and yanked the grubby pillow from under Joanna's head. He gripped it now, at either end, and in that moment she knew what he was planning to do.

A part of her mind detached herself and remained poised, separated from reality, thinking: So this is how I'm going to die.

'I can't let you go, you know,' he said, his voice becoming suddenly matter-of-fact. 'You're too dangerous.'

'Where's my mother?'

'It's no business of yours.'

'I've a right to know! I want to see my mother.'

'I'm not going to let her go now that I've found her. You've lost her forever, and I'm *glad*.' He moved closer, still holding the pillow, his knuckles sharp as he extended it above her face.

'*No!*' she yelled. 'This isn't going to help. Please, Ryan. Let me try and make it up to you for all you've missed . . .'

The moment stretched between them like a shining sword as they looked into each other's eyes. My half-brother, Joanna thought with shock. My mother's son.

At that moment she heard a commotion in the hallway below. Rapid footsteps, doors being slammed, and Tom Gilbert's unmistakable wheezy voice yelling: 'You've no fucking right to be here!'

Ryan stood poised on the balls of his feet, listening.

He started bringing the pillow down over Joanna's face.

'Get the fucking hell out of here!' they heard Tom roar.

Ryan looked wildly around the room, taking in the pictures of Arabella. His breathing became laboured as if he'd been running. Then he spoke as if he were talking to someone.

'Mum, don't let them take you away from me. Not now. For God's sake, not now. I need you . . .'

Heavy footsteps were racing up the creaking stairs, pounding along the landing. The handle was turned roughly. The door held fast. Joanna could hear someone talking, giving a flurry of commands.

Then suddenly the door was forced open and DI Walsh strode into the room, followed by DS Chambers and several uniformed policemen. He glanced swiftly at Joanna, lying trussed up on the bed. In a dream she watched as Ryan was seized and, after a struggle during which he screamed and kicked, finally handcuffed between two large uniformed policemen.

Then she was being untied herself, the rope cut away from her wrists and ankles, and a sympathetic WPC was rubbing her skin to bring back the circulation.

She sat up slowly, hearing Walsh say the familiar words she'd so often heard on television police dramas; 'Ryan Andrew Gilbert, I am arresting you in connection with the murder of Arabella Mary Webster . . .'

Joanna started to cry then, for the mother she'd lost and for the half-brother who was deranged, as well as from the sheer relief of being rescued just when she'd thought she was going to die.

'Are you all right?' the WPC asked in concern.

'Where's Freddie?' Joanna asked immediately, wiping her cheeks with numbed fingertips. 'He's my boyfriend and he was with me. Is he all right? Ryan attacked him and he fell.' Her voice was edging towards hysteria. 'If anything has happened to him . . .'

'I came straight up here so I'm not sure.'

'Oh, God! Can you find out?' Joanna turned in anguish to Chambers who was standing in the middle of the room, looking at the walls in silent shock. 'Where's my boyfriend? He fell down the stairs. I've got to go to him, he may be badly hurt.'

'Why don't we go downstairs?' the WPC suggested helpfully. 'D'you think you can manage?'

Joanna got to her feet. She was stiff and aching, but all she wanted was to get to Freddie. 'I'm OK,' she insisted, hobbling to the door. She was only saved from falling by the strong arms of one of the uniformed policemen who was milling around.

Ryan was being led away just ahead of her, his arms gripped on either side, his face now expressionless. He did not look back at her.

'We'll let them go ahead,' the WPC suggested.

They waited until they heard the heavy clumping of feet recede and fade away.

'OK now? Do you think you can do it?'

'Yes. I have to get to Freddie. He's only here because of me, and I'm terrified something's happened to him.'

There was no sign of Freddie at the bottom of the stairs. Joanna was led into the kitchen, and saw the Gilberts seated at the table, surrounded by policemen.

Walsh was talking on his mobile. There was no sign of Ryan.

'Where's Freddie?' Joanna demanded, but no one seemed to hear as police walkie-talkies crackled and buzzed and a dozen officers seemed to be talking into them at once.

Suddenly Tom Gilbert saw Joanna. 'I did warn you on the phone to leave things alone,' he said, shaking his head accusingly. 'If you'd stopped searching, none of this would have fucking happened.'

Joanna looked at this alcoholic wreck of a man and then at his wife, weeping silently into a crumpled tissue, and felt total disgust. So they'd known all along what Ryan had done and yet they'd continued to protect him.

'Where's Freddie? What have you done with him?'

'I'm here, Jo,' said a calm voice. 'And I'm fine.'

She spun round as he came through the door behind her. Apart from a slight gash on his forehead he seemed unhurt. She rushed to him, taking his face tenderly in her hands, looking searchingly into his eyes as if she could hardly believe he was all right.

'Are you sure?' she kept repeating. 'Oh, God, are you sure?'

He nodded, holding her close. 'Yes. Nothing but a few bruises. What about you? Has he hurt you, Jo?'

'I'm OK.' Her voice was wobbly.

They heard Walsh give orders for the Gilberts to be taken to the police station in Taunton for further questioning. Then he came over to where Joanna and Freddie were standing.

'Are you two all right?' he asked. 'It was a shock to

find you here. Why didn't you tell me you were coming? I didn't bargain on you turning up.' He sounded coldly angry.

'Why are *you* here?' Joanna countered. They moved to sit in the chairs vacated by the Gilberts and Walsh perched on the edge of the table.

He glanced at Freddie's head, ignoring her question. 'You should have that seen to.'

'It's nothing, just a nick.'

Joanna leaned forward. 'What made you suddenly decide to come here?' she asked again.

Walsh's face was impassive. 'A few days ago we were given a positive lead by the Somerset Constabulary. Someone in the village of Roxwell had reported to the police several weeks ago that something strange was going on up at the Manor. Ryan Gilbert, apparently, was spotted night after night, sitting in the forest glade at the bottom of their garden, talking to himself. They were aware we'd been making enquiries in the Gwent area about your mother. They also, of course, were able to identify the drawing of Roxwell Manor on the headed writing paper, and so eventually, we all put two and two together.' He paused and looked at Freddie. 'When my officers and I saw your car in the woods just now, I guessed you'd arrived at the same conclusion by other means. You could have hindered us from getting an arrest, you know. And you put yourselves in grave danger,' he added severely.

Joanna sat in shocked silence.

Freddie spoke aggressively. 'Why didn't you tell Joanna any of this? She's been to hell and back trying to find out what happened to her mother. Have you *any* idea what she's been going through?'

'We had to be sure of our facts, first. You must understand we can't give out information without verifying our suspicions.'

'Were Mr and Mrs Gilbert involved, too?' Joanna asked in a small voice.

'Not initially, we believe,' Walsh replied. 'Only when they realised what Ryan had done and in order to protect him. We have two new statements; one from a window cleaner who works in the Knightsbridge area and who has been off sick, declaring that on the morning in question whilst cleaning the windows of a house opposite Eric Webster's, he saw a man answering Ryan's description jump into your mother's car, seconds after she did, and he was holding something up to her throat. Moments later the car sped off with her at the wheel. The second statement came from an attendant at a petrol station on the M4. On that same day, he saw a blonde woman in a dark green Jaguar try to get out of the driver's seat, and she was dragged back into the car by a dark-haired young man. He thought it was a domestic quarrel at the time.'

Joanna and Freddie stared at him, trying to take in what he was saying. Everyone, except DS Chambers and the three local policemen had gone by now and the house was eerily quiet after the commotion.

'Then his foster parents discovered what he'd done,' Walsh continued. 'Ryan's been in and out of trouble since he was about eight. Petty criminal stuff, and later more serious accusations of cruelty to animals. When

Tom and Connie Gilbert got wind of the fact that we suspected something, they went out of their way to obstruct us. Hence the threatening calls, I'm afraid.'

Joanna stiffened, wondering how much worse this was all going to get.

'But Joanna had already made the link between the letters to her mother signed "R" and this house,' protested Freddie.

Walsh nodded. 'Quite. But before we acted we had to explore the connection between Ryan and Arabella Webster. There had to be a motive for what he did, and when we discovered from someone in the village that he was fostered by the Gilberts as a baby, we made some more enquiries.' Walsh stopped suddenly and looked askance at Freddie. 'I don't know whether you . . .?'

Joanna intercepted the look. 'Yes, he's told me everything,' she said quietly. 'Except this.' She looked at Freddie. 'Did you know she'd had a baby at fifteen?'

He shook his head. 'I'd never heard that.'

'It's more than likely she never told anyone,' Walsh explained.

'How did Ryan find out who his real mother was?' Freddie asked.

Joanna spoke. 'Ryan just told me Arabella left him when he was ten days old. He said Tom had told him.'

Walsh nodded. 'That's what we heard, and apparently the fostering was privately organised by Arabella's late mother, who was adamant she should get rid of the baby. The Gilberts were willing to take him on, as they wanted a child and couldn't have one.'

The poor child, Joanna reflected with a pang.

Walsh was still talking. '. . . seems to have formed a sick obsession with Arabella.'

'As can be seen from the room upstairs,' Freddie added.

Walsh nodded.

'And now he believes she *is* with him,' added Joanna.

'What happens next?' Freddie asked.

Walsh turned his head away in an effort not to intrude on Joanna's distress. 'We've already found her car in a lock-up garage round the back of the house. That gave us the evidence we needed to carry out an arrest tonight. All we have to do now is go to the spot where Ryan was seen every night, carrying on a soliloquy.'

Dawn, Sunday 7 November

'. . . Ma! What terrible thing have you done?' Joanna, unable to sleep, had crawled out of bed. Wrapping a spare blanket around her shoulders, she went and stood in the window, looking out at the slowly awakening town from their room in the Rising Sun.

'Have you any idea what you did? How *could* you just have dumped your baby on the Gilberts? No matter what your mother said. Didn't you care at all? Did you ever think about him? Wonder what he was like?

'I phoned Dad when it was all over last night and asked him . . . but he had no idea. He was as shocked as me. He said your mother would have forced you to give the baby away. He said she was strait-laced and very religious so she'd never have let you have an abortion. Even so . . . Even so, Ma, how could you have done this? The very thought makes me want to weep.

'And it makes me realise . . . just as Ryan said . . . that you would have kept him if you'd been married. So does that mean you only kept Louise and me because we weren't a social inconvenience? Would you have given us away, too, if . . .

'Oh, Ma, I can never think of you in the same way now. That's the worst thing of all. I can sort of get used to knowing what you did . . . in order to have nice things and go to wonderful places. I can even understand you getting drugs for your clients, because they pressured you, though I don't approve . . .

'But *this*? I feel I've lost you now. Just as Ryan did, all those years ago.'

'Babe?' The voice from the bed was muffled.

Joanna turned slowly. 'Hi, Freddie,' she said softly.

'What are you doing? Come back to bed before you freeze to death.'

Morning, Sunday 7 November

'Mum, it's all over, isn't it? Our long talks, our evenings together, sitting under the trees at the bottom of the garden . . . I was so happy then, for the first time in my life.

'I don't know what's going to happen now. Maybe I don't care any more. There's nothing to look forward to, is there?

'*You've let me down from the beginning. I realise that now. You never wanted me. I was just an embarrassment to you.*

'*Still . . . being together was wonderful while it lasted. A lifetime squeezed into a few weeks, that's what it was.*'

Twelve

As Joanna was getting ready to leave for work, DI Walsh phoned to say he wanted to see her right away.

'I'd like to fill you in on what's been happening before the media get hold of it,' he explained.

She felt herself grow cold and her stomach tighten, her body reacting to the pressure of the past weeks while her mind refused to believe there was worse to come. What could possibly be worse than what had already happened? Unless of course . . .

It was only eight-thirty. Freddie had left for work but her father would still be at home, having breakfast with Victoria and Louise who had returned from Brittany the previous week.

'Dad? It's me,' Joanna said when she got through.

'Hello, sweetheart. Is anything wrong?' He knew instantly from her voice that she was worried.

'No, not really. It's just that DI Walsh wants to see me . . . and, well, I get nervous every time I speak to

295

him. Such awful memories, you know. I don't suppose it's anything, though.'

'Would you like me to come with you?'

There was a pause before she answered. 'Could you, Dad? Would you mind?' She sounded grateful.

'I'll pick you up in . . . what . . . fifteen minutes? Will that be OK?'

'It would be wonderful. I want to tell you what's happening with Arabella Designs, too. We can discuss it on the way.'

Joanna was waiting on the front steps of her building when Jeremy turned up in his slightly battered Golf V5. She jumped into the passenger seat beside him and kissed him on the cheek.

'Thanks, Dad. Just the thought of going back to the police station again, and seeing DI Walsh . . . God, I wonder when the whole thing will be over?'

'I'm sure it won't be long now, Jo. Tell me about the company. What are your plans?'

'The German company Eleanor was in contact with got back to me last week. They seem to have been following what's been going on in the press, and phoned me to ask if we would consider an offer of financial backing? They're very impressed by our client list and the general goodwill we've generated since London Fashion Week. We're thrashing out a deal at the moment with Ma's lawyers and accountants, and her present backers are considering the take-over. They might do quite well out of it. It looks as if the German company will appoint a talented designer, and a manager to run the business side for a period of three years, and then we can assess the situation further. It would mean that Rosie and all the girls could be kept on, and the company will still trade as Arabella Designs. In three years' time I can either sell outright to them, or have them continue to be our backers, whilst I take over as business manager myself.'

Jeremy glanced at her. What a long way she's come, he thought, almost sadly. No longer a carefree girl, but a woman who has had to come to terms with the reality of a fatally flawed mother.

'Sounds interesting,' he said. 'And what about you? Will you continue to do the PR?'

Joanna looked down at her hands. 'I want to go to art school,' she said quietly.

Jeremy thumped the steering wheel with the heel of his hand. 'I'm delighted to hear it,' he said. 'Good for you. You should have gone in the first place, like I wanted you to.'

'I know, Dad,' she said, smiling. 'But . . . well, Ma somehow made it impossible for me to turn down the chance of working for her.'

'I know,' he agreed. They arrived at the police station, and he slipped into a parking space just as another car drew out. 'But you've got your own life back now, haven't you?'

Detective Inspector Walsh looked well. He greeted Joanna and Jeremy in a friendly manner, seeming relaxed, like a man who has arrived at his destination after a long and difficult journey.

They sat in chairs opposite him as he took his place

297

behind his desk. Leaning forward on his elbows, fingers interlaced, he looked at them levelly. 'I won't beat about the bush,' he began. 'I wanted you to be the first to know that we've found Arabella . . .'

For a breathtaking instant Joanna thought he meant . . .

'. . . her body was found yesterday afternoon, buried in a forest glade at the bottom of the garden of Roxwell Manor.'

It was said. Somewhere in the middle of Joanna's chest there was a strange sensation as if something there had suddenly withered and died.

'Forensic have done a positive identification from her dental records. They estimate she died approximately eight weeks ago,' Walsh continued in a purposefully flat, matter-of-fact voice.

It was a small point but Joanna couldn't let it go.

'What about the tapes? The last one arrived less than three weeks ago. She must have been alive then?'

He looked at her sympathetically. 'I think they were made within days of her being abducted then sent to you much later so you would think she was still alive. Ryan Gilbert, of course, wanted the search to be called off, and that's why he delayed sending them to you.'

He looked down at his papers again. 'We now know that Ryan was in London on the day the first tape was hand delivered to your home. We have also learned that he had to drive to the Gwent area on October the twelfth, delivering something to Mrs Gilbert's sister, and that's when he mailed the second tape.'

'But why did my mother co-operate? Why did she

298

make those tapes? She sounded really happy in them, as if everything was all right?'

Walsh sighed. 'We believe Ryan promised her she'd be released if she recorded them. We've found out he kept her captive in her own car in the lock-up garage for maybe several days. There's evidence he took her food and drink.' He stopped abruptly, seeing the pain in Joanna's eyes.

'Has he confessed to any of this?' Jeremy asked, wishing his daughter could have been shielded from these details.

'Like most psychopaths he is denying everything, maintaining an arrogant front and treating us with utter contempt. Tom and Connie Gilbert, on the other hand, have decided to come clean and be co-operative. It's almost as if they're relieved everything's out in the open at last. They both realised what he'd done, but too late. Mistakenly, they tried to protect him, knowing he was mentally unbalanced. As you know, Tom Gilbert even went to the lengths of making those threatening phone calls. They realise now how misguided they were. Connie Gilbert loves Ryan, in her own way, and felt she must be to blame for his behaviour. He was a disruptive child, and Tom Gilbert's heavy drinking didn't help because it led him to become violent with the boy and knock him around. Several years ago Mrs Gilbert had a nervous breakdown. I gather she's never been the same since.'

Joanna covered her face with her hands, thinking how different her own childhood had been from her half-brother's. And wondering if things would have been different if Arabella had kept him.

'That's terrible,' she heard Jeremy say.

Walsh nodded. 'They felt guilty because he wasn't their natural child and overcompensated in their treatment of him, thinking he might be instinctively missing his own mother without realising it.'

'Oh, he realised it all right,' Joanna said. 'I know how he felt. He told me.'

'Their big mistake was not telling him he'd been fostered by them when he was small so that he grew up accustomed to the idea. He flipped completely when he was told. He said they'd ruined his life and that, no matter what, he was going up to London where he'd live with his real mother. From what I gather from Mrs Gilbert, he turned up at Arabella's place of work, and she rejected him outright. He apparently returned to Roxwell in a terrible state.'

Tears sprang to Joanna's eyes. 'What a hideous situation! How desperately hurt he must have been.'

Walsh nodded. 'Yes.' He shuffled the papers on his desk to give her time to recover herself.

'So,' Jeremy continued, 'she was taken at knife-point and made to drive to Somerset?'

'That's correct. But we know there is no way she went willingly. A carving knife went missing from the Gilberts' kitchen the day before she disappeared. The pathologist found a series of little cuts to the side of her chest, level with her heart, and to her throat. They match the serrated edge of the knife.'

Joanna closed her eyes, imagining that long awful journey with Ryan by Arabella's side, threatening her with a gleaming blade.

She hardly dared ask and yet she had to know. 'And in the end . . . was she stabbed?'

Walsh shot Jeremy a quick look. He nodded slowly.

'She was strangled with her own scarf,' Walsh said quietly. 'I'm afraid all these details will appear in the newspapers, and that is why I wanted you to be prepared.'

'Thank you,' Joanna said faintly.

'It's a tragedy for all of you,' the Inspector continued. 'If the Gilberts hadn't been such a dysfunctional couple they might have done something to avert this tragedy, but they'd become largely immune to Ryan's behaviour, denying even to themselves that he'd been unbalanced ever since he was small. They were also in deep financial trouble and trying to sell that rundown old house, but in recent weeks Ryan was desperate to stay. And now we know why. So far as he was concerned, his real mother was there now. And of course Tom Gilbert was drinking himself into a stupor on a daily basis while his wife . . . well, you met her. She's scared of her own shadow.' He leaned back in his chair. 'That about wraps it up,' he concluded. 'Ryan will eventually be sectioned under the Mental Health Act.'

He smiled then for the first time. 'You've had a terrible time, Joanna, and you've been very brave. I just hope you'll be able to put this nightmare behind you and get on with the rest of your life.'

She didn't answer. So many things were going on in her head. But it was too late to do anything for her tortured half-brother, consumed by his psychotic obsession, believing the only way he could have

301

Arabella and make her his was by killing her. The thing he most loved . . .

Joanna bit the inside of her cheek until it hurt, in an effort to control her emotions. Then she rose.

'Thank you for everything,' she said, reaching across the desk to shake Walsh's hand.

'You'll be all right,' he told her, getting up and coming round to the front of his desk. 'You'll manage. You're a strong young woman.' He was gazing at her with undisguised admiration. 'Remember, we have excellent counsellors in our victim support team, if you feel in need of them.'

'Thanks,' she said again. Jeremy and Walsh shook hands.

Outside in the street, Jeremy put his arm around her. 'Shall I take you home, sweetheart? Or are you going to work?'

'Neither, Dad. I want to go and see Eric and settle things with him. You know you and Victoria said at the weekend you'd be prepared to look after Louise permanently now Ma's dead?'

It was the first time she'd said those actual words. She looked at Jeremy in sudden horror.

His gaze was steady, reassuring. He'd taken that fact on board weeks ago.

'Not "prepared" to look after Louise, but wanting to. Longing to,' he corrected her gently. 'We love the child and she has a real home with us as I hope Eric will agree. He's always doing lecture tours and travelling around the place. Louise needs mothering and security.'

'And Caspar,' Joanna added. 'She's always begged to have a dog.'

'And Caspar. But don't let him think we're trying to take Louise away from him. We'll talk to him ourselves, of course, but please do reassure him that he will have complete access to Louise at all times.'

'I will, Dad. I will.' She hugged him and kissed his cheek. 'Thank you for coming today. I'll ring you later.'

Hailing a passing taxi, she gave the driver Eric's address.

Mrs Holmes opened the door. Her expression became hostile when she saw who it was.

'Good morning, Mrs Holmes. I'd like to see the Professor, please. Is he in?'

'I'll go and ask him,' she replied tartly, shutting the door in Joanna's face again.

It was several minutes before she returned, announc-ing grudgingly, 'The Professor's in his study. He's busy but he says he'll see you.'

'Thank you.' Joanna crossed the familiar threshold of her former home, instantly missing the energised atmos-phere her mother had created when they'd lived here. Now even the air seemed stale, as if all the oxygen had been drained from it by those who had long since departed. The ornamental wall lights were switched off to save electricity and there were no flowers.

Eric was seated behind his pristine desk, his back to the window which overlooked the garden. He glanced up when she entered but did not rise. As always his appear-ance was immaculate, as if he'd been polished and

303

pressed, brushed and smoothed, from head to toe.

'Good morning, Eric,' Joanna said, no longer his stammering teenage stepdaughter.

'Yes?' His face was pale and waxy, eyes beady. That habitual arrogance was still there, displayed like a banner. 'What do you want?'

'I don't want anything, Eric,' she replied politely, taking the same diplomatic line as DI Walsh. 'I've come to tell you before you see it in the newspapers that they've found Arabella's body.'

He stiffened visibly. 'So?'

'They've arrested the man who killed her.'

'How remarkable,' he said scornfully. 'I presume that means they realise they made a mistake when they accused me?'

She looked at him levelly. 'That's exactly what it means and I for one am very sorry it happened.'

He raised his chin, stretching his neck out of a smooth white collar. 'One of her ex-lovers, I presume?'

'Her son, actually.'

Eric looked completely blank, astonishment showing in every line of his face. 'Her *son*?' he repeated almost stupidly.

'It's a long story, but that's not why I've come here. I wanted to talk to you about Louise. She and Victoria have returned to London. She's longing to see you, and I think, if it's all right with you, we should arrange for her to spend some time with you soon. She's really been missing you and her visits here.'

Eric's face softened and became suffused with colour. For a moment Joanna thought he was going to weep.

'Yes . . . yes,' he stammered. 'Whenever she can. I'm not going up to Oxford until Tuesday week and after that . . .' His voice trailed off and he frowned worriedly.

'For the rest of the time,' Joanna continued carefully, 'would you be agreeable to her living with my father and Victoria? They both absolutely adore Louise, having no children of their own, and she's so happy with them – happier than she'd be with me since I'm soon going to art school. But I will be seeing a lot of her, and keeping an eye on her, too. I think she's got to the age when she needs someone there all the time who can give her motherly care.' She paused, purposely stressing Victoria's future role with Louise rather than Jeremy's.

Seeing Eric's mood mellow, she added lightly; 'There's also the attraction of Caspar, their Border Terrier, whom she's mad about.'

Eric was nodding, and for the first time in her life Joanna saw a look of vulnerability in his eyes.

'Yes,' he said again. 'I have been very worried about Louise's future. I'm not really equipped to look after a child full-time.' There he paused and eventually added: 'There's no question they'd want to adopt her, though, is there? I couldn't let that happen.'

'No question of that at all,' Joanna said firmly. 'And Louise doesn't know any of this yet. Unfortunately she saw an English newspaper when she and Victoria took a trip to St Malo and now realises Arabella has been murdered. It's the one thing we all wanted to keep from her and that's why she was taken to Brittany, but I suppose she had to be told sooner or later. Now it's been confirmed . . .' her voice broke for a moment and she took a deep breath before continuing '. . . I think she's hoping Victoria will continue to look after her, but she does keep asking to see you.'

Eric rose and glanced out of the window at his garden, restored to its previous formal charm by a professional contracting firm. 'Lunch on Sunday, perhaps? Could you drop her off?'

'That would be perfect. I know she'll be thrilled.'

He wavered, as if he wanted to say something but wasn't quite sure whether he should. Joanna hesitated, too. She'd never liked Eric, never got on with him, but he was Louise's father. They were all going to have to deal with him in future. The more amicable their relationship, the better for all concerned.

'What is it, Eric?' she asked gently.

'That quarrel . . . the one I had with Arabella the day she disappeared,' he began, avoiding her eyes.

'Yes?'

'It's true, you know. We had a dreadful fight. She threw a valuable bronze statuette at me. Of course it looked very suspicious from the police's point of view. But it was about Louise, you see.'

Eric turned to look at her then, and in the light of all she'd found out about her mother in the past few weeks Joanna was able to treat her former stepfather with understanding if nothing else.

'What about Louise?'

'Arabella threatened she'd never let me have Louise to stay again. She said she'd never even let me *see* my daughter unless I paid off her huge mortgage, although

I'd given her the money to buy the flat outright in the first place. She also wanted another fifty thousand pounds a year, on top of the seventy thousand I was already giving her. I just don't have that sort of money, Joanna. But she meant it. Or Louise was to be out of bounds to me. I lost my temper and shouted at her, I admit it, so she flounced out of the house . . . and that was that.'

'It was indeed,' Joanna replied slowly. 'While I think of it, Eric, my mother left a will, leaving everything jointly to Louise and myself. If it's all right with you, I want to sell her flat and put all the proceeds in trust for Louise.'

'Isn't that rather too generous, Joanna?'

She smiled. 'No. It's about starting again with a clean slate. It's what I want.'

'Well, that's very good of you. Well done.' He saw her out, smiling with genuine warmth for once. As they left the study they saw Mrs Holmes, busily polishing the hall table that had obviously been polished once already that morning.

'Lunch on Sunday, Mrs Holmes,' Eric announced. 'Roast chicken and all the trimmings, I think. Louise is coming to see me.'

Afternoon, Thursday 11 November

For the past two days the media had gone to town on the discovery of Arabella's body. The fact that her secret son had been charged with her murder added a new layer of sensation to what was already a front-page story.

Joanna refused to read the newspapers which were indulging in typical overkill, the editors relishing this opportunity to fill their pages with as much material on Arabella Webster as they could lay their hands on, whether relevant or not.

As they milked the story, squeezing every fact from it they could to attract readers, experts were commissioned to give their views. Articles by psychiatrists and psychologists examined the effects of adopting, fostering or abandoning babies.

The pictorial spreads showed photographs of Arabella looking particularly glamorous and flighty, in sharp contrast to snapshots of Ryan taken at various stages of his life, from a toddler sitting on the front steps of Roxwell Manor to a teenager standing sullenly with a school group.

In all the pictures he looked puny, undersized and unsmiling; a tragic misfit among his peer group. A boy who had been rejected by his real mother and had never come to terms with being fostered. Everyone seemed to have an opinion about 'loners', examples of 'low self-esteem', and children who were 'insecure from birth'.

A lot was also made of Tom Gilbert's being an alcoholic, and Connie Gilbert's having had a breakdown because she couldn't cope.

Arabella herself didn't escape criticism, either. Much was made of her 'genius as a fashion designer', but in several articles she was portrayed as a deeply selfish woman who cared only for her image.

Most surprising, however, was an interview in the *Daily Telegraph* with Connie Gilbert, who had been absolved of guilt by the police in connection with the murder and had now spoken freely to a journalist.

'It was Arabella's mother who came to us when she discovered her fifteen-year-old daughter was pregnant. She was distraught and disgusted at what had happened. She was naturally prudish and didn't approve of abortion because of her religious beliefs. Arabella was made to feel she'd done something indescribably dirty. Her own mother had told her she deserved to be in the gutter. Sex had always been a taboo subject in their family, I gather, viewed as something rather shameful and sordid.

'I believe,' Connie was further quoted as saying, 'that Arabella was left feeling both unclean and deeply damaged by having to give up her baby. This, I think, shaped her at an early age into becoming someone who grabbed everything she could for herself, to compensate for losing Ryan. When her mother died the following year and her father soon afterwards, I think Arabella blocked the whole episode out of her mind and set herself on a course of self-destruction, although that's not what it looked like.'

The article concluded with a final quote from Connie, in which she said: 'Arabella took out her own inner sense of loss and worthlessness on everyone else. She used and abused people, and rode roughshod over anyone who got in her way. She became greedy and rapacious, almost as an act of revenge for what life had done to her. I feel sorry for her ex-husbands and her other children. But most of all I feel dreadfully sorry for Ryan.'

This was an article Joanna felt compelled to read, and when she did, the final pieces of the jigsaw slotted into place.

At a stroke it helped her understand the black and white of her mother's character, the fatal emotional flaw brought about by her own mother's attitude when the teenage Arabella had been expecting Ryan; the terrible legacy she'd left behind of people whose lives had been scarred by her.

Jeremy, on whom she'd walked out after four years of marriage; Eric, whom she'd married for his money before walking out on him, too; Louise, who now came from a broken home; and Eleanor, who had been the most cruelly taunted and abused of all.

And Joanna herself? She gave a faint smile. She had Freddie. And she had her father. And she was going to art school at last. Not too badly damaged after all.

'There's someone here who insists on seeing you,' Alice announced as she hurried into Joanna's office. 'She's down in the showroom. I've told her you're not seeing anyone . . .'

'Is she a journalist?' Joanna cut in. 'Tell her I'm not seeing *any* journalists.'

Alice shook her head. 'I did ask her that but she got quite rude and said "Certainly not". She's refusing to budge. I thought she was going to follow me up here just now.'

Joanna frowned. 'What's her name?'

'Mrs Andrews.'

Shocked, Joanna leaned back in her seat and closed

her eyes for a moment. Eleanor's mother. What the hell did she want?

'Shall I go and ask her what it's about?' Alice enquired helpfully, not recognising the name.

'Thanks, but I'd better see her myself. She probably wants to blame me for Eleanor's breakdown.' Joanna rose, smoothed down the legs of her black trousers with the flat of her hands, and straightened her jacket.

Mrs Andrews, small and shrewish, was sitting on the edge of a seat in a corner of the showroom, a woman in her seventies with a deeply lined, embittered face. She was wearing a plain black overcoat and her white hair was cut severely short.

'Good morning,' Joanna said politely. 'I gather you wished to see me? What can I do for you?'

Dark eyes glared balefully up at her, so reminiscent of Eleanor's. 'Hasn't your family done enough damage to us already?'

Joanna remained standing. 'I'm sorry, I had no option but to ask Eleanor to leave.'

'It's not poor Eleanor I'm talking about, though God knows your mother made her life hell for years and years . . .'

'She could always have left. No one forced her to stay.'

'She couldn't have left! Eleanor loved her job, it meant the world to her. Anyway, she'd no idea what Arabella was *really* like,' Mrs Andrews retorted waspishly.

Joanna looked straight into the old woman's spiteful eyes. 'Oh, yes, she did,' she said quietly.

'No, she didn't. Eleanor put her on a pedestal.

Thought she was wonderful. She would have done anything for your mother, and what did she get in return?
Arabella used her, like she used everyone. Eleanor didn't
know the half of it because I never told her. She never
knew how much I suffered. She never knew why her
father committed suicide, imagining it was general
depression. She never knew that my life was ruined, too.'

Joanna felt icy cold and bewildered, her mind spinning
in numbed circles. 'I don't know what you're talking
about,' she said defensively. 'My mother and Eleanor were
at the same school, but they weren't even in the same form
because Eleanor was two years older, and my mother
certainly never knew you or your husband.'

But Mrs Andrews wasn't listening. She was wound up
like a machine, her thin lips working furiously. 'I've
known what your mother was like for the past twenty-
five years, and now at last she's been punished for what
she did. Just retribution has been served . . . and by her
own son, too. What a perfect ending to that bitch's life!'
she added with bitter triumph.

Joanna reached for the back of a nearby chair, gripping
it with both hands. The atmosphere in the quiet showroom
was suddenly fraught with tension. Outside in the street
she could see some photographers glancing in from time
to time through the glass door, clearly hoping something
was up, so they could keep the story running.

'I cannot allow you to talk about Arabella like that.
She is dead and what has happened has nothing
whatsoever to do with you. I'd like you to leave . . .'

'*It has everything to do with me!*' the older woman
suddenly shouted. 'Didn't you ask yourself, even once,

312

who Ryan's father was? Arabella seduced *my husband* when she was fifteen! It was at the school's sports day. We'd gone down to see Eleanor. I had to go to the bathroom and on my way I heard a noise coming from one of the dormitories.' She paused, her face a white mask of tragedy.

'I caught them red-handed, Hugo and Arabella. But I was so ashamed I crept away and never told anyone. When Arabella realised she was pregnant a few weeks later she was expelled, of course. I heard about it from Eleanor. That's when Hugo . . . killed himself.'

Joanna stood stock still, feeling sick, not doubting for a moment that what Mrs Andrews had said was true. What was it Eleanor had said? 'Arabella used to flirt with all the fathers on Sports Day, but especially with mine . . . She'd laughed in my face when I told her I loved her.' The appalling clarity of what had happened, and Arabella's sheer cruelty stunned her now.

'Arabella deprived me of a husband and Eleanor of a father,' Mrs Andrews was saying. 'She'd bewitched Hugo, of course. He was fatally besotted with her.'

And she bewitched your daughter, too, thought Joanna. The irony of it suddenly seemed terribly fitting.

Would she ever really know her mother at all? Or had Arabella bewitched everyone who knew her? She looked at Mrs Andrews, and thought of poor demented Ryan.

'I'm sorry,' she said simply. There wasn't really anything else she could say.